It was one-fifteen in the morning. Dinner had been a great success: good food, bright conversation, and the new couple next door seemed attractive and amusing. Now the newcomers had left, and the Parkers, the Radnors, and the Jablonskis, old neighbors and old friends, settled down for a nightcap, like generals in a war room appraising a new tactical development.

"Well," Tom Parker sighed, "if we have to have fags for neighbors, I'm glad they're decent ones."

"Tom!" Ethel said in astonishment and horror. "You think . . . they're . . . homosexuals?"

"Ethel," Tom said, "if a married man and woman moved into the neighborhood and came to dinner, and after they'd left somebody said, 'I bet she's a cold fish in bed,' you'd giggle your head off. Well, a new couple **has** moved into the neighborhood, and we're discussing their sex life. So what?"

"Well, it bothers me," said Joe Jablonski.

And indeed it bothered all of them, each in a different way.

Neighbors

A novel by Russell O'Neil

PAPERBACK LIBRARY

NEW YORK

PAPERBACK LIBRARY EDITION

First Printing: May, 1972

Copyright © 1972 by Russell O'Neil

All rights reserved

Library of Congress Catalog Card Number: 72-76805

For Mark

Paperback Library is a division of Coronet Communications, Inc.
Its trademark, consisting of the words "Paperback Library"
accompanied by an open book, is registered in the United States
Patent Office. *Coronet Communications, Inc., 315 Park Avenue
South, New York, N.Y. 10010.*

CHAPTER I

These were quite unextraordinary people, drawn together—reluctantly at first—by mere geography rather than by common interests or instant mutual affection. They all lived on what they called "the property." It had once been the Robinson Cartwright estate of ten acres, dominated by the fifteen-room Cartwright mansion. Three two-acre parcels had been sold off when Mrs. Robinson Cartwright had gone into seclusion twelve years ago. The remaining four acres formed a sea of lawn dotted with trees and topiary and azaleas surrounding the original house. Even when the three new owners had built their houses, "the property" remained an entity; if not a separate community, surely a separate neighborhood within a community.

Each husband and wife agreed privately that building on the property and meeting the other two families had been a happy accident. The Radnors had built first, and within their first year there, the Jablonskis had started construction. Before the Jablonskis had finished their house, the Parkers had laid the foundation for theirs.

Peg Jablonski (née Kelly) had put it pretty well when she said to her husband after two months on the property, "I've got to admit I was a little worried. You know what it was like, Joe? It was like when you wanted to go to Sea Island, Georgia, on our honeymoon, and I wasn't sure I wanted to go there. But we met the nicest people and had the best time of our life. It was the same thing here. I wasn't very sure of the Radnors when we built, but now I feel like I've known 'em since I was born." What Peg meant, but did not, could not say, was that she had been concerned that a Mick bride and a Polack groom from New Jersey might have been outclassed at Sea Island, Georgia, which would have embarrassed Peg and ruined her one-and-only honeymoon. It was not an attack on the snobbishness of others, but a fear of her own—and Joe's—inadequacy.

Cynthia Radnor had a different problem in the beginning. She and Herb had met the Jablonskis before the Jablonskis had broken ground for their house. The vague self-doubt was born instantly and incubated in Cynthia's mind for months. She said to Herb one night after dinner, "Do you think we and the Jablonskis will be all right?"

"What do you mean, 'all right'?" Herb asked.

"I'm afraid they'll think I try to be . . . grand. I'm sorry, but it is me, and I'm not going to change. I just don't want the Jablonskis to think I'm . . . putting them down."

"You just said the important thing. It *is* you. Be yourself, and I'll be myself, and if we all get along, great. If we don't, I'm sure we and the Jablonskis are civilized enough to live in peaceful coexistence."

"The property's too small for that. I want us to be friends."

"So do I. All we can do is try."

"Yes." Cynthia's very wealthy family had gone broke in 1929, and they had spent the thirties—Cynthia's

6

childhood—trying to live as if they had not. The struggle left Cynthia both with marks of good breeding and scars of economic hardship, and the struggle was still going on. It was not neurotic or compulsive or submerged in her subconscious mind. She simply believed that the good life was the best life, and she wanted to have it and to share it with others.

By the time the Parkers had moved in, the Radnors and the Jablonskis were already fast friends. Cynthia and Peg had met the Parkers' moving van like a kind of personalized Welcome Wagon. They had put themselves utterly at the disposal of the new neighbors, having previously arranged their own domestic affairs to free them for such service. Cynthia had had lunch waiting in her dining room for the Parkers, and for their moving men on a picnic table on the back lawn. The women had unpacked and arranged furniture and run errands with such efficiency that they had been able to send Tom Parker back to his New York office by early afternoon, at which time dinner for six was already being prepared in the Jablonski kitchen. The Parkers had never forgotten their welcome to the neighborhood, and their gratitude continuously oiled the wheels of neighborliness. Now, ten years later the lubricant continued to run thick and free, and despite brief periods of pique and consequent coolness, the adult members of each family considered the adult members of the other two families their closest friends.

They knew each other well enough for genial insults. They could generate genuine laughter among themselves with just the punch line of a joke, the details of which they had shared long ago and which were no longer necessary to the humor. They knew each other's capacity for alcohol and the names and ages of each other's children. They could identify each other by voice alone. Being together forced each of them to become a quite specific person, a known, prejudged person, recognized, accepted and, with qualifications, liked by all the others. And at such times, they all recognized, accepted and, with qualifications, liked themselves. They were good for each other.

Their dinner parties were always informal. The men never wore ties. The women dressed to be pretty, but they were always accessorized cautiously, as if they might be asked to help in the kitchen. Invariably they offered each other such help, and invariably it was graciously declined by the hostess, who at the moment was Cynthia.

They had their drinks—the women two, the men three—in the living room and talked about local politics, incidents at the office, a Broadway musical, their children. Herb explained that David, his fifteen-year-old son, was at a rock concert in Newark. Peg told a "funny sayings" story about their six-year-old daughter. Then Mrs. Turner, the cleaning woman who had stayed on to help with dinner, came into the living room and told Cynthia that dinner was ready. She was greeted warmly by the guests, for none of them except Cynthia could comfortably treat another human being as a servant.

Dinner was served family style. Mrs. Turner brought the food to the table in serving dishes, and the diners helped themselves, passing each dish from person to person. It was not until everyone had been served and they had begun to eat that the subject currently most important to them was brought up. It was as if there was a tacit conspiracy to save the topic for the right moment. The inevitable, with all its devastating surprise, had occurred. Two months ago, Mrs. Robinson Cartwright had died, and none of them knew what provisions had been made in regard to her house.

For the Radnors and the Jablonskis and the Parkers this was not a cause for mere gossip or curiosity. The situation was dire, for their way of life was at stake. There was no immediate loss to them in Mrs. Cartwright's death. Indeed, Cynthia was the only one of them who had ever seen her or talked to her. No one ever entered or left Mrs. Cartwright's house except the housekeeper and an occasional tradesman. It was the gain they feared. Five years ago, the Quinn mansion in nearby Ramsey had been bought by an organization called the Manufacturers' Association and turned into a private club. The consequences to *that* neighborhood had been automobile traffic at virtually all hours of the day and night, occasional late, noisy parties, and a general air of commerce hanging over the area. Now it could happen to them.

Since no one ever visited Mrs. Cartwright, it was the consensus among the neighbors that she had no living relatives and that the house must be up for sale. Yet there were no "for sale" signs and no sale advertisements in the local newspapers. The house simply sat there, dominating the property more in its emptiness than it had when it had been occupied. The not knowing was maddening. Then, today, a man had come to look at the house.

Ethel had seen him first, and she had called the others immediately. Neither Peg nor Cynthia kept a constant watch at their windows. They peeked out occasionally, hoping to catch a glimpse of the stranger. They both saw him when he came out of the house into the back garden. They saw that he was tall, graying at the temples, good looking and well-dressed. He stood for a long moment just looking around. Then he went back inside. They also saw the Mercedes-Benz parked in the driveway of the house.

"I just cannot stop wondering who that man was today," Ethel said.

"You may as well stop wondering, Ethel," Tom Parker said. "He could have been anything, anybody. A lawyer, a real estate man . . ."

"A real estate man?" Ethel said. "In a Mercedes?"

"In a Rolls-Royce the way land is today," Joe Jablonski said.

"Not only could he be any of those things," Herb said, "he could be a relative, and heir—*the* heir."

Tom put down his knife and fork and said, "Herb, do you really think there could be an heir? I mean, twelve years without one visitor. Either she didn't have any

9

relatives or she had relatives she didn't like well enough to see."

"Maybe she left it to charity," Joe said.

"If she did," Peg said, "I hope it wasn't the A.S.P.C.A."

"Well, it's better if she left it to a charity than if some developer gets a hold of it." In spite of just a high school education, Joe Jablonski owned a construction company, and he knew about such things as real estate and land developers. The others listened to him intently. "Some eager-beaver developer gets a hold of that land, he'll turn it into a drive-in movie."

"Not the way it's zoned," Herb Radnor said. Herb was principal of the George Washington High School of Hainesdale, New Jersey—where they all lived—and he constantly defended the general morality of the community.

"You know the right people and got the right money," Joe said, "that can be arranged."

Herb smiled and shook his head. "Someday I'm going to force you to make those vague allegations specific."

"What?" Joe said. "And lose my access to the sources?" It was a small joke they often played out publicly. Privately, Joe believed Herb to be hopelessly naïve, and Herb believed Joe to countenance corruption. Neither expected his friends to be without faults.

"I don't think he was that kind of a man," Ethel said.

"What?" Tom said. "What kind of a man?"

"He didn't look like a land developer or a real estate man. He looked . . . dignified."

"Then he certainly could have been a relative of Mrs. Cartwright's," Cynthia said.

"I know I've told you a hundred times, but that makes me so envious," Ethel said. "I mean that you knew her, you were actually in the house."

"I didn't *know* her, Ethel," Cynthia said. "One invitation to tea to tell me it would be the *last* invitation to tea isn't knowing her."

"She must've been quite a bitch," Joe said.

"No," Cynthia said. "Oh, I'm sure she was formidable, but she was a genuine lady. Even when she was telling me she never wanted to see me again, it wasn't insulting. Somehow she made it clear that she had . . . retired . . . for good reasons that were none of my business, and she did not want me to try to be neighborly, because she simply did not see people . . . ever. She was perfectly honest and open. And those pearls!"

"I'll bet they were beautiful!" Ethel said.

"They were real," Cynthia said.

"You know, Joe, you're lucky," Tom said. "Your wife is a realist. Ethel and Cynthia are both romantics. This gray-sideburned, distingué gentleman who looked at the house is probably a junior account executive at Doyle, Dane who can't afford to buy the house." Tom was an assistant account executive at another advertising agency. "Those two think he's . . . Heathcliff or something. Whatever he is, we can't do anything about it. Why don't we talk about something else?"

The subject was changed, first to gardening, since it was May (what would become of Mrs. Cartwright's azaleas?); then to children again (had Mrs. Cartwright ever had any?); then to property taxes (imagine the taxes *she* had to pay!); then to dessert. An hour and a half later, the guests went home.

Coming from New York City, the half-hour drive from the west end of the George Washington Bridge to Hainesdale, New Jersey, is unremarkable except for the vulgarity of the landscape. The land is absolutely flat and scarred by decades of the digging and scratching of industry. U.S. 4 is a corridor seemingly cut between two rows of gas stations and stores and places-to-eat, all screaming out their commercial messages in a variety of grotesque effects. The exit to Route 17 is a barren stretch of land which leads to a madhouse of signs instructing drivers to sections of shopping centers: EXIT D— LORD AND TAYLOR.

EXIT E—BAMBERGER'S. EXIT B2—NEWMAN CARPET. After that, there's the corridor again with the gas stations and stores and places-to-eat.

Suddenly there are trees alongside the road, and there are only occasional islands of merchandising. And at the towns—Hohokus, Upper Saddle River, Allendale, Ramsey—there are exits. The exits are made up of ramps and access roads and overpasses and underpasses where there once were acres of trees. And once off the highway, there are the towns. George Carr turned off Route 17 at the Hainesdale exit, remembering when none of the ugliness existed.

George found it difficult to believe that an eighth of a mile of road could have returned him from the ugliness to the green villages of his childhood. The countryside was a blanket of little towns, indistinguishable from each other except for the small signs that announced their boundary lines. They were marred here and there by new, squat little houses, painted pink or blue or yellow and looking like whores pretending they liked themselves. But there were the old houses, too, the ones he remembered. Great white clapboard houses that sat on their banked green lawns like matriarchs, proud of themselves and of the generations they had bred and sheltered.

And everywhere there were trees. It was as if each settling family had taken just enough land for its own needs and left the rest of the forest intact. There were evergreens, not long free of snow. There were maples and oaks and willows and weeping birches and copper beaches, all thick with the early, hopeful foliage of May. George tried to summon up a sense of homecoming.

He pulled into the semicircular gravel driveway and stopped the car. The sun had reached the peak of the gentle hill to the east and had just begun to burn off the morning mist. The white pillared façade of the house was bathed in rose-gold light, and the panes of the fan window above the Georgian door were tinted pink. It was a handsome, imposing house.

George went inside for the second time in twenty-nine years. As he had yesterday, he stood for a moment in the downstairs hall. The absolute sameness of it made it seem haunted. He wondered if present winds could blow away the lingering atmosphere of his childhood, or if his vivid memories would persist and make it impossible for him to live there.

He was also trying to achieve some realization that the house and everything in it were now his, not in the sense that it had been "my house" as a child, but that he alone owned it. He was counting on esthetic values to win the battle.

The furniture in the house, which had set his lifelong taste for elegance, was all good and English and antique. It had been arranged decades ago in hospitable, but not quite informal groups and had never since been changed. The fabrics were mostly bright prints, which gave the house an agreeable ambivalence. Where the floors showed at the edges of the thick Oriental rugs, they were stained almost black and glowed with a deep, rich patina of wax. George considered the irony of it: if it had been a stranger's house, a house he had never seen before, he could have moved in as naturally as a nesting bird.

He heard the sound of the moving van in the driveway. It was bringing his clothing, personal effects and the furniture from his New York apartment, which was to be stored in the attic. He explained this to the moving men, and they started unloading.

It was just past noon when the movers finished, and George thanked them, paid them and tipped them. He closed the door and turned back into the hall, which was now crowded with cartons, all securely double-taped and elaborately marked with George's coding, indicating the nature of the contents and their eventual destination. George was a thorough and meticulous man.

He went upstairs and into the master bedroom. It, too, was the same as he remembered it. The memory was remarkably indelible, considering the few times he had been there. It was exactly like Mrs. Robinson Cartwright: elegant and understated, yet with a strength which was almost palpable. He heard another car in the driveway, looked out the window and saw that it was the red Porsche.

He opened the door just as Gian-Carlo reached it, carrying his two suitcases. "Gian-Carlo," George said. "What kept you? I was beginning to worry."

"I am sorry," Gian-Carlo said. "So many things happened at the apartment . . . at the last minute . . ."

"Of course. I understand. Your sitting room and bedroom are back that way, just off the kitchen. Unpack and get yourself straightened out before we tackle this." He nodded toward the stacks of cartons.

Gian-Carlo smiled and started toward the kitchen. The doorbell rang. George said, "I'll get it, Gianni. You go on." He opened the door. Ethel Parker stood on the front step, holding before her with both hands like an offering, something in a brown paper bag.

"Hello," she said with a smile that seemed to have been embossed on her face. "My husband and I are your neighbors. I'm Ethel Parker."

"Hello," George said with a lack of astonishment that almost frightened Ethel. "I'm George Carr. Won't you come in?"

All morning Ethel had rehearsed saying, *Oh, no. I don't want to intrude*. Instead, she stepped across the threshold into the entrance hall. She resisted the impulse to look around and said, "I know what moving day's like, so I thought you might be able to put this casserole to use. It's macaroni and ham and cheese. Just pop it in the oven for twenty minutes. It's a great lunch."

"That's very kind of you," George said. He took the casserole from her and put it on a small table by the door. "Anything that saves time is a blessing."

"Oh, I know how it is," Ethel said sympathetically. She smiled at him expectantly for a moment. "Well . . . if there's anything I can do, just let me know."

14

"I will. And I'm really grateful for the casserole."

"Don't mention it."

George opened the door for her and she left. As he closed the door, he thought to himself, *Oh, what the hell. I may as well start right away.* He opened the door again.

"Mrs. Parker," he called to Ethel, who was no more than five feet from the door. She turned back to him. "I have an idea. Why don't you stay and have lunch with me?"

"Oh, you needn't take the time," Ethel said.

"I'd enjoy it. Please. I'll have Gian-Carlo put the casserole in the oven, and we'll have a drink while we wait."

"Well . . . my kids are at school and . . ." She shrugged ungraciously and happily and went back into the house.

George picked up the casserole and said, "If you'll wait just a minute, I'll take this into the kitchen. Excuse me."

As soon as George had gone, Ethel looked around her like a goldfish in a new aquarium. She was debating whether to take a few steps up the stairs when George came back, carrying a thermos bucket.

"Now, let's have our drink," he said, inviting Ethel into the drawing room with a gesture.

"What a beautiful house!" Ethel said on the way.

"Thank you," George said. "Even though I had nothing to do with it."

They went down the three steps into the drawing room. It was predominantly green and yellow and was filled with sunlight.

"Why don't you sit there, it's very comfortable," George said, indicating a wing chair near the fireplace.

"Thank you," Ethel said.

"What would you like? I think the bar's well-stocked," he said, opening the doors of an armoire. "I'm having a martini, but if that's too strong for you for lunch, I can make a daiquiri or a . . ."

"Is a Manhattan too much trouble?"

15

"Not at all." He made the drinks quickly and efficiently and took the Manhattan to Ethel. Then he sat on the green velvet settee opposite her. He lifted his glass and said, "Cheers."

Ethel lifted her glass and said, "Welcome." They drank.

"I don't know much about present Hainesdale society," George said. "What should we be, Mrs. Parker and Mr. Carr or Ethel and George?"

"Oh, Ethel and George, certainly!" Ethel said, pointing at him with her glass. "We're very informal."

"Good. Which house is yours?"

"Over there," she said, pointing toward the front of the house. "The split-level gray one. I'm allowed to say it because all the neighbors admit it. It's the one with the prettiest grounds. Except this one, of course."

"Including this one, I think. It doesn't seem to me that too much has been done about the grounds here."

"Oh, Mrs. Cartwright had a gardener every day. Three times a week in the winter."

"But not for the last two months."

"Well, no, not since she . . . died. No."

There was a knock at the open double doors of the drawing room. Ethel turned with a look of slight astonishment to see Gian-Carlo standing in the doorway. The astonishment and its expression grew. Gian-Carlo, even without his name, was obviously Italian. His skin was the color of sunlight and olives. His hair was black and was cut so that the waves, instead of cresting, lay in crescent-shaped curls, thick all the way to the collar of his white cotton jacket. His eyes were large and brown, and his wide mouth was a mass of curves. Ethel's immediate impression—at least the only one she allowed herself—was that he was probably twenty years old.

"Excuse me, sir," Gian-Carlo said. "Is there anything I can do?"

"How's the casserole, Gian-Carlo?" George asked.

"In the oven, sir."

"Is three hundred and twenty-five degrees okay, Ethel? We can take our time."

"Perfect," Ethel said, tearing her eyes from Gian-Carlo.

"Did you find some lettuce?" George asked Gian-Carlo.

"Yesterday I ordered some things by telephone from a near market. Lettuce was one thing and arugala."

"Beautiful," George said. "I'll ring when we're ready. I think there's a call bell in here. If there isn't, I'll come and get you." Gian-Carlo left them. "Gian-Carlo's marvelous," George said, shaking his head. "I didn't tell him to order anything from the market. If he thinks of something that ought to be done, he just goes ahead and does it."

"Marvelous is right!" Ethel said. "My maid Mildred wouldn't report a fire in the kitchen if you didn't tell her to."

George laughed. Then he said, "I've been told there are only three other houses on what used to be the estate."

"Yes. There's ours," she said, pointing again toward the east, "and the Radnors'," pointing north, "and the Jablonskis' " pointing northeast. "Oh, you'll love Cynthia! Cynthia Radnor. I know you will. You'll like Peg, too."

"We're all very close, aren't we?" George said. "I mean, you can see the other houses from the one you're in."

"Yes, you can. Oh, we're close, all right."

"I've just had another idea. After all, we are all going to be neighbors. Why don't I take the plunge? Do you think Mrs. Radnor and Mrs. . . . ."

"Jablonski."

". . . Mrs. Jablonski would think it were . . . well, forward if I asked them to join us? The casserole's plenty for four."

"No. I guess they wouldn't," Ethel said.

"Do you think they'd be able to come over . . . on such short notice?"

"Oh, yes," Ethel said excitedly. "Cynthia's boy is at school, and Peg's sister Helen helps out every day. They'd come." Ethel had a very satisfying image of her friends entering the Cartwright house and finding her already comfortably ensconced in the wing chair.

George got up and went to the phone across the room. "I'd give odds you know the numbers."

"Three seven two, one o eight one. That's Cynthia."

George dialed and waited. "Is this Mrs. Radnor? . . . This is George Carr, your new neighbor. I hope you'll forgive my forwardness, but the plain fact of the matter is that Mrs. Parker—Ethel—kindly brought me a casserole for my lunch, and we've decided we might as well get to know each other all at once. Could you come over reasonably soon for a drink and some lunch? . . . Yes, now. I know it seems. . . I'm delighted . . . Don't even think about it. It's just a drink and a bite to eat. The house is full of unpacked cardboard boxes. It couldn't be more informal . . . Wonderful. Goodbye."

George hung up and looked at Ethel. She said, "Three seven two, four four two three."

"Mrs. Jablonski?" George said when the call was completed. "My name is George Carr. I just moved into the Cartwright house . . . Yes. I was wondering if you'd be free to come over for lunch. I know it seems odd, but Ethel Parker is here and Mrs. Radnor is coming, too. I thought we might all get to know each other . . . No, it's strictly come-as-you-are. It just kind of happened . . . Good . . . We'll see you in a few minutes, then. Goodbye." He hung up and turned to Ethel again. "Well. They're both coming."

"Yes. I knew they would."

Cynthia and Peg saw each other from a distance as each of them stepped over the perimeter of the Cartwright lawn. Aside from conducting a title search, there was no way of knowing where one neighbor's lawn began and another's ended, but there was a tacit recognition of the extent of Mrs. Cartwright's property. They all knew, for

18

example, when a roqueted croquet ball had passed the line onto Mrs. Cartwright's lawn, or when one of the younger children strayed across the boundary. Now Cynthia and Peg crossed that lawn, waving to each other as they drew closer together. Neither of them quite said it, but they were acutely aware that they were there by invitation.

Cynthia said, "Hi, Peg. Isn't this weird?"

"Yeah. The first day and all. But leave it to Ethel to start something."

They reached the door and rang. The house was so well and thickly constructed that they couldn't hear the doorbell ring inside. After a moment, Gian-Carlo opened the door. "Good afternoon," he said.

Peg looked startled and Cynthia said, "Mr. Carr expects us." She stepped inside. "It's Mrs. Radnor and Mrs. Jablonski."

Cynthia thought they might have to wait while they were announced, but Gian-Carlo said, "Mr. Carr is in the drawing room. It's this way, please."

As they walked down the three steps, George was already on his feet, crossing the room to meet them. "It's really very good of you to come on such short notice. You're Mrs. Radnor, and you're Mrs. Jablonski."

Cynthia extended her hand and George took it in the compromise grip that is somewhere between hand-kissing and hand-shaking. "It's good of *you* to ask us . . . and on the first day."

"Hello," Peg said.

"I'm delighted to meet you both. Sit down and I'll get you a drink. What would you like?"

"The bar's well-stocked," Ethel said.

"Ethel," Cynthia said, "it was so thoughtful of you to bring lunch to Mr. Carr."

"Wasn't it?" George said. "Oh, incidentally, Ethel and I have decided to be on a first-name basis. I much prefer it if it's all right with you."

"Of course," Cynthia said.

19

"Everybody calls me Peg," Peg said.

"About the drinks," George said.

"Would a martini be any trouble?" Cynthia asked.

"It would simply be *another* martini. I'm already having one. Peg?"

"Same," she said. She didn't want a martini, but she knew how much less trouble it was when all the kids had the same thing for lunch.

George made and served the drinks and returned to the settee. He got up again immediately, saying, "I forgot to tell Gian-Carlo about lunch. Now, where is that call bell? Maybe I can find it by instinct." He closed his eyes for a moment, then opened them and said, "It's over there."

He walked across the room and pressed the small pearl button imbedded in the wall. "But does it still work?"

They waited and in a moment Gian-Carlo appeared in the doorway. "Yes, sir?" he said.

"It works," George said. "That's a good sign. Gian-Carlo, we'll be four for lunch instead of two." He grinned and said, "I thought you'd like to know."

Gian-Carlo smiled an absolute sunrise of a smile and said, "Thank you, sir." He bowed slightly and went away.

"George," Cynthia said. "You must have a quick mind. It's your first day in the house, and you seem to know it quite well."

The words of explanation were already forming in George's mind when he realized that these women knew nothing about his situation and must have been speculating for a long time. "I was *born* in this house," he said. "Janet Cartwright was my aunt, actually my mother's aunt. I didn't buy the house. Aunt Janet left it to me."

There was a moment of silence before Cynthia said, "I admit we were wondering."

"That was stupid of me. I just assumed that you . . . Anyway, I lived here till I was fifteen."

"And I thought *we* were welcoming *you*," Ethel said.

"In a way we are," Cynthia said. "But we're welcoming you home."

"We didn't know old Mrs. Cartwright had any relatives," Peg said. "Nobody ever came to visit or anything."

"No," George said. "I'm the last of the family. That casserole must be ready." He got up and went to the call bell again.

Lunch was served in the dining room, which, like the rest of the house, had a cozy formality. The surface of the mahogany dining table glowed in response to the faintest light. It was set with white bone china, crystal wine glasses and the heavy family silver, which was, fortunately for George, monogrammed with a "C." Gian-Carlo served lunch—the casserole, French bread and a green salad—anonymously and with flourishes. George asked about the ladies' husbands and children and houses, which seemed entirely proper. The ladies asked George virtually nothing, which, in some strange way, also seemed entirely proper. They were all willing, if not content, to let the story of George's life unroll in its own way and its own time, just as they would have enjoyed a popular novel at the author's chosen pace. Gian-Carlo brought them strawberries in wine for dessert. They went back to the drawing room for coffee.

They talked for twenty minutes more about things which only superficially concerned them. Then, looking at her watch, Peg said, "My God, I've got to get home!"

"I guess we all have," Cynthia said. She got up. "George, it was a lovely lunch. I think better impromptu this way than if you'd planned it. Anyway, I hope it proved how welcome you are."

George was standing now, too. "I'll tell you the truth. I feel better now that I've met you all."

"Oh, come on!" Ethel said. "We were just as scared of you as you were of us."

Cynthia looked at Ethel and smiled, and they went up the steps from the drawing room into the front hall.

Cynthia said to George, "You know, you've only met

half of us. You haven't met the boys. Herb and I are having the Parkers and the Jablonskis to dinner on Friday night. Would you come?"

"On Friday?" George said. "I'd be delighted."

"Wonderful," Cynthia said. "Seven o'clock. You know which house?"

"Yes. Ethel explained it to me. Thank you."

"Well, we'll see you on Friday then," Cynthia said.

George opened the door, and with appropriate expressions of thanks and goodbye, the ladies left. Gian-Carlo came into the hall from the kitchen.

George said, "I think it'll be all right, Gianni."

"No," Gian-Carlo answered, shaking his head. *"Mai."*

The geographical location of the ladies' houses dictated that they had only a moment together before their paths separated.

"Well," Ethel said, as if it were a statement.

"Well what?" Peg asked.

"I thought he was charming," Ethel said.

"Yes, I guess he was," Peg said. "And how about him being Mrs. Cartwright's nephew?"

"We should have guessed, really," Cynthia said. "If they can help it, people don't let houses like that get out of the family."

"What did you think of him?" Ethel asked Cynthia.

"What you thought. He's charming."

"I wonder if he has a family," Peg said.

"I suppose eventually he'll volunteer the information," Cynthia said.

"And that Gian-Carlo!" Ethel said.

"Talk to you later," Peg said as she moved away toward her house. Ethel and Cynthia smiled, and they parted.

George and Gian-Carlo spent the rest of the afternoon unpacking cardboard boxes and putting their contents away. Of his own things, George used only what he was very fond of: an antique student lamp, his leather desk set, a small campaign chest, a number of art objects collected in traveling. Their greatest difficulty was storage space. There was plenty of it, but it was filled with the earthly possessions of generations of departed Cartwrights. Just after six o'clock, Gian-Carlo came downstairs with an empty box and found George standing in the hall looking at the remaining cartons.

"We haven't even made a dent, Gianni," George said.

"Made a dent?" Gianni said.

"It's an expression that means we haven't got very much of the job done."

"Oh. We have worked hard."

"You bet your ass we have. To hell with it. Let's have something simple for dinner. We can eat in the kitchen and then get some sleep. Christ, we've been up since dawn! I'm too old for this kind of thing. I should have hired a mover who does all this for you."

"Maybe I could 'make a dent' alone."

"No, no. You've worked hard enough."

"I know you like to have things finished."

"Like a fussy old lady, huh?" Gian-Carlo smiled at him. "You stop making fun of me. If you think I'm bad, you should have known Aunt Janet. I'm going to have a drink." He started down the hall, then turned back. "Oh, I put booze in the kitchen for you. Did you find it?"

"Yes. Thank you."

George took his martini upstairs. He had chosen a bedroom which hadn't been occupied when he had lived in the house. He didn't even know the name of its last occupant. His own previous bedroom was on the third floor. George rarely allowed sentimentality to inconvenience him.

He showered, shaved and changed and went downstairs to watch the evening news on television. At eight o'clock, he and Gian-Carlo had chopped steak and a salad in the kitchen. Then they retired, George to his anonymous room upstairs, Gian-Carlo to his small suite off the kitchen.

George was awakened by the sound of a car pulling into

23

the driveway. He switched on the bedlight and saw that it was two-thirty. By the time he had put on a robe and gone downstairs, Gian-Carlo was coming into the hall. The doorbell rang, and George opened the door.

"Michael!" he said. "What's happened?"

"They canceled the tour," Michael said and shrugged.

"Oh, Christ, I'm sorry. Come in. Come in."

Michael came into the hall, put down his flight bag and he and George embraced briefly. Michael reached out and tousled Gian-Carlo's hair. "How are you, Gianni?"

"I am fine. The new house is very beautiful."

"If those two Chippendale side chairs are an example, it certainly is," Michael said.

"You have more luggage?"

"Don't bother till morning, Gianni. I have everything I need here in the flight bag."

"Michael," George said patiently, "don't leave it in the car all night."

"Oh. You're right." He handed the car keys to Gian-Carlo and said, "Would you mind, Gianni? They're in the trunk."

"Are you hungry?" George asked.

"No, just tired. But I'd like a drink."

"Come on," George said.

Michael looked around the drawing room for a moment. "Mrs. Cartwright or somebody had very good taste."

"Oh, that was Aunt Janet," George assured him. "*That* she had." He took a large brandy to Michael and had a small one himself. "Sit down and tell me what happened."

"It's very simple. After eight weeks of touring with practically no business, they realized there wasn't going to be any business. The play barely made it on Broadway, and people in the provinces just didn't want to see it. Everybody in the company hated everybody else. It was a nightmare. So this afternoon they announced that when we closed our split-week in New Haven tonight, we wouldn't be going on. I think everybody stifled an impulse to applaud."

"It's too bad."

"I really don't care, George. It was a rotten play, and I'd really rather be working on the novel. This way I'll just get started earlier."

"Champing at the bit, are you?"

"Yes."

"But why didn't you call?"

"Because I lost the phone number," Michael said exasperatedly. "I remembered the address, but couldn't remember the number. You know it's unlisted, and so was our old one, so you don't get the new one when you dial the old one. I called a dozen people in New York I thought might have it. They weren't home. The line was busy. No, they didn't have it. So finally tonight when we closed, I couldn't stand another minute in that town or that company. I said, Fuck it, and got in the car. And here I am."

George sighed and said quietly, "Why didn't you send a wire?"

Michael looked at him blankly. He smiled and said, "You know ... I really didn't think of that."

"That's my boy," George said.

Gian-Carlo came to the drawing room doorway and said, "Can I get you anything?"

"No, thanks, Gianni. Michael isn't hungry. Go on back to bed."

"Good night," Gianni said. "Welcome home, Michael."

"Thank you, Gianni. Good night."

"Oh, Christ!" George said when Gian-Carlo had gone. "I just thought of something. I accepted a dinner invitation for Friday night."

"What's the matter? I'm not good enough to go along?"

"It's with the neighbors."

"I'm not good enough to go along."

"I'll call tomorrow and . . ."

"George, no sweat. They don't even know I'm here."

"By eight o'clock tomorrow morning, they'll see the car and know *somebody's* here."

25

"I don't *want* to go."

"Oh? Michael, don't do your dumb blonde role and tell me you forgot or misunderstood. We agreed when we decided to move out here that we'd have to have . . . ought to have some kind of social intercourse with the neighbors."

"What if I don't like them?"

"Find out."

"I mean, if we took a house at Fire Island Pines, and we didn't like the guys next door, we wouldn't see them. We wouldn't have to see them."

"That's entirely different, and you know it. We're not spending a summer here; we're going to live here."

"George, we came out here so that I could have the peace and quiet to work on the book, not to socialize."

"Nonsense. You've never written a word after five o'clock in the evening."

Michael took out a cigarette and without lighting it, as if the idea had come to him more quickly than he had expected, he said, "It's the way it happened that's wrong, George."

"You don't know how it happened."

"It's obvious. You met the ladies of the neighborhood, and . . ."

"They were here to lunch."

"Well! They strike like lightning. Anyway, you didn't tell them anything. There was no need to. You didn't know I was going to be here. They asked you to dinner, and you accepted."

"And now I call and cancel a day in advance because my friend has arrived unexpectedly. And they say, 'Bring him.'"

"Because they feel they can't say anything else. Look, George, if they'd come over here today and met us both and said, 'You dear, sweet boys must come to dinner,' all right. That's their problem. But this way, they invite the intriguing new bachelor—and I'll bet you didn't even tell them that much—and he arrives with his fag lover. I

26

don't want it to start that way. On the other hand, if they met you, they already know, don't they?"

Michael smiled, but George did not smile back. It was not that he was in any way insulted by the joke, but that Michael was still reneging on their agreement.

"Try to remember, Michael. Try to remember all the things we said before we made the decision. We gave up the sandy homosexual communes years ago. Our circle of close friends is small. They all have more than one home, and they travel a great deal, as we do. We are infrequently all in the same place at the same time. We're close enough here to New York to see our friends when they're there. But we agreed we could only live here if we were in reasonable harmony with the immediate neighbors. Well, Friday night is the beginning."

"But you're going to have to *explain* me."

"So what? You're my friend. You've come out here to write a novel. You're going to share the house with me. It's a hell of a lot simpler to explain you than it would be to explain why I came without you, now that you're here. We have to start somewhere."

"All right, all right." He lit the cigarette.

"Besides, you'll probably have a marvelous time performing."

"Probably bore them to death. And they'll bore me."

"You're never bored when you're performing."

"Neither is the audience."

"You see? Everybody's happy." They both laughed and George said, "Let's go to bed. The beds are all made up. Pick your room."

"You mind if I come up later? I want to say a proper good night to Gian-Carlo."

George shook his head and said, "You'll never change. See you tomorrow. Good night."

"Good night."

George went upstairs.

CHAPTER II

Tom Parker selected his new dark-blue suit with the double-breasted jacket and slightly belled trousers, a pale blue shirt and a blue rep tie. He tried it all out before the full-length mirror and was completely satisfied with the effect. He came downstairs for breakfast and hung the jacket in the guest closet. He had just set foot in the kitchen when Ethel said, "There's a car there, Tom!"

Tom shook his head in mock confusion and said, "There's a car *where,* dear?"

"At the Cartwright house," she said. "At George Carr's house."

"As I remember, there were two cars there yesterday."

"I mean *another* car."

"That makes three," he said and sat down at what Ethel called the breakfast nook. It consisted of a square pine table and two pine settees placed by the three kitchen windows. It was comfortable and quite attractive.

"But somebody must have arrived during the night."

"Maybe it was Amahl and the night visitors."

"Tom, be serious."

"About what? You know, it's too bad the old lady died. At least she stayed home. You have enough trouble keeping up with the comings and goings of the Radnors and the Jablonskis. Are you really going to try to keep up with the George Carr household, too?"

"You'd think I spied on them or something."

"Well, there aren't any field glasses or anything like that, but . . ."

"It's just natural curiosity."

Tom grinned and said, "Sure." He opened the newspaper that lay next to his orange juice. Ethel went to the stove and started Tom's eggs.

It was seven-fifteen and, except for Ethel's excitement at the mysterious car, everything was normal at the Parkers'. When the eggs were finished, Ethel would sit in the breakfast nook and have coffee while Tom ate, read the paper and talked to her at the same time. Then she would pour Tom's second cup of coffee and go upstairs to wake the children for school. Tom would finish his coffee, put on his suit jacket and call goodbye to Ethel and Jonathan and Susie. He would go outside and get the eight o'clock bus for New York, which stopped right in front of the house. Ethel would get the kids ready and at nine o'clock, when the school station wagon would pick them up, Mildred, the colored woman who helped with the housework, would arrive. But there was the mysterious car.

This morning Ethel did not finish her coffee. Instead, she went into the living room and telephoned the Jablonskis' number. "Hello," Peg said.

"Peg, it's Ethel. Did you see . . ."

"I saw it. I also heard it at two-thirty this morning when it pulled in. It woke me."

"Who do you suppose it is?"

"Now, how would I know, Ethel?"

"I just thought maybe you saw somebody, or . . ."

"With the baby . . . and Joe and three kids to get off in

30

the morning? I'm lucky if I have a chance to see myself in the mirror."

"Maybe there's a Mrs. Carr."

"Here comes Joe. He'll be yelling for his breakfast in a minute. I'll talk to you later."

"All right. Bye."

Peg hung up, and Joe said, "Who the hell was that?"

"Ethel."

"At seven-thirty? What'd she want?"

They went into the kitchen. "You know Ethel. A car pulled up at the Cartwright house in the middle of the night, and Ethel's not going to have a minute's peace until she finds out who was in it."

"You wouldn't say she was nosey or anything."

"It's just Ethel. Come on, breakfast's about ready."

In the huge kitchen, Joe sat at the big formica-topped table and Peg went to the stove. Joe's company, the Hainesdale Construction Co., Inc., had built the house, and, naturally, Joe himself had supervised the construction. As a professional favor, an architect with whom Joe often worked had designed the house specifically according to the Jablonskis' needs, present and future. It was a large, rambling ranch-type house, and it was a marvel of efficiency and modernity. It had cost Joe about half its actual worth. They could easily have afforded it even at full cost, but the Jablonskis were not people to live up to their means. They spent whatever they needed to spend to be what they considered comfortable. But their standards of comfort had been established during the Depression when they had both been young children in large, impoverished families, Joe's first-generation Polish and Peg's what she herself cheerfully described as shanty Irish. Now that they were more affluent than they had ever expected to be, thrift was still deeply ingrained in them. They knew the difference between satisfaction and self-indulgence.

For breakfast Joe always had juice, cereal, ham and eggs, toast and coffee. Owner or not, he spent most of his working time on the construction sites, and except for personal and nearly obsessive financial checks, he left the office work to others. He needed nourishment for both jobs.

"I don't know how Ethel ever gets any housework done," Peg was saying. "I mean, even with Mildred to help out. She's on that telephone about every other minute."

"Yeah, but Ethel's a good kid."

"Now, you know I'm fond of Ethel. I didn't mean it that way."

Joe grinned and said, "I bet you the Radnor's phone is ringing right now."

He was right, of course. Cynthia picked up the kitchen extension and said, "Hello."

"Cynthia, this is Ethel. Have you seen the extra car in the driveway?"

Ethel's inquisitiveness was accepted good-naturedly by all the others. "Yes, Ethel, I've seen it."

"I'm dying to know whose it is."

"I know you are, dear, but I'm afraid I can't help you."

"Are you going over there today?"

"Am I what?" Cynthia said incredulously.

"I just meant are you going over there for any reason."

"Of course I'm not. Ethel, it was very sweet of you to take the casserole over yesterday, but we don't want to make pests of ourselves, do we?"

"I wouldn't dream of it!" Ethel said.

"I'll call you later. I'm a little late with breakfast."

"Fine. Bye."

"Goodbye."

They both hung up, and it was at that moment that Ethel remembered that her casserole dish was still in George Carr's kitchen.

Herb came into the kitchen and looked around. "I thought I heard you talking to David."

"It was the telephone."

"At this hour?"

"Yes. And when I'm behind schedule and you have an early meeting."

Herb went into the dining room. The Radnors never ate in the kitchen. "It could only have been Ethel."

"It was," Cynthia said, bringing a glass of orange juice to Herb.

"Don't bother with the egg," Herb said. "I really only want toast and coffee. My stomach's a little upset."

"Did you take something?"

"Yes. I took two brandies after dinner last night. That's what did it. Someday I'll learn that brandy and I are not friendly."

"I'll get you some Pepto . . ."

"No, no. It'll be all right."

"Are you sure?"

"Positive."

Cynthia went back into the kitchen, and David came downstairs and into the dining room. "Morning, Dad," he said. "Morning, Mother," he called toward the kitchen.

"I have a meeting, Dave," Herb said. "Do you want to go with me or wait and have your mother drive you?"

"I think I'll wait. I have some work to do before I leave."

He sat at the table. Cynthia came in and David said, "Can you take me to school, Mother? Dad's going early."

"Of course, dear." She put the toast rack before Herb and sat. David was already putting milk on his cereal.

"What on earth did Ethel want?" Herb asked.

"I suppose she wanted to play twenty questions about the extra car in George Carr's driveway."

"Oh, for God's sake!" Herb said. He took a piece of toast and turned his attention to the sheaf of papers by his plate.

David laughed and said, "Mrs. Parker ought to write a column for the *Ridgewood News*."

"All right, David," Cynthia said. "Let's not be rude."

"I wasn't being rude. She'd make one hell of a gossip columnist."

33

Cynthia and Herb had already lost the battle of the mild expletive. They had been reluctant about it at first, but they turned defeat into victory by being defensively proud of their progressiveness.

Herb chuckled and without looking up from his papers said, "Maybe you should go into the job placement field, Dave."

"You may both stop making fun of Ethel," Cynthia said.

"Mom, we're not making fun of her. We're just recognizing her qualifications."

Names were an issue in the Radnor family. Cynthia refused to use a diminutive of David and winced when anyone else did. Herb refused, except in moments of parental severity, to call his son David. Herb hated "Herbert," although it was essential to his public dignity. It had taken him three years to break Cynthia in to the use of the shorter form. While they were dating, Herb had thought it one of those touching, private, lovers' things to call Cynthia "Thia." She had endured as long as she could (until they were married), then insisted on a return to the original. David had gone directly from "Mama" to "Mother" for normal usage. "Mom" indicated a somewhat deeper level of emotion—humor, annoyance, conviviality. Any deeper emotion than these—anger, sadness, frustration—required "Mother" again. Herb was inalterably "Dad."

When Herb left at seven-forty-five, Cynthia saw him to the door and went back to the dining room to sit with David as he finished his breakfast. She liked these mornings that gave them an hour alone together. David was in every way precocious. When he was six years old, people began remarking that he was like a miniature adult. Now, at fifteen, there was an eerie whisper of maturity in everything he did. He was five feet, ten inches tall, wore his dark hair long and spoke more or less in teenage argot. But there was an air of completeness about him, a firmness of jaw and of purpose, a poise and certainty in behavior. His eyes were dark brown and always intense. He was more a handsome young man than a good-looking boy. His I.Q. was 130. He was the only sophomore on the high school basketball team. He had not an enemy in his class. With such advantages, his range of activities was wide and his schedule heavy. Cynthia, who adored him, seemed to see him less and less.

"What's on your agenda for the day?" she asked.

"Classes till four," he said. "Then a staff meeting of *The Clarion*. If there's time after that, Bobby Geary and I are going to try to finish the new arrangement for the group. But I don't think there'll be time, so I'll probably go over to Bobby's tonight and work on it."

"Quite a day."

"And tomorrow's worse. First day of exams."

"Oh? Shouldn't you be staying home tonight in that case?"

David smiled at her. "Come on, Mother, give me credit. You know I'm ready without cramming."

She smiled back. "Yes. I know you are."

"But I'm not ready for my first class this morning." He looked at his watch and got up from the table. "I just have time."

Cynthia watched him leave the dining room and stared into the emptiness he left. She felt a deep sadness. With David, her only son, the inevitable drawing away into adulthood had begun so early. There was no lack of closeness between them. David loved her and unashamedly expressed his love in many ways: with truly thoughtful, personal presents on holidays and birthdays, with frequent recountings of the private events of his life, with general and unfailing considerations. But filial dependence was almost totally gone. He rarely sought advice from either Herb or her. He made his own decisions, almost invariably right ones. Orphaned, David would have survived nicely. For these things, Cynthia was proud of him. Her pride shone like a patina over her invisible regret.

She finished her coffee and went into the kitchen and

glanced out toward the Cartwright house. There was no sign of life.

In fact, the Carr household was already astir. George Carr rose every morning, regardless of season or day of the week, at home or traveling, at seven A.M. Gian-Carlo did not appear until George had already begun making coffee.

"I am sorry, George," he said. "I slept over." His eyes were not quite open.

"Overslept," George said. "Up rather late, huh?" Gian-Carlo didn't answer, and when George turned to him, there was a wounded look in his eyes. "I was kidding, Gianni. Really. There's no jealousy among us. Each of us has his own relationship with the other. That's all. No sweat."

They had breakfast and went back to work on the cardboard cartons. George knew that Michael would sleep late and felt that he deserved to. George held the American attitude toward sleep: it should be indulged in for essential rejuvenation. But sleep outside its normal schedule was either earned or vaguely sinful. Whether he had been asleep or not, George's instinctive answer to the telephone question, "Did I wake you?" was always, "No, of course not," as if it were shameful to be caught sleeping. Michael could sleep anywhere at any time under almost any circumstances without a shadow of guilt. George envied him.

Today there was an advantage to Michael's sleeping late. George could get the whole business of the dinner party settled without having to repeat last night's discussion with him. At ten-fifteen, he called Cynthia.

After inquiries into each other's state of being, George said, "I'm afraid we're going to have to make some adjustment about Friday night." George would not play the game he had described to Michael. He would not open with the announcement that he could not come to dinner because a friend had arrived and wait for the inevitable invitation.

36

"I hope it's nothing that'll prevent your being here," Cynthia said.

"I hope not, too. It's just that my friend Michael Kaye has arrived unexpectedly, and I really couldn't leave him behind. If another guest is in any way inconvenient, I can take a rain check. But I know he'd love to come if it really isn't any trouble."

"As a matter of fact," Cynthia said unhesitatingly, "it would round out the party to an even number."

George wondered if she knew she had said it would make four couples instead of three and an extra man, or if she meant to say that. "Please be honest, Cynthia. I would understand completely if . . ."

"Don't be silly, George. One more for roast beef isn't going to make the slightest difference. And we have to meet each other's friends."

"Particularly in this case, since Michael will be sharing the house with me."

The pause was almost imperceptible. "Well, then, how can there be any question? He's a neighbor."

"You know, I feel at home already. You're very gracious."

"Nonsense. Just come, both of you."

"It really isn't inconvenient? Because . . ."

"George, stop it. You and . . ."

"Michael. Michael Kaye."

"You and Michael are expected. It'll be fun."

"Thank you, Cynthia."

"There's nothing to thank me for. See you on Friday at seven."

"Wonderful. Goodbye."

"Goodbye."

Gian-Carlo came into the drawing room as George hung up. He was carrying the casserole dish just as Ethel had carried it the day before. "I will take this back to the lady who brought it. Where does she live?"

George looked at him for so long a moment that Gian-Carlo was embarrassed. When the look of embarrassement began to turn to a look of annoyance, George said, "You are something else, Gianni. You want to take it back to her before she comes to get it. Are you protecting us from the local harpies?"

"Please tell me where the lady lives and her name."

"Gianni, they're going to come here, all of them. And we're going to go there. It has to be that way." He waited, but Gian-Carlo said nothing. He was staring into the casserole dish. "You can't do anything about it." He waited again for a long time. "You're a pain in the ass when you play dumb Italian boy." He waited again. "She's Mrs. Parker. It's the gray house, over there."

Without looking at George, Gian-Carlo turned away, left the house and crossed the lawn toward the Parkers'. He did not notice how lovely the morning was. The grass was still beaded with dew, and the trees were as still as the dead. Sounds—the bark of a dog, an automobile horn, the whir of a lawnmower—hung separately in the air. Gardens were beginning everywhere, and the sun touched everything. But Gian-Carlo saw none of it, because he was afraid—for George, for Michael and for himself.

Ethel was already headed for the front door, a cashmere cardigan over her shoulders, when Gian-Carlo rang. She hid her surprise behind a gorgeous smile.

"Good morning, Mrs. Parker. I am returning your dish. Mr. Carr asked me to thank you."

"I thank you for returning it."

Gian-Carlo smiled and turned away. Ethel closed the door and looked down at the casserole as if it were a naughty child. The phone rang and she answered. It was Cynthia.

"You know I'm not very good at gossip," she said, "but I wanted to ease your pain. I know who's at George Carr's."

Ethel was disappointed at not having found out first, but the prospect of finding out at all was too exciting for the disappointment to matter much. "Oh! Who is it? Tell me!"

"His name's Michael Kaye. He's going to share the house with George."

"He's going to share the house with George," Ethel said with precisely the same inflection.

"They're both coming to dinner tomorrow."

"Oh. Then we'll meet him." Her voice was toneless.

"Yes. I just thought you'd want to know."

"Of course. I'll call Peg," Ethel said as if it were her duty.

"All right. Goodbye."

Gian-Carlo was back at the house by the time this conversation ended. George and Michael were in the kitchen. Michael was making instant coffee, and George was sitting at the kitchen table, where the servants had eaten when he was a child.

"Good morning, Gianni," Michael said.

"Good morning," Gianni said cheerlessly.

"Well," George said, "how was Mrs. Parker?"

"She thanked me for returning the dish."

"And was she enraged that you robbed her of her excuse for a visit?"

Gianni picked up one of the cardboard boxes that had mistakenly been put into the kitchen. He held it before him and stared at George in an almost childishly belligerent way. "I have work. Excuse me."

When Gianni left the kitchen, Michael sat at the table with George and said, "Maybe Gianni's right. You know, oil and water."

"Please don't start again. Oh, we're both invited for Friday night."

"No grass growing under Uncle George's feet, is there?"

"Michael . . ."

"All right, all right. But don't forget, I know these people. I grew up with them Oh, I know how to make them like me. I'm not worried about that."

"You'll charm them within an inch of their lives."

"Until it occurs to them that we sleep together. Then we may have a problem. Not as big a problem as when

39

it occurs to them that we also sleep with Gian-Carlo, but a problem. And it will occur to them."

"Of course it will. I think they'll ignore it. They're not children, Michael."

"Ah, but they can be very childish. You're the only person I've ever known who didn't have a childish streak in him somewhere."

"Thank you. Anyway, that includes Gianni, and that's exactly what he's being."

"I suppose so. You don't think it's enough to make him leave, do you?"

"No, of course not."

"Doesn't want to leave Uncle George, huh? Daddy. Father figure."

"Something like that. I suspect you have rather a lot to do with it, too."

"You can hardly blame him. If I'd been hustling the streets of Rome since I was eleven, and you came along and said, 'Let me take you home with me and . . . and comfort you,' I think you'd be my father figure, too."

"Oh? I thought I was."

"Hah!"

"Come on, finish your coffee. You are not going to get out of helping unpack the boxes."

"Yes, Daddy."

"And that will be enough of that."

Herb greeted George and Michael at the door with genuine warmth. "Hello. I'm Herb Radnor." He extended his hand and said, "You're George Carr and you're Michael Kaye."

"Cynthia's been describing me," George said as he shook hands. "It's nice to meet you."

"Hello," Michael said.

George and Michael were wearing tweed jackets, George with a dotted silk ascot, Michael with a cowboy-tied scarf. Cynthia had called George and warned him about the informal attire.

"We're all so glad you could come," Herb said as he took them into the living room. "Drinks before anything else. What would you like?"

"A martini for me," George said.

"The same," Michael said.

"On the rocks?"

"I'm afraid not," George said. "It's so much easier on the rocks, I always feel I ought to apologize."

"It's no trouble at all. Both up?" Michael nodded. "Please sit down. Cynthia'll be in in a minute. Excuse me." He went into the dining room where he kept the liquor on a small side table. He was back very soon with the martinis.

George raised his glass and said, "Cheers." He sipped the drink and said, "Now I really feel at home. Gordon's gin."

"You have an extraordinary sense of taste," Herb said.

"Not really. If it were any other brand, I couldn't identify it. I just know when it *isn't* Gordon's."

Herb liked George immediately. He liked his open yet decorous manner. He liked the subtlety of the compliment about the gin. He liked his poise and assurance.

Cynthia came in from the kitchen, and George and Michael stood up to greet her.

"George," she said, extending her hand. "I'm so glad you could come."

"So are we," he said. "I want you to meet Michael Kaye."

"Hello," Cynthia said, extending her hand.

"Cynthia. For Mount Cynthus on the island of Delos, where there was a shrine to Apollo. It's one of my favorite names."

Cynthia seemed almost embarrassed. She smiled and said, "Thank you."

"I'm just showing off," Michael said. "The meanings and origins of names is a hobby of mine."

"That's very interesting," Cynthia said, suddenly relaxing again. "What's Herbert?"

41

"Ah, Herbert," Michael said. "Herbert, Herb, Bert, Bertie. Glory of the army." George noted with satisfaction that Michael was off and running. "Very noble name, Herbert. Very august."

"And very apt," Herb said. They all laughed. "What's Michael, by the way?"

"Michael is really a form of the Hebrew Micah. It means 'Who is like God.' Sometimes," he said, reading it as a question, "it's, 'Who is like God?' with a question mark, but I always do it the flattering way. You won't believe George, Georgie, Geordie."

"What is it?" Cynthia said.

"'Tiller of the soil,'" Michael said. "Tiller of the yacht, I might believe, but 'tiller of the *soil* . . .'"

"Wrong image," Cynthia said.

"Absolutely," Michael agreed.

The doorbell rang then and Herb answered it and brought the Parkers into the room. George was markedly relieved at seeing that Tom was wearing a scarf loosely pulled through a leather ring. When the introductions were made and Herb had begun making drinks, Cynthia said, "Come on, Michael. What about Ethel and Thomas?"

"*Thomas*?" Tom said. "What the hell is this 'Thomas' suddenly?"

"You'll see," Cynthia said. "Go on, Michael."

"You're embarrassing me," Michael said.

"Somehow I don't believe that," Cynthia told him.

Michael laughed and said, "All right. Ethel, Ethlind, Ethelinda, all Anglo-Saxon. They mean 'noble.'"

"Oh, that's my Ethel to a T," Tom said.

"I am noble," Ethel said. "I mean, my motives are noble."

"Your motives for what, dear?" Tom asked.

"For . . . everything."

"Oh," Tom said.

"Thomas, Tom, Tommy is, curiously enough, a Hebrew name," Michael went on. "And it means a twin."

"A twin I am not."

"Maybe it means in a spiritual sense," Herb said, handing Tom a martini.

"You mean maybe inside me I have a spiritual twin?"

"Something like that."

"Sounds like schizophrenia," Tom said. "Cheers."

The Jablonskis arrived, and the process was repeated. Cynthia asked Michael to "do" Margaret and Joseph.

"Margaret is a Greek name. Maybe the Greeks liked it, but nobody else seems to. I mean, aside from Margaret Mead, do you know anybody who's actually called Margaret? Listen to the nicknames: Greta, Mag, Madge, Maggie, Margie, Marjory, Meg, Meta, Peg, Peggy. If you're going to name somebody something, why not stick to it?"

"Oh, how I agree with you!" Cynthia said. "I've given up trying to get people to call David 'David.' "

"David, whom I call 'Dave,' is our son," Herb explained.

" 'David' is my all-time favorite name," Michael said. "For your sake, Cynthia, I'll skip the diminutives, but it's Hebrew and it means 'beloved.' "

"I didn't know that," Cynthia said.

"But it's certainly appropriate," Herb added.

"All right, so I dote on my only child. It's a mother's privilege."

Tom said, "It should be explained to George and Michael that David is fifteen, is bright, is an accomplished rock musician and composer, is the most popular boy in his class, and is handsome enough to knock dead any woman from the age of twelve to seventy. So Cynthia likes him. Surprise."

"He sounds formidable," George said.

"What does Margaret mean?" Peg asked.

"I'm sorry," Michael said. "We got sidetracked. Margaret means 'a pearl.' "

"Peg's a pearl," Joe said. "I've always said Peg's a pearl."

"And Joseph," Michael said. "Joseph is a very interest-

43

ing name. It's Hebrew, of course, and it means, 'He shall add.'"

"Right," Peg said. "He shall add his books every two days."

"I've also added four kids to us," Joe said.

"And I had nothing to do with it?" Peg said.

"You did your part."

"Thanks."

Joe explained to George and Michael. "I've got a construction business where I'm not in the office much, and, believe me, you've got to watch everybody. I don't mean they're trying to steal from you, but you've got to keep an eye on the books. Peg's always kidding me about it."

"You've got a thing about the books, Joe," Peg said. "What do you do?" she said, turning to Michael.

"Well, until two days ago, I was an actor."

"Really?" Ethel said, delightedly.

"We just closed a national tour in New Haven, 'unexpectedly' I think is the right word. The play was *Putting It All Together*."

"We saw that on Broadway," Tom said.

"When I wasn't in it," Michael said. "They hired me for the road. Life's like that."

"Oh, that's terrible," Cynthia said.

"Not really," Michael said. "I'm not a very good actor, so I don't care too much about it. I really want to write. Fiction. I had a couple of novels published years ago, and I never got over it. That's why George and I came out here, so I can write my novel."

"I'm going to have to go around the house in bedroom slippers again." George knew instantly that he should not have said it. It was too intimate, too like *their* domestic conversation. He hurried to cover the error. "I suspect that Michael is normally partially deaf, but when he's working on a book, he can hear a cat walking in Los Angeles. It disturbs his concentration."

"That's a slight exaggeration," Michael said, falling into the trap. "You're just noisy around the house."

George and Michael could no more have avoided talking like a married couple than the other pairs in the room. They had lived together in the intimacies of marriage—the first enthusiasms, the evolution of habits, the infidelities, the mellow maturity—for eighteen years. They knew each other better than any two mere male friends could know each other, and hiding the knowledge would have required a minute-by-minute effort. But the oddity of such conversation was as unmistakable as were its implications.

"I understand you grew up here, George," Herb said.

"Right across the lawn."

"Did you go through our glorious public school system?"

"No, I didn't. I went to the Whitmore School till I was fifteen. Then military academy. Then Princeton. Then the market."

"Oh, you're in the market?" Tom said.

"Not any more," George said, clearly indicating his lack of regret. "I had nine long years of it. When my mother died, twelve years ago, it became unnecessary for me to go on with it. I'm afraid I just quit."

"Good for you!" Tom said.

George smiled and said, "I don't know that it was very admirable. Oh, if I wrote or painted or something like that, I'm sure I would have gone on doing it. But when I found myself with enough money to live on for the rest of my life, it seemed an awful waste to stay chained to a broker's desk." There was nothing pretentious or boastful in George's saying it. It was simply part of the necessary exchange of social information.

"It would have been criminal," Cynthia added.

"It would have been goddamn crazy," Joe said. "But I can't imagine what it would be like not to do *something*."

"It's very pleasant, really," George said. Everyone laughed.

"Wait till David finds out we have a writer on the premises," Herb said.

"Does he want to write?" Michael asked.

"He's not sure. His trouble is—and I'm neither kidding nor bragging—his trouble is he's too versatile. He does too many things well. He has too many choices. But writing is certainly one of them."

Tom said, "Our Jonathan is ten, and the only things he does well is anything you really don't want him to do." They laughed again.

"How many do you have?" George asked.

"Two," Ethel said. "There's Jonathan and Susie. She's eight."

"We have four," Peg said. "Eddy, Chrisie, Peggy and Joey, Jr. Six, eight, ten and twelve."

The congeniality continued to escalate throughout the evening. Herb had been circulating constantly, not waiting to make another round of drinks, but filling each glass as it became empty. They drank three bottles of Beaujolais with the roast beef, and even Mrs. Turner couldn't help laughing with them as she served dinner.

George and Michael were so much an integral part of it that when Tom complained that their newspaper boy hadn't thrown the paper within ten feet of the house for a year, Michael was able to say, "Sounds like Jonathan."

"Oh, no!" Tom said. "Jonathan would leave it on the curb." There was more of the warm, relaxed laughter.

By the time they came back into the living room for coffee and after-dinner drinks, they had all had a good deal to drink. No one was drunk, but certainly no one was entirely sober. They told risqué jokes, a pastime at which Michael excelled, and the laughter became more frequent and almost raucous. They were almost able to touch each other physically in fellowship.

The others protested loudly at George's first suggestion that he and Michael leave—it was twelve-thirty—and George agreed to one more drink. Socially George was both sensitive and subtle. He knew that on this first night, he and Michael should go home first and leave the other

46

three couples together. Michael had no such sensitivity. He would stay as long as George was willing to stay, and, had it not been the first night, much longer than that.

At one o'clock, George went into the kitchen to collect Michael, who was talking animatedly with Herb and Joe.

"Aw, come on, George," Joe said. "One more for the road."

"Tomorrow's Saturday," Herb said.

"Shit, Herb," Joe said, "every day's Saturday for George. Come on."

"I'm gonna have one little half drink, George," Michael said.

"All right, I'll have a *half* drink, too."

"Way to go," Joe said. "Come on. I'll make 'em."

As Joe and Michael went into the dining room, George said to Herb, "If you knew the things still to be done to my house . . ."

"That's right. It is your house now, isn't it? Happy about it?"

"I don't know, Herb. A lot of memories."

"Pleasant?"

"Some. Some not. I keep forgetting, you didn't know Aunt Janet."

"I keep getting the feeling you didn't like her."

"Aunt Janet was above being liked or disliked. You were either assimilated by her or . . . or you weren't assimilated by her."

"And you decided not to be."

"I don't think I had a choice. Anyway, I think you and Cynthia for being such good neighbors. Maybe that'll make the difference."

"I truly hope it does."

Joe came into the kitchen with a full cognac for George and said, "Come on. The girls want us in the living room. Women's lib or something."

They went back to the living room and talked for another fifteen minutes, until George announced with a soft finality that he and Michael were leaving. After another ten minutes of goodbyes, they left. The last sound of the departure ceremony was Tom's voice ringing out through the darkness and the grassy smells of spring: "Take a Bromo before you go to bed!" as George and Michael crossed the lawn.

It was late for them to be up and still drinking, but the neighbors settled down for a nightcap, like generals in a war room appraising a new tactical development. Tom sighed and said, "Well, if we have to have fags for neighbors, I'm glad they're decent ones."

"Tom!" Ethel said in astonishment and horror.

"What?"

"How can you say such a thing?"

Ethel was, of course, the only one to whom the possibility had not occurred. For each of the other five, the single realization had a different meaning, a different significance. Those differences seemed to be explained by the conversation, but they were not.

"Because it's true. I'm not insulting them."

"You mean . . . you think . . . they're . . . homosexuals? That they sleep . . ." She hunched her shoulders and shook her head, unable to go on.

"Ethel, they're forty. They're bachelors. They live together. They're a little too . . . sophisticated. They're fags, honey."

"It doesn't bother you?" Joe asked Tom in a flat, academic way.

"No. Who cares?" Tom said. "As long as they don't do it in the streets and frighten the horses."

"Tom! Stop it!" Ethel said.

"Ethel," Tom said patiently, "if a new couple moved into the . . . I mean a married couple . . . if a married man and woman moved into the neighborhood and came to dinner, and after they left somebody said, 'I bet she's a cold fish in bed,' you'd giggle your head off. What's the difference? A new couple *has* moved into the neighborhood, and we're just discussing their sex life. So what?"

"Well, it bothers me," Joe said.

"Why?" Tom asked.

"It . . . just bothers me." Then louder, "What the hell do you mean, 'Why?' "

"There's been homosexuality, forbidden or otherwise, in almost every recorded civilization," Herb said rather absently.

"That's useful to know," Tom said sarcastically.

"I just meant that it isn't a new problem."

"Well, it's a new problem to me," Joe said.

"Yes," Peg agreed. "And I'm not sure I know what to do about it."

"Are you saying you didn't like them?" Cynthia said challengingly.

Peg hesitated, then said, "No. I admit it. I liked 'em both. I enjoyed them."

"You *admit* it? That's generous of you, Peg," Tom said.

"What are you? Defending 'em?" Joe asked.

"I'm not defending anybody or anything. For Christ's sake, Joe, they're here. They seem like nice enough guys. What the hell?"

Although none of them quite realized it, they were in parliamentary debate to decide whether or not to accept George and Michael. There would be no final vote, but there would be tacit agreement to accept or reject them. And there would be no stalking out of the assembly when the silent decision was reached. This thing had to be unanimous. Dissenters were required to follow the majority. The unspoken rules by which they lived were far more binding than the rules of their explicit social code.

"Don't get me wrong, Tom," Joe said in boozey earnestness. "I don't condemn anybody for bein' what they are. Jews are born Jews, whites are born white, and colored are born black. But that doesn't have anything to do with decidin' to have sex a certain way."

"Don't be too sure it isn't the same thing," Herb said. "Nobody knows for certain whether homosexuals are born or made."

"Why don't we stop talking about it?" Ethel said. Her usually piping voice was shrill.

"That's not a hell of a good idea," Peg said. "But I don't like the talk either."

"I don't see what there is to talk about," Herb said. "We have two new neighbors, two men who live together. They came to dinner and couldn't have been nicer. They were interesting, they were funny, they have damn good manners. Where they fit, they'll be invited. Where they don't, they won't."

"For instance?" Joe asked.

"Well, I don't think I'd ask them to a church supper." Herb raised an eyebrow and grinned. When he had too much to drink, Herb often became sly and wore a continual expression of knowing something no one else did.

"All I can say is they're welcome in our house," Tom said. He did not look at Ethel, and she did not look at him.

"Obviously they're welcome here, or we wouldn't have asked them," Cynthia said.

"As long as they stay in line, sure," Joe said.

"You know, maybe I'm compensating," Tom said, leaning back in his chair and staring at the ceiling as he often did in the drama of drunkenness. He snapped his head downward and looked into the faces of the others, pausing for a moment at each one. He only did this when he was absolutely sincere, and he was forgiven for the performance. "I've fired guys for being queer. I didn't want to, but it's agency policy. I was *told* to. But I know guys still working in the agency are queer as a three-dollar bill. What am I supposed to do, squeal on 'em?"

"How could you possibly *know?*" Ethel asked.

"You can tell," Joe told her. "I can spot one a mile away."

Herb giggled and said, "That's funny. I mean, how do you know you haven't seen somebody who's a fag, and you didn't know it?"

"I've heard it takes one to know one," Cynthia said.

Joe was leaning forward in his chair, his elbows on his knees, his drink in both hands. He looked up at Cynthia, and the muscles of his neck tightened into columns of flesh. For an instant his eyes were narrowed in anger. He said, "Don't screw around about that, Cynthia."

"Remember the story about the two women who meet in a bar?" Tom said. "First one said, 'What'd you do to your hair?' Second one said, 'Nothin', why?' 'Looks like a wig,' first one says. 'It is a wig,' second one says. 'You'd never know!' Like the fags. How do you know if you see one and don't know it?"

"*I* can tell," Joe insisted.

"By their high-heel pumps, huh, Joe?" Tom asked.

Through Tom's laughter, Peg said, "I wonder if they do that?"

"Do what?" Ethel asked.

"I wonder if they wear women's dresses around the house like I hear some of them do."

Herb shook his head and said, "Really, Peg."

"Can you see George in a wig and a slinky satin evening dress?" Tom said.

"He'd be the chiffon type," Cynthia added, and they all laughed. "Now, Michael would be the Jinx Falkenberg type—white halter top and tennis shorts . . . with an overskirt, of course."

"I think you're all terrible," Ethel said.

"Oh, come on, Ethel," Cynthia said. "It's all in fun."

"Well, I don't think it's funny."

"Hey," Peg said, "what about that . . . uh, Gian-Carlo? What'd he wear?"

"A Pucci, of course," Cynthia said, and they all laughed again, except Joe, who didn't understand the joke.

"Do you think he's one, too? Joe asked.

"Wait'll you see him in his Pucci, and you'll know," Tom said. "Joe, would he be working for them if he weren't?"

"I guess not."

"Tom, it's late. We ought to go home," Ethel said.

"Okay, honey." He drained his glass and stood up.

"It was a wonderful dinner, Cynthia," Ethel said.

"Great," Tom said. "We thank you both."

Tom went to the window and looked out toward the big house. "Is that the ghost of Mrs. Cartwright I see, or is it George in drag?"

"Oh, you don't see anybody!" Ethel said.

"No, but there are lights on downstairs."

"What do you suppose they're doing up so late?" Ethel asked. "They went home so long ago."

"Probably the same thing we were doing," Cynthia said, looking out the window across the lawn. "And I'd give anything in the world to be a fly on the wall."

They were doing exactly that. When they reached their own front door, Michael had said, "Georgie, one of my greatest charms is my ability to admit it when I'm wrong. I had a very good time. They're nice people."

"They are, aren't they?"

"Of course, they wouldn't do for every day, but . . ."

George grinned and said, "You're incorrigible."

As George opened the door and they went inside, Michael said, "Seriously, I liked them, and I think they liked us. But I think the reservations are probably mutual. I don't think they'd want us all the time any more than we'd want them. But as long as we still have our own friends, and they have their own thing, it just might work."

"That sounds something like what I've been trying to tell you."

Michael looked down the hall and said, "Hey, look. There's a light under the kitchen door. Gianni must still be up. Let's go and tell him about tonight."

"What makes you think he wants to hear?"

"I don't. Let's tell him anyway."

Gianni was sitting at the kitchen table, shining his four pairs of shoes. They were lined up precisely on the table before him as if awaiting the order to march. He was wearing just a pair of lime green velour trousers, and the muscles of his bare torso were taut with effort. He did not look up when George and Michael came in. His petulance was their punishment for wooing the neighbors, for he knew that even in Rome, where the attitude of "sex is sex" was said to prevail, where male prostitution in the young was said to be morally justified by poverty and was absolvable by sacrament, the stigma of the *finocchio* remained. He had borne it and suffered the loneliness it brought.

"Hello," Michael said.

Without looking up, Gianni said, "Good evening."

Michael and George exchanged glances. Gianni was always formal with them when he was in any way upset. "We had a good time."

"That's good." He brushed more vigorously.

"Want to hear about it?" George asked. Gianni often waited up for them and, provided they were reasonably sober, were not fighting and had come home alone, they would all sit together and have a drink as Gianni listened happily to the details of a party or a play. Privately they each thought it was childish, and each of them thoroughly enjoyed it.

"No, thank you," Gianni said.

"Come on, Gianni," Michael said. "We'll have a brandy, and we'll tell you all about the dinner party. Some of it's funny. Come on."

"No, thank you. I am tired." He put down a shoe and picked up another.

"Don't be mad," Michael said.

"I am not mad."

"Well, don't be upset or whatever you are. Come on in with us and have a drink and talk."

"I don't want to."

"Okay, smart-ass. We're going into the drawing room, and we'd like some drinks poured if you don't mind." He went to the kitchen doorway, stopped and turned to Gianni. "Come on."

Gianni stared at him for a moment with a hard, unreadable look in his eyes. "Yes. In a minute."

Michael left. George looked at Gianni for a moment, but Gianni did not return the look. George followed Michael into the drawing room. Michael was slouched carelessly in an armchair.

"That wasn't very nice," George said.

"What?" Michael said, as if in surprise. "Oh, for Christ's sake, George! He wants to be here just as much as we want him to. He just wants to be coaxed, and I'm too tired to coax him."

"He has a right not to be here."

"George, I said I did it because he *wants* to be here. It was just a shortcut. Two minutes after he gets here, he'll be giggling like a school girl."

"It still wasn't very nice."

George was looking over Michael's head toward the drawing room doorway. Michael continued to look at George for a moment, then sat up and turned toward the door. Gian-Carlo was standing there completely dressed in black, striped trousers, a white shirt and black bow tie, and his short, starched white jacket. He held a silver tray in his outstretched hand, and a small, white, neatly folded towel hung over his arm. There was silence as he came down the steps and crossed the room to the bar. He stopped and turned around. "Cognac, Michael, sir?"

As the silence resumed, neither George nor Michael could quite look Gianni in the eye. Michael put his elbow on the arm of his chair and put his head in his hand. After a moment, he said, "All right. You've succeeded. I'm thoroughly ashamed of myself." He looked up at Gianni. "But I swear to God I only did it to make you do something I thought you wanted to do. I swear it, Gianni."

"Yes, Michael sir. Cognac?"

"Gianni, I'm sorry. I apologize. I bow to you. Now, stop being silly and come on over and sit down."

"Come on, Gianni," George said.

It was, as Michael had said, exactly what Gianni wanted to do. His expression became petulant for a moment, then, in spite of his effort to prevent it, his sunrise smile lit up his face. "You are very mean, Michael."

"I'll get the drinks," George said, starting for the bar.

"No, let me do it," Gianni said. "Cognac?"

"Cognac, George, sir," George said. "Yes."

Michael said, "Gianni, I know you think we shouldn't have anything to do with the neighbors, but there's nothing we can do about it. And we found out tonight they're very nice people."

"I did not say they were not nice," Gianni answered, handing him a brandy. "A dog can be a nice dog, and a cat can be a nice cat, but don't put them together."

"Old Italian proverb," Michael said disgustedly.

"No. I made it up."

"You are clever. Look. These people are well-mannered, decent . . ."

"Michael," George said. "None of that makes any difference. Gianni obviously thinks no two homosexuals should try to mix socially with provincial suburban families. You're not going to change his mind. If we continue to get along with them, he's wrong. If we don't, he's right."

"You don't believe in debate, George."

"Not when it's pointless. What did you think of Tom Parker?"

"Best of the lot," Michael said. "No. I don't mean that. I guess he's just closer to what I am than the other two. But what in the hell do you suppose he talks to Ethel about?"

"Maybe she's good in bed."

"Oh, no! She doesn't understand sex. Absolutely not."

"It's a subject on which I trust your every instinct. Now, Cynthia is almost my kind of girl."

"And you are completely her kind of man. Well, not quite completely. She was fascinated by him, Gianni."

"The strange thing is I think Herb more than anyone else felt an immediate fondness for me."

"He did. But I don't think it's so strange. You're kind of academic by nature."

55

"I'm not sure I like that."

"You know," Michael said, "as hard as I try, I cannot picture any of those people in bed together. I know they're supposed to be the ones who can't picture *our* sex life. But I'll be goddamned if I can see Herb screwing Cynthia, for instance."

"I can see Joe screwing Peg." George said.

"Yeah. Yeah, that's right on."

"Ethel and Tom would be complex. It would be such a different thing for each of them."

"Ethel's about as complex as an amoeba."

"That's not what I meant."

"And what about David? I can hardly wait to clap eyes on *him*."

"I was wondering when you'd get around to that," George said. Then to Gianni, "David is the Radnors' fifteen-year-old son."

"Oh, and I suppose you aren't in the least bit curious."

"Children are not my cup of tea."

"What am I, a child molester?"

"Knowing your proclivities, I must say I admire your restraint."

"Thanks." Gianni was grinning broadly and suppressing his laughter. "You weren't a child, goddamn it," Michael said. "I don't think you were ever a child."

"I liked it a lot when we suddenly started talking like Dorothy and Dick. Touché, Gianni."

"I don't know what that means."

"Without realizing it, we were talking like a man and wife."

Gianni nodded in understanding, but he did not smile.

"I wonder . . ." Michael stopped to laugh quietly to himself. "I wonder what would have happened if we'd really let go—like a couple of real old married queens." He raised the pitch of his voice and somehow softened its texture. The result was more feline than feminine. " 'In the eighteen years we've been together, I've *never* met a *sweeter* man than Georgie.' Can you see Joe Jablonski's face?" George was laughing at the image of Joe, and Gianni was laughing at Michael. " 'Ethel, that is the *cutest* dress. It's so *right* for you. We *love* the house, of course, but those kitchen curtins *have* to go! Red and white checks? Nobody's done that since Rose Cumming died.' Can you see them? They'd be absolutely speechless with embarrassment."

Through his laughter, George said, "Embarrassment and God knows what else."

"It would almost be worth it."

"It would. It would. And Gianni would love it."

"It's such a goddamned charade. They know we're queer, we know we're queer; but we have to pretend not to be, and they have to pretend they don't know. Christ!"

"It is better to pretend," Gianni said.

"Is it, Gianni?" George said.

"Yes. It is easier for everybody."

"Oh, it's easier. But I wonder if it's better."

"The truth is not always good."

"I'll drink to that," Michael said, raising his glass.

As they were finishing their brandy, the Parkers and the Jablonskis were crossing the lawn toward their homes. Ethel and Tom apologized to the baby-sitter for being so late, looked in on the children and went to their own room.

As they were undressing, Ethel said, "Tom."

Tom was taking off his trousers. "What?"

"You never did anything like that, did you?"

He stopped, balanced on one leg, and said, "Did anything like what?"

"You know. Like George and Michael."

"Oh, for God's sake, Ethel!" He returned to undressing.

"You didn't, did you?"

"Of course not. Oh, I guess there were the usual kids' things." He felt her staring at him and turned to her. "Well, it's perfectly normal for little boys to want to see other little boys' dingies." She was still staring. "First of all, you want be sure other little boys have them. I mean,

57

it could be some kind of grotesque growth that belongs to you alone. Well, when two little boys see each other's dingies, they touch each other's dingies. It's perfectly normal."

"What . . . did you . . . do?"

"Do? Holy Christ, Ethel, I don't know what we did!"

"How could you not remember?"

"Ethel. I couldn't have been more than ten years old. Not only was it not homosexual, it wasn't even sexual. It was the normal, healthy curiosity of a little boy. However, if you're interested in something that *is* sexual, I've had just enough booze to be very horny."

"Did it happen more than once?"

"Did you hear me?"

"I'd rather not . . . tonight, Tom. I don't even want to think about sex."

"Because of George and Michael?"

"I guess so. Yes."

"That's ridiculous."

"There's something so . . . sinister about it."

"Sinister?"

"Yes."

"Ethel, you'd better go to bed. I really think you're cracking up."

"I'm just . . . shocked, that's all."

"Yeah? You're my wife, and you're denying me your bed because as a ten-year-old I touched another ten-year-old's prick. You're cracking . . ."

"Stop talking like that!"

He looked at her for a moment, then said, "Go to bed, Ethel." He folded his trousers meticulously and put them on a pants hanger.

By the time Peg finished the rounds of the children's room and returned to the bedroom, Joe was undressed and getting into bed. His clothes were thrown over a chair near the bed; Peg would hang them up in the morning. She looked at Joe's naked body (he always slept in the nude) with satisfaction. It was a squarish body,

58

broad at the shoulders and chest and with almost no discernible waistline. Joe was in no way fat; his body was simply solid and straight. His chest was hard and rounded and covered with thick blond hair, which continued down his torso in a narrow path to the explosion of darker pubic hair. Peg liked everything physical about her husband. She was proud of the manual nature of his work and of his number-one standing in the bowling league. She liked the whole idea of his sleeping naked. She was virtually addicted to his body, and her own body, full-busted and broad-hipped, seemed made for receiving his.

Joe lay on his back with his hands clasped behind his head, watching Peg undress.

"What'd you really think of the two new guys?" Peg asked as she hung up her dress.

"What d'you mean?"

"If I knew, I wouldn't have asked ya."

They certainly never put on airs for anybody, but their speech was always more colloquial when they were alone together.

"I just think you didn't say what you really thought."

"I liked 'em good enough. But imagine not doin' anything at all. Christ, that's something I never even thought about."

"You were too busy makin' a livin'."

"Yeah. But I wonder what it'd be like. I mean, what would you do with yourself all day?"

"You'd go nuts, that's what you'd do."

"Yeah. You're right. I couldn't do it. Besides, there's somethin' . . . I don't know."

"*I* know. There's somethin' wrong about it. A man not doin' anything for a livin'. No job, no nothin'. No family, no kids to work for. It's . . . unmanly."

"What'd you expect?"

"That's what I was askin' you about. What'd you think about them bein' queer?"

"Look, Peg, they're here, and it looks like we're gonna

59

be seein' 'em. They were okay tonight, weren't they? Why think about it at all?"

"I can't help thinkin' about it." She slipped her rayon nightgown over her head, fastened it and got into bed. She turned out the light. "Tell me what you think, Joe."

"I'm tellin' you, I don't think about it. I don't want to. Not if we're gonna be seein' 'em. Two grown men, together. It'd make me sick if I thought about it."

Joe was lying on his side now, facing Peg. She shifted her body slightly as a pretext for letting her hand brush Joe's partial erection.

"I *knew* you felt like that about it," she said. She let her hand touch him again fleetingly.

"How would you like a little fuck, lover?" Joe asked.

"Not tonight, honey." Then she grabbed his now complete erection. "Wow! You really got a hard on!"

"Come on. Lemme put it in." He started to roll toward her, pulling her nightgown up.

"No, Joe," she said, futilely pushing against his body.

"Yes," he said on a quiet inhalation of breath. "I'm gonna fuck you like you never been fucked before."

"Don't Joe! It hurts! It hurts too much! It's too big!"

"When it's all in there up to the balls, it won't hurt anymore." He was on top of her now, with her nightgown pulled up.

"Oh, don't Joe!" she pleaded, pushing at his shoulders with her hands. "Don't stick that big cock in me! Don't Joe!" She reached down and took hold of his hard-on and began to massage it.

"Yeah, baby, guide it in."

"No Joe. I'll jerk you off. I'll just. . . ."

"Come on, honey," he said breathlessly. "Put it in."

"Wait, Joe. C'mere." She put her hands on his hips and pulled him up toward her head. He slid up automatically until his crotch hovered above her face. She took the erection in her mouth, and Joe, making quiet moaning sounds, moved his hips slightly forward and back. Suddenly he pulled out of her mouth, slid down the length of her body and with one sure, vigorous thrust rammed inside her. She let out a strangled, guttural scream and beat at his shoulders with her fists.

"Oh, God, stop, Joe! Don't screw me! Don't rape me, Joe!"

But he went on with all his strength, pushing himself as far into her as he could, then all the way out, then in again as he was supposed to. And Peg protested, muttering, "Oh, God! Oh, God!" as if the ritual were a religious one. When the reality of her ecstasy murdered the fantasy, she put her arms around him and moved against him in perfect counterpoint. The ritual ended, as it was meant to, in mutual, coordinated orgasm; and five minutes later, they were both asleep.

Cynthia and Herb were still emptying ashtrays and washing glasses when David came home at two A.M. David seemed surprised to find them still up, and Herb was displeased at the lateness of the hour.

Looking at his watch, he said, "This is a fine time for you to be getting home."

"I'm sorry, Dad. I just . . ."

"I think your mother and I are very fair with you, Dave . . . perhaps to a fault. I wouldn't want to see you take advantage of our lenience."

"Dad, I'm really sorry. It's just that . . ."

"I want you to listen to me for a minute. We've always tried to base our relationship with you on mutual respect and honesty. But you have to do your part, too. If we're to trust you, you must trust us, too. Trust our judgment and respect it."

Since the age of ten, David had recognized his father's tendency to present clichés as profundities. At first he was puzzled by it, then maddened; but he had eventually learned to play the game well. He countered Herb's banality with simple honesty and exaggerated earnestness. It was a measure of Herb's blind preoccupation with his image to the world that he did not realize that there were few psychological games at which his fifteen-year-old son

61

could not beat him; for David knew when they were playing them, and Herb did not.

"I do," David said. "And I know you trust me. That's why I didn't think you'd be worried or anything." Herb realized suddenly that they hadn't been worried. They rarely worried about David. "It was just that that rotten old heap of Jim Gerber's broke down on the way home from the gig in Mahwah. We tried for an hour to fix it ourselves, but we couldn't. Then it was another half hour before Nick Gambone got there from the garage. He just let Jim's car sit there and drove us all home. I'm sorry. I really am."

"We know those things can't be helped, David," Cynthia said. "But you are only fifteen years old, and two o'clock is just too late. You understand that."

"Sure."

"All right, Davey. No punishment this time." Herb wondered for an instant when was the last time there had been punishment, when it had seemed necessary. "Accidents will happen. Go on up to bed."

"Okay. Good night, Dad." He kissed Cynthia on the cheek. "Good night, Mother." He went upstairs, and his parents followed shortly.

As they got ready for bed, Cynthia said, "I think the evening was a complete success."

"Complete. And dinner was excellent."

"I think the Parkers and the Jablonskis enjoyed it, too, don't you?"

"They seemed to. They certainly stayed late enough."

"I must say George and Michael appeared to have a good time."

"Why wouldn't they? We're quite civilized people."

"There's no reason why they wouldn't. But I'm sure their life in New York was very different from life in Hainesdale."

"No doubt. But since they've chosen life in Hainesdale, we have to assume that they prefer it."

"I think that's probably what they're trying to find out."

"Well, no one's going to make any special effort on their behalf. If they fit in, fine. If they don't. . . ."

"Somehow I think they will."

"It seems likely if tonight is any indication."

Herb went into the bathroom and put on his pajamas. He came out and got into bed.

Cynthia came to bed, switched off the bed light and said, "Good night."

"Good night, dear."

George and Michael had moved their things into a large, second-floor bedroom with twin beds. They lay in the darkness, their conversation about the evening trailing off into desultory half-sentences.

"All in all, it was pleasant enough," George said.

"Um. Might even work out in the long run."

"Strange group, though. So little in common."

"Including us."

They were quiet for a moment. "Sleepy, Mike?"

"And drunk. The brandy got to me."

"It always does. All right. Sleep well."

"You too. Good night."

"Good night."

CHAPTER III

On the following Friday morning, Mrs. Turner arrived at the Radnors' and began cleaning. At ten-thirty, Cynthia, wearing a pale pink jersey suit, went out to the breezeway to get into the Pinto to drive to New York. It was a routine trip, and she had been wondering all morning why she was apprehensive about it. She was about to slide into the driver's seat in that proudly aware and graceful way so few women know, when she heard Ethel calling her from across the lawn. She turned her head and saw Ethel running toward her, waving both arms frantically. From Ethel's excessive excitement, Cynthia knew there was nothing much wrong.

"Cynthia! Cynthia! Wait!" Ethel was shouting. Cynthia waited.

"I'm glad I caught you," Ethel said breathlessly as she reached Cynthia. "This detergent thing is reaching a crisis! Are you going in to New York? Mildred refuses to use non-phosphate detergents for the laundry. She says things just don't get clean. Now that you're not allowed to buy the regular ones around here, I'm in a crisis. Tom bought them for me the last time . . . and he said that's what it was, the *last time*. Would you, Cynthia? I'd like more, but I can't ask you to carry more than about ten." She was counting out money from the pocket of her shirt. "Ten Tides. Just regulars. You'd never be able to manage economy size."

"No, Ethel," Cynthia said. "I'm sorry, but no."

Ethel seemed stunned. "No? Why . . . not?"

"I may be too lazy or too selfish to do anything to help the cause of ecology, but I'm certainly not going to go out of my way to set it back."

Ethel was clearly offended. "I don't think it's asking for too much to want clean clothes."

"All right. But I don't think using a non-phosphate detergent is so much of a sacrifice."

"You think I'm being dishonest or something, don't you?" Cynthia didn't answer. "You don't seem to mind smuggling cigarettes to your New York friends."

"To each his own," Cynthia said. "I really don't want to argue about it."

"Then you won't get the Tide for me?"

"No."

"Well."

Ethel stuffed the money back into her pocket, did a military turn and stalked off across the lawn. As Cynthia watched her go, she felt she was suffocating right there in the bright morning sunshine. She got into the car.

As she left the cloistered village for the declamatory vulgarity of Route 17, she was willing to admit that forces which she didn't understand—astrological machinations, ESP, chemical imbalances—but was willing to admit the existence of, might be working within her being. She had been suffering this condition, or at least been aware of it, for the last few days. Obviously it could be connected to the arrival of the new neighbors, but, at first, that seemed too facile. Yet George Carr was a thoughtful

66

man, and perhaps his thoughtfulness had nudged her out of a dull complacency as a well-cleaned room in a neighbor's house might remind a woman of her own unwaxed kitchen floor.

Yes. That was it. George Carr at the age of forty-whatever-it-was was still a creature of change. He was willing to move into an inherited house in a new neighborhood which was probably hostile to his life-style, with no intention of changing that life-style, and simply to find out what the consequences would be. But George Carr was not married. At least, he was not married in any way which necessitated his rounding out his spouse's public image. That was the difference: she was not free to undertake the same kind of adventures as George Carr. She had a well-defined husband to whose definition she was obliged to contribute whatever wisdom she could. George Carr had no such obligations.

Still, she was moved to wonder how she would behave if her obligations were nonexistent or were different from the ones she owned. Would she be adventurous? Would she take risks? Would she have the courage to behave as she pleased at any given moment, or would she seek out a set of foregone conditions which would make her behavior obligatory as it was now? She didn't know. She decided she was a sociological agnostic and chuckled aloud at the thought.

Yes. It was George Carr. And it was quite simple. In wondering what George would think of her, she began to wonder what she thought of herself. Since yesterday afternoon, she had gone about her daily chores with decided scrutiny, trying to look at them and at herself from the outside. She applied the same scrutiny to dinner, to her conversations with Herb and David. Now, as she drove toward New York, she tried to apply it to what she was about to do.

She had reached Route 17, and the traffic required her full attention. She thought about none of this again until she had left the car at the garage and taken a cab to the hotel. Perhaps in the past she had deliberately avoided thinking about the single aspects of her afternoons in town, but now they came at her in a steady stream of small, separate realizations. The name of the hotel, the room number of the suite, the name of the agency that rented it, the colors and textures of the furnishings, and finally the very nature of her being there.

She let herself into the suite and sat down. She was sure her scrutiny would continue and become more intense. She was sure she would examine her motives, her emotions, her passion; and she wondered how the examination would affect her performance. She wondered, too, if it would affect Tom Parker's.

He was there exactly on time. He did not kiss her, but touched her face in greeting as he always did in the suite, and she touched his hand in return.

He was fixing drinks for them when she said, "Tom, do you ever wonder about us . . . think about us?"

"I don't think I know what you mean," he said.

"Do you . . . just come here . . . and forget about it till the next time?"

"Of course not." He gave her the drink. "I think about it. I remember it. I . . . look forward to it."

"Do you? I've been thinking . . ."

"Cynthia. I always hate this because it sounds so . . . awful. But I have a meeting. It just came up about an hour ago. There was no way of letting you know."

"Oh." She was annoyed, but she knew it was not Tom's fault. She knew, too, that unless he really wanted to be with her, it would have been easier for him to say he had no time at all. She got up and went into the bedroom.

She had been wrong about her examination's intruding. It was the same as always. No matter what frame of mind she was in at the beginning, her complete physical involvement with Tom's body drove away the mood. The twenty-five minutes they spent in bed were entirely, blissfully carnal. Their coitus was entirely free of the emotional involvements which had always blessed, then dissipating, cursed her love-making—all love-making, she believed. Sex with Tom was like the most elaborate and satisfying masturbation: guiltless and instantly gratifying. Yet it was free of the burden of fantasy. It was the best, the most fulfilling sex Cynthia had ever had. Within a moment after it was over, her mind returned to her earlier considerations. That this was possible was part of the magic of the sex.

"May we finish our drinks?" she asked when they came into the sitting room again.

"Sure we can finish our drinks," Tom said. There was unmistakable resentment in his voice.

She sat down again, picked up her drink and said, "I started to ask you before if you ever thought about us. If you ever think about why we do it."

"I know why I do it. I thought you did, too."

"I mean underneath the obvious reason."

"Why does there have to be a reason underneath the obvious reason?" He was still standing, but aside from that, showed no signs of anxiety at prolonging the interview.

"Maybe we don't question ourselves enough."

He looked down at his drink and smiled and frowned at the same time. "Cynthia, do you want to call a halt?"

She hesitated as if she were not sure. "No."

"Then why don't we just . . . just drink up?"

"Because . . ." She looked about the room in a defensive way. "Because I think I've begun to ask myself some questions."

"Okay. Ask yourself till the cows come home. But don't ask me." She looked hurt. "Cynthia, look. I don't want to lose this. I don't know what I'd do without it. I don't even know what I *did* without it. It means . . ."

"*It* means . . . or *I* mean?"

"*It* means." He frowned again without the smile and shook his head. "The first time we were here together, we got a little smashed. Remember? I told you that Ethel

69

was lousy in bed, and you told me Herb was lousy in bed. And . . ."

"I said he was impotent."

"How many guys do you know who are impotent and great in the sack? You see?" he said in response to her look of annoyance. "All of a sudden it sounds like I'm accusing you of sleeping with every man in Ridgefield County. That's what comes of all the questions. To you, sleeping with Herb is like sleeping alone. To me, sleeping with Ethel *is* sleeping alone. We said that the first time, and we laughed about it. Then we had another drink and made it together. Today was just as good for me as that first time. Why do you want to screw it up?"

"I'm only asking what's to come of it," she insisted. "What it means inside our lives."

The muscles of his face started to form an expression of exasperation, but he looked at his watch instead of allowing the feeling to show. "Cynthia, I want to stay married to Ethel. I don't anymore know why than you know why you want to stay married to Herb. We both know he's a colossal pain in the ass, but there's something underneath that that . . ." He stopped for a moment, then went on. "Ethel's my girl. It's just exactly that corny. I still call her that . . . less than I used to, but now and then. Whenever she does something infuriatingly stupid, which is infuriatingly often, all she has to do is say, 'Am I still your girl?' and ten thousand memories come back all at once. Not memories of the college prom or moonlight on a lake. Memories of Jonathan's tonsillectomy . . . and being in the delivery room while she was having Susie. And the car stalling in a blizzard in New Hampshire. The realities of half a lifetime come flooding back, and I can't take Ethel away from those realities without . . . I don't know, without destroying them, I guess. It takes a long time to make somebody that much a part of your life, and I don't think I want to go through it again. Maybe I'm just afraid it would end up the same way in the long run. Anyway, for as long as we both enjoy it, I want this to go on. As soon as one of us doesn't want it anymore, it's time to stop." He smiled the growingly anachronistic college boy smile and said, "Or until we get caught."

"Oh, yes. That would be lovely." She got up and executed all the little feminine movements of collecting herself. She checked the contents of her handbag, smoothed her skirt, put a hand to her hair. "I suppose that's all you have to say. I mean, even if there were more time, that would be all you'd have to say."

"Yes."

She looked at him blankly for a moment. "I'll leave first."

When she got to the door, Tom said, "Cynthia, who's the best lay you ever had?"

Without looking at him, she said, "You."

"And the same goes for me. What do you want?"

"I'll call you at the office when I'm going to be free," she said.

"Good."

She stopped for a moment in the corridor outside the door of the suite and told herself that in spite of her scrutiny, nothing had changed. She also told herself that that was because she probably didn't want it to change. Before she reached the elevators, she was recalling the name of the hotel, the number of the suite, the name of Tom's agency.

Inside the suite, Tom washed the two glasses, threw the unused ice into the sink and put on the double-breasted jacket of his blue suit. Then he straightened his tie and went back to the office.

That evening George went over to the Jablonskis' before Michael. In spite of his dedication to straightforwardness with the neighbors, George now and then did such little obeisances to the false god of decorum. For either of them to appear occasionally alone, George believed,

71

relieved the nagging implication of their appearing constantly together.

The Jablonskis' back yard—it was in no sense a garden —came into George's view as he rounded a corner of the house. Cynthia and Herb were already there with their son, David. They stood together in a little group. Joe was at the big, efficient barbeque with its hooded oven and temperature gauge. Peg was crossing the rectangular flagstone patio with a tray of glasses. The flagstones were the only domestic extravagance Peg had insisted on, and now that it was done, Joe was glad she had.

"Hey, George!" Joe yelled, looking up from the fire and seeing George over the Radnors' heads. "Come on in."

"You haven't met David, have you?" Cynthia said.

"No." George extended his hand. "Nice to meet you, David."

"Thanks, Mr. Carr. I'm glad to meet you."

"I think your mother and father will agree we can't have this 'Mr. Carr' business. George."

David smiled and said, "Okay."

Peg joined them and said, "What are you drinking, George?"

"How about a gin and tonic?"

"Joe!" Peg yelled. "A gin and tonic for George!"

"I'm checkin' the baked potatoes!" Joe yelled back. The Jablonskis' back yard was bigger than the Radnors' or the Parkers' gardens, and Peg and Joe seemed to enjoy shouting across the distance. "In a minute!"

"Well, when you get around to it," Peg yelled, "make it three, because Ethel and Tom are here!"

Just as the handshakes and greetings were finished and the drinks were served, Michael arrived. Joe was now finished checking the baked potatoes and got a gin and tonic for him. Cynthia and Herb were the last ones Michael greeted. Again, Cynthia introduced her son.

"Michael, this is my son David."

There was a curious expectancy in the way she presented him, as if she were waiting for the kind of recognition that is the core of nineteenth-century melodrama. She wanted the kindred spirits to embrace in an ecstatic vacuum of sameness. She would have been satisfied to have David be at Michael's age what Michael now was, and to have him go on to be what George at George's age now was. If he could do it without being a homosexual. That she did not wish him.

"Hello, David," Michael said with a combination of enthusiasm and restraint that pleased Cynthia.

They shook hands, and David said, "I think I'm supposed to call you 'Michael.' "

"Yes, I think you are. Besides, I'd feel pretty silly calling you 'Mr. Radnor.' "

The remark and the subsequent laughter elicited all the right responses. It was what Cynthia had expected. It was casual and sufficiently distant for Herb. Tom thought it was what *he* would have said, and Ethel paid no attention to it. Joe didn't hear it. George laughed silently.

As Joe expected, the baked potatoes had been hard when he checked them. It would have been rude to allow less than an hour for drinking before dinner, particularly in warm weather and out-of-doors. None of the neighbors were solitary or secret drinkers, nor did any of them "drink too much" in a clinical sense. Tom admitted that now and then he "drank too much" in a vague social connotation. If Cynthia told a joke that was too risqué, she might say she had had "too much to drink." When Ethel got the giggles, she might say she had had "too much to drink" or "couldn't drink this much." Joe maintained, quite correctly, that he could drink any of them under the table. George and Michael had not been tested, but were presumed to be able to hold their liquor.

The neighbors spent the hour doing what was expected of them. The fifth drink was pushed on them enthusiastically by Joe. They could bring them to the table, he told them. The table was two six-foot-long pine picnic tables put together end-to-end and covered with a scotch-taped

73

pair of paper tablecloths. The tables and the lawn around them had been dappled by the sun when they had been set by Peg and her sister, Helen; but now twilight and scudding gray clouds had darkened the picnic scene. Joe had lit the black, stick-in-the-ground torches, and Peg and Helen had lit the candles on the tables. Helen had managed not to come out into the yard while it was entirely light and now fluttered about her servant's business without need of acknowledgement, let alone introduction. She smiled at everyone like an airline stewardess who expected a crash. The hopeful passengers accepted the smiles and returned them in kind.

There were steak and baked potatoes and casserole of creamed lima beans and carrots and a green salad and Italian bread. There were also wine (endless gallons of Gallo Mountain Burgundy) and beer. This was gilding the alcoholic lily, since everyone except David who sat down at the put-together tables was already drunk in his own fashion and to his own degree. Ethel was giggly. George was cautious. Tom was exuberant. Herb was withdrawn. Cynthia was lofty. Michael was on. Peg and Joe were host and hostess with a kind of magnanimous excess. Helen, having waited for this moment, was at last able to cope with her slightly disabled friends.

"Here's to Peg and Joe for a wonderful dinner," Helen said, lifting her plastic glass of wine.

Michael looked at her in awe, considered a counter-toast and said, "I'll drink to that." The others drank, too.

The texture of the rest of the evening was maintained like a tapestry being woven tightly enough to form an image, but loosely enough for its threads to be pulled out for another time. By the time coffee was served, the guests had split up into groups, then couples, then amoebic clusters which an individual could leave or enter without disruption. Between the leaving and the arrival, there was even time for solitude. In such a moment, Michael found David in a corner of the back yard.

"What's the matter? Bored by the over-thirty set?"

74

Michael could see David's smile in the torchlight. It was a warm, winning, confident smile. "No. Just thinking."

"You're not supposed to think too much at a party. It spoils the fun. "Michael turned and looked at the others behind him. He turned back to David and said, "At least, not at this kind of party."

"It sounds like *you're* bored."

Michael grinned at him almost in apology. "I didn't mean it that way. Some parties are all booze and jokes and laughing. After a while it has to get to be an effort." He shook his head. "But dead sober it must really be a drag."

David laughed quietly and said, "Well . . ."

"Why are we being honored with your presence, anyway? I'm sorry. After a certain number of drinks, I manage to make everything I say sound sarcastic." Since he had reached the age of twenty-five, Michael had found it easier to talk to people younger than he than to his peers. He was aware of this and thought perhaps it was an attempt to stay youthful. But he knew that he enjoyed being honest and felt comfortable being honest with young people. His attempts at total honesty with people his own age were often met with tolerance or ridicule or stunning astonishment. On the morning after, he often repeated such conversations to himself, searching for the source of his suspicion that he had behaved like a drunken fool. Even when he found nothing foolish in what he had said, the suspicion lingered.

"I wanted to come," David said. "I do every now and then."

"Because you really want to, or as a token of peace?"

"A little of both, I guess. Mother and Dad never make me go out with them. Or stay home when they have a party. I'm always welcome if I want to be there, and it's always okay if I don't. Sometimes I want to be there."

"That's the most sensible answer I've ever heard to the generation gap. Or isn't there one for you?"

"Sure there is. You hear a lot about kids resenting their parents' double standards. *I* think you hear it more from adults talking about kids than from kids themselves. Anyway—I hope it's all right for me to say this—I don't particularly like the way my parents behave toward the end of these parties. I guess they're kind of smashed. But at least they don't behave any different because I'm here. If they did, that would really be dishonest."

"I guess that applies to me, too."

"What?"

"I mean, you mustn't like my behavior, either."

David was deeply embarrassed. "Hey, I didn't mean . . ."

"Forget it. I was kidding," Michael said, but he hadn't been. "I'm not your father. That makes a difference. God knows, booze doesn't always bring out the best in us."

"I guess not."

Michael looked straight at him in the shifting firelight. "I suppose you prefer grass."

David was only mildly startled. "Why . . . why do you ask me that?"

"You aren't afraid of incriminating yourself with *me*?"

After a moment, David said, "No. No, I guess not."

Michael, sobered somehow by the conversation, decided he was being too openly ingratiating. "You know, it used to be that whenever I talked to young people, I hastened to tell them I smoke grass fairly frequently—which is true. You know, show them I'm on their side. Then I read somewhere that kids think anybody over thirty who smokes is sick. So I stopped that little gambit."

David laughed loudly. "That's ridiculous."

"I thought so, but who am I to argue with the kids?"

"Okay. I smoke sometimes. And since we're being so honest, I guess I'll tell you why I came tonight."

"Oh? Good."

"I wanted to meet you. Mother told me you're working on a novel."

"Aha! You came to pick my meager brain."

"Not exactly."

"Is that what you want to do? Be a writer?"

"I don't know. I'm scared of it, I guess." Michael didn't answer, and after a moment, David went on. "I'm sure my mother told you I was very bright."

"She did. Or *somebody* did."

"Okay. Take math. With a math problem, there's always a right answer. Anyway, till you get into higher forms, theoretical things. You know you're looking for one thing. If you don't find it the first time, if you solve an equation wrong, like it's no big deal. Somebody shows you your mistake, and you do it again right."

"May I point out something? You can't solve an equation wrong. You can either solve it or not solve it. There are absolutes, even in semantics."

David looked puzzled. "You mean you can't have a wrong solution?"

"When you're talking about algebraic equations, the phrase 'wrong solution' is contradictory. If you have two plus two equals, and you put down five, you have not solved the problem. You said there's only one right answer. There's only one solution. Anything but that one solution isn't a solution at all."

"I don't know if I understand."

"Let's say the problem is . . . well . . . let's say the problem is which college to go to. Harvard, Berkeley, Penn State, Grinnell. There's more than one solution. Some solutions are more satisfactory than others. But none is necessarily right or wrong. You might solve the problem more or less satisfactorily and still have a solution. But not in math. You either have *the* solution, or you don't."

The irrepressible smile was there again. "That's wild!"

"I was just being pedantic. You were going to tell me why writing scares you."

"Because I'm not ashamed to show a teacher an equation I solved wro . . . I mean, an equation I didn't solve, but . . ."

77

"You learn fast."

". . . but I'd be ashamed to show anybody something I wrote that was . . . terrible."

"David, it ought to be the other way around. If there is no absolute answer, nobody can blame you for not finding one. But if there is one, and you don't find it, you're a dumb-dumb."

David nodded enthusiastically and said, "Yeah, you're right. But I was talking about picking a career. I *know* I can learn how to be a mathematician . . . or a physicist or a chemist. There are answers, and the whole point is to find them. But at least you know they're there. Yeah. That's it. I'd be afraid to commit myself to . . . to spending my life looking for answers that maybe aren't even there."

"The answers are there just as surely in art as in science."

"Are they? If I submit an algebra test, and Mr. Anderson says there are three problems wrong, they're wrong. If I submit a composition to Miss Sperling in English Lit. and she gives it a B-minus, I can still think it's perfect. And I can say, 'Who the hell is she to judge?'"

"That's simply because the scientific answers are universal. The artistic answers are an integral part of the person who offers them. The challenge is greater . . . and the rewards usually less."

"Then how do I ever know if my personal answers are the right ones?"

"Shit, David, you don't want solutions. You want standards. You want to be judged by a qualified authority. David is right. Or David is wrong. Instant success."

"Or instant failure."

The conversation had built quickly to a strange intensity.

"Oh, for Christ's sake!"

"Which means you don't know what I'm talking about."

"Yes, I do. You don't want to find out after ten years

78

that you're a failure. You want to find out right away . . . so you'll have time to start over."

"Right on."

"Well, that isn't the way things are."

"Well, that's the way they should be."

"Ah, the wisdom of the young. There shouldn't be death or pain or sorrow or agony of any kind. Why do young people always think they can be eliminated?"

"You can't eliminate them if you just accept them."

"Tell me your plans for getting rid of death."

"Aw, come on."

"Instant childhood."

"Instant over-thirty."

"Balls, David."

"Same to you Michael."

Herb said, "You seem to be in some kind of disagreement." He was not swirling his drink, but the ice clinked against the glass loudly.

Absolutely without guile, Michael said, "You'd be proud of us, Herb. We've been having an absolutely academic discussion."

"Some of the terms of which I would be reluctant to introduce into my curricula," Herb said.

Michael winked, pointed a finger and looked directly at David. "Now, *that* is pedantic." Instantly he regretted having said it and wondered if he would have to have another accusative conversation with himself in the morning.

Herb turned to David and said, "We're leaving in a few minutes. Come back and say good night to Peg and Joe." He walked away then, skirting an azalea bush by an unnecessarily wide margin, and returned to the others. He left an uneasy silence behind him.

"I think your father's uptight."

"Without the 'up,'" David said. "Doesn't he think I don't know what balls are?"

"He thinks you shouldn't use the word publicly as an expletive. And he's right."

79

"Sure he is. So from now on, when *I* get uptight, I'll say 'foot' or 'finger' or 'eyebrow.' I won't say 'balls' or 'shit' or 'prick' or 'fuck' or 'cunt.' "

"Okay. Let's go back."

Michael started to walk away. David said, "I'm sorry. I was showing off." Then the smile again. "After all, I'm only a kid."

Michael turned back. He smiled, too, and said, "Oh . . . eyebrow it. Hey, do you have something you've written that you'd be ashamed to show to me?"

"Sure."

"But you're going to show it to me anyway."

"I'll show you mine if you'll show me yours."

Michael knew the torchlight was behind him. David could not see his blushing. "You drive a hard bargain." The blush heightened. "Traditionally, novelists do not show their work in progress. However, I'll trade you." He didn't seem to be able to say anything right.

"Will you?"

"It seems to me I said I would. Call me, and we'll exchange manuscripts."

"Like tomorrow?"

Michael smiled at him and said, "Like tomorrow." Then they started across the yard toward the others.

David was still young enough that his own enthusiasms did not seem gauche to him. He called Michael the morning after the Jablonskis' party. Michael carefully hid his amusement and took the call with the same seriousness with which David made it.

When he had hung up, he had said to George, "David Radnor's coming over in a few minutes."

George looked at him with open astonishment and said, "Why?"

"Guess. He wants me to read something he's written."

"*That* again."

"It's inevitable. You know, he's really a very nice kid."

"And straight as a dye."

80

"Absolutely."

"A fact which I trust you will keep foremost in your mind."

"George, do you think I'm crazy or something? Do you really think I'm crazy enough to make a pass at Herb and Cynthia's fifteen-year-old son? Or anybody else's fifteen-year-old son?"

"Which question do you want answered first?" Michael looked at him disgustedly. "I think if you could have sex with an attractive fifteen-year-old boy without fear of the consequences, you would."

"All right. I probably would."

"You *certainly* would. I don't think anything in the world could induce you to make a pass at David Radnor. But what if he makes a pass at you?"

"But we both know he's not going to do that, don't we, George?"

"Do we? He's a nice ripe, confused fifteen-year-old. What if he did? Would you take the risk of his having misgivings after the fact?"

"No. Of course not. Sometimes you treat me like a juvenile delinquent."

"I just wanted to be sure."

"You couldn't be sure without asking me?"

"I'm sorry. I suppose I could have."

David arrived to deliver his work fifteen minutes later and stayed for an hour talking to Michael in the study. Neither of them deliberately reactivated the conversation of the night before, but it was reactivated. It seemed that any chance remark could plunge them into immediately deep conversation, conversation from which neither of them had any desire to extricate himself. George came into the room to tell Michael that lunch was ready. David was neither physically nor mentally so much a child as to be sent home at mealtime. George invited him to stay for lunch. David hesitated for a brief moment during which George feared he would accept. Then, saying that lunch was probably ready at home at that very moment, he left. Michael went to the door with him.

"I'll call you as soon as I've read it," he said.

David hesitated, then said, "Could we ... work it out some other way?"

"What do you mean?"

"Well ... Mother and Dad haven't read any of it yet. And I don't think I want them to yet."

"You mean they don't even know you're writing at all?"

"Oh, they know. I mean, they know I write for the school paper and that stuff. But they don't know about this."

Michael smiled and said, "Okay. I'll try to read them tonight or tomorrow morning. Why don't you come over tomorrow after lunch?"

"Thanks. That'd be great."

George spent the afternoon in the garden. As a child, he had spent hours with his Aunt Janet's gardener, watching and learning. The old man had allowed him to try his hand at many things—putting in the early bulbs, pruning the roses, transplanting begonias to a more healthful site—for the most part secretly. For Aunt Janet did not approve of George's gardening. It was both unmasculine and beneath his station. He had never since had a garden of his own, but had never lost his ardent desire for one. Now it was as if he had been denied food, then set free at a banquet. He had rehired Mrs. Cartwright's new gardener, not the old friend of long ago, but a man just as dedicated. Ever since his aunt's retirement, the garden had been a matter of routine. It had been designed so that there was something in bloom from May to September, but it had been planted year after year exactly the same way. George was changing all that with the enthusiastic approval of the gardener. They moved the daffodils and tulips closer to the house so that they could be seen more easily from the terrace. They bordered the flower beds with French marigolds. They dug up circles of lawn around the boles of all the trees and planted myrtle. They littered the lawn almost at random with crocuses. They put in Canterbury bells and redbuds and azaleas. And in a stroke of delicious malice, George put in cucumbers, whose roots, George fantasized, reached deep and far into the earth—under the turnpike, under the stream and the lake, under the country club golf course, all the way to Fairview Cemetery, where they tickled Aunt Janet's remains into spinning in their grave at the vulgarity of vegetables.

With a vise-like grip of discipline, Michael worked on his novel in the study, which had become his room. He worked well, even with David's unread work sitting on some delicate branch of his brain like a bird in a tree. At four o'clock, he put aside his own work and eagerly picked up David's. He opened the large envelope as if it were a suddenly found attic trunk. And he found its contents, like the contents of most suddenly found attic trunks, disappointing.

There were three rather long short stories. Michael suspected from their length that they were overwritten. Reading the first one confirmed his suspicion. He put it aside and began the second, which suffered from exactly the same flaws as the first. But as he read, he was filled with a growing ambivalence. Again and again he winced at technical errors, at careless language, at self-indulgence with favorite themes. But always his deep interest survived the interruptions. By the time he had finished the third story, he knew he was in the presence of a rare phenomenon: a genuine writer who had not yet learned his craft.

Michael believed in a mysterious alchemy of creativity. Without certain specifics in physical construction, it is impossible to be an opera singer; and no amount of instruction or training will accomplish it. He believed something like this to be true of writing. He did not know the nature of this required nucleus in a writer. It was surely not as simple as an inquiring mind or keen powers of observation. It was an inexplicable psychological predilection, but he believed he could recognize it when it was there. And he was certain he recognized it in David's work.

Michael reread the first story. He was very excited now, not only at his discovery, but at the prospect of the part he might play in the development of a talent he was sure was far greater than his own. He had often been asked by young people to read their work—plays by other actors, the writing of young men he was sexually involved with. Invariably the request triggered a fantasy in which Michael found an embryonic talent and nurtured it into full growth, to fame, perhaps even to greatness. His own gratification—the age-old joy of the teacher, the impresario, the surrogate father—could be sweet beyond any satisfaction he would ever know in his own work. This was the first time there had been even a possibility of it.

Unlike David, Michael kept his enthusiasm in check. When George asked him about it, he calmly told him the work showed promise. They had dinner, watched television for a while and went to bed.

The next day was the most perfect of the entire spring. From the moment of dawn, the sunlight spread itself across the earth uninterrupted by a single cloud. It touched everything, lawns and gardens and trees and houses, with an almost glaring vividness. A mild breeze made the trees shimmer in the brightness. It was so beautiful that George refused to let Michael sleep through it. They got up very early and had breakfast on the terrace and read *The New York Times*.

None of the three Radnors believed in God, and none of them knew this about each other. But they believed, to varying degrees, in Herb's obligation as principal to keep up appearances. So they attended morning service on Sundays at Calvary Episcopal Church of Hainesdale and, though they were hardly pillars of the church, they were active in its social schedule.

From the terrace, George and Michael could see one end of the front of the Radnors' house, including the front

84

door. They saw the Radnors leaving for church. They waved, and George and Michael waved back. Cynthia and Herb moved out of view, and David lingered for a moment. Michael waved again, and David waved back. Michael knew he had understood the invitation was confirmed.

David arrived shortly after they had finished lunch. George had gone back to the garden, and Michael was in the study when Gianni showed David in.

"Hello, David," Michael said.

"Hi. Have you had a chance to read any of it?"

Michael smiled. "I've read all of it. And I want to talk to you about it."

"Great."

"But it's such a beautiful day, why don't we go for a walk? I haven't taken a walk since we moved in."

"Sure. We can walk through the country club."

"Me? A non-member?"

"Be my guest. There's a lot of land there they don't even use. It's just woods. It's like being in the country."

"David, we're already in the country."

"All right, I know. But this is like there were no towns around."

"Sounds great. Let's go."

Although Michael hadn't been there, he knew where the country club was. Outside the house he started in that direction.

"Could we go this way?" David said.

Michael looked puzzled and said, "Sure. If you want to."

"Look. It's just that . . . I didn't tell Mother and Dad where I was going. They don't know about the writing yet . . . and I didn't feel like telling them. I wasn't going to lie to them about it. So I . . . just didn't say anything."

Michael looked annoyed, but turned in the direction David had indicated.

As they crossed the front lawn of the country club, the fieldstone clubhouse was on their right. The putting greens and tees and the golf course were on the left. Before them was a small lake with a wooden dock and diving boards and rowboats. Farther out a raft swayed in the almost motionless water. It was an absolutely accurate Hollywood version of a middle-class country club.

But behind the clubhouse, the land rose gently in a series of small hills. They were as David had described them. They were thickly wooded and obviously unused for any official purpose. The forest began with the abruptness of a mountain's timber line, and ten feet beyond that, one felt a sense of cool remoteness. After thirty feet, the country club and the suburbia around it disappeared magically. Only an occasional distant siren or the drone of a single-engine airplane intruded on the illusion.

"You're right, David. It *is* like being in the country. No. No, it's more like being in a wilderness. That's even better."

"I've been coming here since I was about nine years old. I don't think I'm really a solitary person . . . I mean, I like school and composing and playing music for people and dancing. Things that have to do with other people. But when I really want to be alone, I come here. I wrote a lot of that stuff here."

At the top of the hill, there was a sudden clearing, and in it a mass of rock rose ten feet high. The rock was leveled off in at least a dozen different places, forming natural seats. They sat and looked down across the sloping forest. Rabbits scurried here and there through the brush, and birds sang everywhere above them.

"I told you I read the stories," Michael said.

"Yeah." There was a silence. "What did you think?"

"First of all—and most important—I think you're a writer."

"Wow!"

"I'm so sure of it, I think it would be a terrible thing if you *didn't* write."

"You're not just being nice to me?"

"I had hoped you'd know I wouldn't do that."

"Okay."

"David, do you want to be a writer?"

"I told you, I don't know."

"When you find out, let me know."

"I guess I was hoping you could help me to find out."

Michael wanted to bite out his tongue. "All right, so I'm a smartass. I'm sorry."

"I wasn't putting you down. I . . ."

"Never mind. Look, we were honest with each other at the Jablonskis'. Let's continue to be. Writing is such a hell of a hard business. The putting yourself on the line. The . . ." He looked away as if he thought David hadn't been listening.

"What's wrong?"

"Just that I'm not saying what I want to say. Which is one of the things that's wrong with your writing. What I want to say is that I would rather be a really fine writer than anything else in the world, and I'm not going to be. I think you might . . . I think you could be. I didn't want to get involved in it if it was going to turn out to be a . . . an adolescent diversion."

"Michael . . ."

"Wait a minute. I realize now that I ought to do exactly what you said: help you find out if you want to write. I mean, making writing a way of life. I'm willing to make the necessary commitment to help you find out, if you'll make it, too."

"I'll make it."

There it was again: the undiluted and irresistible eagerness in the eyes; the eagerness which slips away from all of us like a coastline giving way to an ocean, until the country of the spirit is diminished almost without our knowing it.

"Okay. Within reason, we must be as honest with each other as we can."

"What do you mean, 'within reason'? Either we're honest or we're not."

Michael rubbed his forehead as if he were trying to

erase the frown. "Uh . . . there's a girl in one of your stories called 'Cathy.' "

"Yeah."

"I think she exists."

The word came more slowly this time. "Yeah."

"And the relationship you describe in the story more or less exists between you and her."

"All right."

"She ever gone down on you? She ever give you head?" David's expression was everything Michael had hoped it would be. "You want to be honest about that? You see, I have no right to ask the question, so you have no obligation to give me an honest answer. The most honest thing you could do is to tell me it's none of my business. Let's rephrase the commitment. We'll never be *dis*honest with each other."

"Agreed."

"Ah, the young are so good at ritual."

"Could we have a . . . sub-commitment? You won't talk down to me."

"In your own words, 'Wow!' "

"You're still doing it. Could I ask you a question?"

"Sure."

"You're uptight about your age, aren't you?"

"Yes."

"You seem very young to me."

"As opposed to immature." David looked away. "I'm sorry. I meant to say thank you."

David still didn't look at him. "Yes, she's gone down on me. We love each other." Instantly the image came to Michael, and his excitement was quite nearly unbearable.

"You didn't have to do that. You really didn't."

"I know."

They were quiet for a moment. "You want to talk about that story?"

David smiled at him. "Sure."

"Eventually we'll go over the story together, and I'll point out some minor technical flaws that you seem to be hung up on. But they're not important, because you can learn to overcome them. The *major* technical flaw in the story about Cathy is a . . . a stylistic ambivalence. You start with a classic literary device: the omniscient narrator. He sees, knows and tells all. He has no identity, no personality and no part in the story. Then suddenly you say, 'Now I, David Radnor, am going to make a comment about all this.' And immediately you intrude on what you've already admitted is the reader's privacy. One way or the other, but not both. Are you still with me?"

"Yes."

They talked then for a long time about style and technique and discipline as they applied to David's story. They each talked with growing intensity. David was accustomed to compliments and commendations from adults, but he was being treated now with a new respect. They were talking exclusively and eagerly about *his* work. Michael recognized ideas which David thought were so deeply buried in the story that he was amazed at the recognition.

"You seem to keep holding back," Michael said. "You talk about what you want to talk about up to a point. Then suddenly there's this fakey, evasive writing. Maybe you're not ready to talk about whatever it is you're trying to talk about."

"Maybe . . . maybe I was trying to make them . . . acceptable for my mother and father."

"Okay. But if you're not ready to write honestly for your mother and father, you're not ready to write. You're not ready to say it."

"What do you think I was trying to say?"

"Don't you want to wait till you put it into the story?"

"I'd like to hear what you think."

"I think, among other things, you're trying to say that you and Cathy—whoever she is in real life—think you want to be lovers for the rest of your lives, but you don't want to make any formal commitment like marriage."

89

"Are you sure I didn't say it? I mean, you got it."

"Oh, it's in there somewhere. But you make the reader dig it out. Most readers won't take the trouble. The responsibility for saying it is yours, not theirs. You know, I think the two things are hooked up together in some way. Your reluctance to say what you have to say, and your changes in style."

"You think I should rewrite it?"

"Yes."

"You think I could get it published?"

"No. But that doesn't mean you shouldn't rewrite it. It's a paradox. Short stories are far harder to write than novels. There's no margin for error in a short story. It has to be virtually perfect. Yet most writers start out with short stories. They have to, I guess. Nobody wants to write a whole novel as an exercise. And speaking of exercises, I'd like you to do something for me. It's an exercise a high school English teacher taught me a long time ago."

"Must have been centuries."

"You're a smart-ass. However. You make two lists on the same piece of paper. One is headed 'I Like,' and the other is headed 'I Love.' The only rules are you've got to use a pencil, and you can't erase. You can change your mind, but you have to leave everything you write."

"It sounds diabolical."

"It can teach you a lot. Will you do it?"

"Sure. How long do the lists have to be?"

"No fewer than ten. After that, it can be as long as you want."

"Okay."

"We should go back."

"Already?"

"The first session should be short so as not to discourage the pupil."

"I'm not discouraged."

"I know. And, David. This nonsense about sneaking

around as far as your mother and father are concerned has to stop. It's ridiculous."

"You think I should show them the writing?"

"You should tell them you'll show it to them when you think it's finished. And you should tell them I'm helping you."

"Yeah. I guess you're right."

"Will you tell me when you think I'm not?"

There was the smile again for just an instant before David said, "Michael, we both know that isn't going to happen, don't we?"

"As I said, smart-ass."

They left the hill then and went back to the property the most direct way. They said goodbye and parted in front of the Radnors' house.

CHAPTER IV

Saturday was just another work day for Joe, and he hated it. It wasn't the work he hated or the being away from his family; he would rather work than anything else he did in life. But with all his employees on time-and-a-half, it was painfully expensive for him. The low clouds scudding across the sky like wads of dirty, gray cotton put him in a worse mood than usual. If it rained, he wouldn't have to pay the wages, but then the work wouldn't get done. He really hated Saturdays.

He arrived at the construction site of the new high school at seven-thirty. Everyone on the job was already there. Joe's Saturday moods were notorious, and even habitual latecomers managed to be on time. On and off through the morning, rain fell in a fine, gray, steamy drizzle, but it was never hard enough to halt work. At noon, Joe told his foreman, Augie Sorrentino, that he was going to grab a sandwich, then attend to some business in Hainesdale. He might be late getting back.

He drove to Hainesdale and had a hero at Tony's

Pizza Parlor. A stranger seeing him sitting at the counter with his chinos and blue workshirt and hard hat would have thought him to be a construction worker on his lunch hour—which, indeed, in a sense he was. But the other sense of him—the executive, proprietor, capitalist sense—a stranger could not have guessed. He ate the unapproachable sandwich and drank beer from a can with a primitive skill. He joked with the waitress in such a way that a stranger, seeing them in mime through the plate-glass window, would have known their jokes were coarse. He finished lunch with a dish of ice cream, a cup of coffee and a cigarette. He took a napkin (his fourth) from the chrome container on the counter, wiped his mouth thoroughly and left. His office was across the street, on the second floor over a dry-cleaning establishment. His "offices" would have been more accurate, but his organization, like Joe himself, was never pretentious.

He let himself in and let the door lock automatically behind him. The office staff rarely worked on Saturdays, and the room was still and gray from the misty light outside. He made his way through the rows of desks and drafting tables and file cabinets toward the end of the long room. There was a line of cubicles there made of knotty pine and glass that looked like slices of ice cubes. As he knew there would be, there was a light on in the cubicle next to his own. He paused for a moment beside the doorless opening, then stuck his head through it and said, "Hi,ya, sexy."

Marion Collins looked up, dropped her pencil and clutched her left breast in astonishment. "Joe! My God, Joe, you scared me half to death!"

Joe laughed and said, "What if I was a nigger rapist from over the Culpsville section? Hah, you'd be in trouble."

"That's why the door's locked, smarty. What are you, issuing keys to nigger rapists these days?"

At thirty-four, Joe's secretary was too young to be called a spinster, although for the last year she had begun to think of herself as one with increasing frequency. She was lumpy rather than fat. There seemed not to be an angle in her entire body. Instead, she was a composition of roundnesses. Within the curved frame of her frosted beehive hairdo, her round face contained large, round eyes, distinct round cheeks, a round and dimpled chin. Her expensive brassiere held her breasts like melons in a cloth sack. Her hips rolled outward from her captured waist. Many men found her voluptuous.

In addition to being Joe's secretary, Marion Collins was the administrative heart of the Hainesdale Construction Company. She superintended every administrative detail she did not actually handle herself. She was a liaison between the four executives. She audited the work of the bookkeeping department. She hired and fired all clerical personnel. She had set up the mail room, ordered the Xerox machine, selected the IBM executive typewriters. She proofread all estimates, in which consequently there were never errors. She handled the entire payroll alone. She was aware of the smallest mistake in the remotest office routine as immediately as she would have been of a wasp buzzing about her tiny office. She was the only person in the company whom Joe trusted entirely.

Marion was not Joe's mistress. He banged her from time to time, always in the office, always after five o'clock or on weekends or on holidays. He had banged her on the drafting tables, against the Xerox machine, on the floor of his office, in the ladies' room and sitting in his swivel chair. The banging had taken place over a period of nine years and was therefore not as frequent as Marion fancied it to be. They never discussed it and never openly arranged it. They never even admitted that they were alone in the office together for any reason other than work.

"What are you doin' here, anyway?" Marion asked. "I thought you were over on the school job."

"I was. Came to get those bids on the Hamilton plant. They ready?"

"They're not even due till Wednesday. Yeah, they're ready."

"Thought I'd look 'em over over the weekend."

Marion riffled through a stack of papers in the OUT basket and handed him the bids he'd asked for.

He went around her desk and pulled her to her feet as he took the papers. He put his hand directly on her crotch and said, "How 'bout a little, honey?"

"Oh, Joe," she said as if he had told her a risqué joke. "Here? Right now? Here?"

"Sure. Why not? I really got hot nuts, baby."

"You *always* got hot nuts, Joe." She giggled, then said, "How 'bout a kiss, Joey?"

Almost without hesitation, Joe kissed her. Her request surprised him. His hand on her crotch was the usual extent of their preliminaries. He couldn't remember the last time he had kissed her. Maybe he kissed her during it and just didn't realize it. No. He didn't kiss her. He wondered if any of the guys did. Some of them must. But he didn't. He wondered why. Wasn't because he didn't like her. She was good lookin' enough. Maybe it had something to do with the places they did it. Like the draftin' table. Man! That was somethin'! And the swivel chair! It was somethin' like Peg's game—which was just as much his game. Come to think of it, he didn't kiss Peg a hell of a lot, either. Christ knows, he liked to fuck, but he liked it a hell of a lot better when there was a . . . a game or the drafting table. It always took the place of the neckin', and he didn't like to neck and fuck at the same time.

He pulled away from the kiss and pulled up her dress.

"Joe!" she screeched. "Right in here?"

"Yeah," he said, working at her underclothes.

"But where? *Where?*"

"On the desk."

"But the papers. . . ."

"Fuck the papers."

"You mean fuck *on* the papers." She giggled again and lay back on her morning's work.

He had been inside her for only a moment when the telephone rang. He reached out to answer it, and she grabbed his wrist.

"Oh, no, Joe! Not while we're . . ."

"Yeah! It'd be a ball. Come on. I want to."

He picked up the receiver and said. "Joe Jablonski." He grinned and winked at Marion. "Oh, hi'ya, Sylvia . . . No She just went out for a sandwich." He was moving slowly deep in and out of Marion. "Maybe she'll be back in a minute. Hey, how's your brother, Chris? . . . Yeah? I bet." Marion wriggled under him impatiently. "Hey, look, Syl. I guess Marion's not comin' right back. I'll tell her you called, huh? . . . Yeah. So long."

Joe hung up and laughed loudly. "Hey, that was somethin' else! What'd Sylvia say if she knew we was doin' it right while I was talkin' to her? Man!" The phone calls had happened before, but it was always treated as the first time.

Marion pulled his face down close to her own and held him there. After a moment the phone rang again. "No, Joe. Don't," Marion whispered.

"Aw, come on." Smiling, Joe picked up the phone and said, "Joe Jablonski . . . Augie? How the hell are you doing? Why aren't . . . What? . . . Oh, Christ! Oh, Christ, no! . . . Oh, holy Christ! . . . Five minutes." He hung up and looked down at Marion. He was still inside her. "The. . . the east wall of the school . . . it fell . . .it collapsed!"

Marion made a little wounded sound, and Joe was standing, pulling up his trousers. He was still buckling his belt as he ran through the rows of desks.

Marion called after him, "Wait, Joe! I'll go with you!"

"Stay with the phone!" he shouted, and he was gone.

Joe was on the site in less than five minutes, the fly of his chinos left open in his haste. As he pulled onto the flat, muddy ground surrounding what had so recently been the shell of the new school, his mind tried to reject the reality of what he saw before him. Less than an hour ago, the red brick walls had stood, fresh and clean, their color deepened and warmed by the wetness of the day. The myriad, precise lines of mortar gleamed almost white against the brick. One could hardly see them and not imagine the finished building: many-paned windows shining in the sun; the white cupola on the gray shingled roof; the bronze arrow of the weathervane arrested in flight. Now where the east wall had been, there was only a gigantic pile of rubble. A quarter of the north wall had fallen, leaving an edge as raw and ragged as if a wrecker's ball had hit it. The police were there: a patrol car and the Emergency Squad truck. The Hainesdale Volunteer Fire Department had sent a ladder-truck and a smaller vehicle, both bright and red as checkerboard squares. There was an ambulance from St. Joseph's Hospital. And everywhere there were the men. Joe's men, helmeted and denimed—the animal-poised, physical, usually laughing men—scurrying desperately and to all appearances pointlessly, like suddenly disturbed insects. The vehicles' emergency lights flashed red and yellow in the gray air, which was filled with so many babbling, insignificant voices that the total effect was of illuminated silence. Joe wanted to remain in the car, a mere spectator, ignorant of the details of the terrible event which involved him more than anyone else at the scene.

Then he was running cautiously on the slippery earth, like most of the others, not knowing where to go or what to do. He heard his name being called and turned to see the Fire Chief, Ben Marbin, approaching him, his weathered, basset hound face alert and sad at once.

"There's somebody in there. Under it."

Joe had heard the words in his head a dozen times in a dozen different ways since he left the office. He had not even denied them, for a denial would have admitted the possibility of their truth. Now it was as if he had never heard them before at all, as if the announcement was sudden and unexpected.

He stopped and stared into Ben Marbin's eyes for a moment. "How many?"

It seemed an odd question to Ben. "Just one as far as we know."

"Who?"

Augie Sorrentino was beside him, grasping Joe's arm in a grip which would have hurt most men. Augie was crying. "Joe! Joe, Steve Wyczinski was standin' . . . He's *under* there!"

The detailed picture was in Joe's mind instantly, and it seemed too real, too newspaper-column, human-interest perfect to be possible. He saw Laura Wyczinski, twenty-nine years old, seven months pregnant, mother of Joe and Jerry, aged six and nine. He saw the gray clapboard house they shared with Steve's mother and the flowerless back yard with its manicured lawn. He saw Steve in the blue and gold uniform, shooting a jump-shot from the varnish-gleaming floor of the Hainesdale High School gymnasium. He saw the strong, square, peasant face under the tasseled black cap of graduation. He saw Steve chug-a-lugging a beer after bowling the 273 that clinched the Industrial League's seasonal title. And he knew that Steve was dead. For there was no mine shaft beneath this wreckage, no cave, no geological chamber in which Steve Wyczinski might hide and suck the precious air while rescuers picked at the debris of his tomb. There was only the basement of the building-to-be, filled in with tons of steel and brick and the flat, demolished body of Steve Wyczinski. He was dead surely.

There was no need for delicacy in Steve's exhuming. Joe and Augie and Ben Marbin and the Police Chief and the intern from St. Joseph's conferred and agreed that the man had been crushed to death and that the matter immediately facing them was the retrieving of his body. They watched almost hopefully as the claw of the giant crane bit into the monumental heap an eighth-of-a-ton at a bite. And Steve's fellow-workers watched with the officials. And as time went on, they were joined by newspaper boys on their bikes and housewives from nearby houses and the county coroner and men on their way home from work. And finally by Laura Wyczinski, who stood ripe and trembling, with Joe's arm around her shoulders as the floodlights were moved in.

The deathwatch was faithfully kept. Those unnecessary to the ritual—the firemen, the intern—left the scene. The mere spectators left and were replaced. Steve Wyczinski's co-workers spelled each other in the helplessness, a group leaving for shots and beers and to call home and returning to relieve another group. They would all be there for the final moment.

As it turned out, the final moment was bogus. The engineers decided at what level the crane should be abandoned and a pick-and-shovel crew should take over. Dr. Maxim Faubus, the coroner, wearing hip boots, courtesy of the Hainesdale Construction Company, moved to the edge of the developing crater, peering down for the first sight of the body he knew they would never find enough of to see. Dr. Faubus was a lithe old man. He scrambled down one side of the crater when his instinct told him they were close. He heard the first clank of the shovel on Steve Wyczinski's hard hat and gestured for the diggers to stop. He took a shovel himself then and turned over several shovelfuls of debris. It was as he had known it would be. He soon could not tell when he stopped turning over debris and began turning over a crudely homogenized mixture of flesh and brick and blood and steel and bone and vital fluids.

He held the shovel loosely beside him and said to one of Steve's friends, "Okay. There it is."

"What are you crazy, Doc? There ain't nothin' but . . ."

"For Jesus' sake, get a stretcher down here, boy! And we'll put the hat and the rags and some bones and what-

100

ever else we can find . . . and some bricks to fill it up. Give that poor woman something to mourn. We'll cover it up and keep it from her. See she gets taken home before we even start."

"You son of a bitch, that's his *wife!* You can't . . ."

"There's part of the head in the helmet. You want to take it up and show her? Pretend, you imbecile! Pretend! Now move!"

The gentle conspiracy was maintained over the next three days. Laura Wyczinski had collapsed at the sight of the ascending stretcher, and Joe had carried her to his car and taken her home. The stretcher full of rubble was delivered to the Boyd Funeral Home and disposed of in a wheelbarrow through the back door. Steve's wife and mother were elaborately dissuaded from viewing the remains. A closed-casket viewing was arranged.

The non-viewing took place on Monday evening. Steve's high school graduation photograph in a gold filigreed frame stood on the lid of the closed casket, which was banked with hundreds of gladioli and carnations and roses and lilies and chrysanthemums, filling the room with a thick, sweet, cloying smell. So many relatives and friends and co-workers came to file past the bier that the viewing hour had to be extended beyond the usual nine o'clock. Close relatives sat on rows of folding metal chairs, whispering above the steady moan of weeping. Several aged Polish women who could put Irish keeners to shame sat quietly with handkerchiefs pressed to their lips, their tradition of wailing in disfavor with the young. Laura Wyczinski sat on the first chair in the first row, her two sons beside her, alternately fidgeting, crying and submitting to Laura's embraces. Steve's mother sat next to them, emitting an endless series of low, quiet moans. From time to time, Laura's crying crescendoed into shrieks, and she was led from the room to compose herself. Shortly after 10:00 o'clock, it was over, only to be resumed the next morning for an hour before the requiem Mass at the Church of Our Lady of Perpetual Help, which all the parish kids referred to as "OLPH."

The funeral procession was the longest Hainesdale had seen since fourteen-year-old Billy Moran had drowned in the country club lake three years before. Behind the two Cadillac limousines supplied by the Boyd Funeral Home came the freshly washed and waxed automobiles of the mourners. The six pallbearers were employees of the Hainesdale Construction Company, strong, deft men made awkward by grief in the attendance to the coffin. The ascetic-looking young priest who had celebrated the Mass was intentionally and blessedly brief at the graveside, where Laura Wyczinski collapsed again. Then the mourners dispersed, slowly, reluctantly, as if prolonging the ritual could somehow prolong Steve Wyczinski's already extinguished existence.

Joe and Peg and their children went home with the remaining Wyczinskis, where a post-funeral feast had been prepared by female neighbors whose attendance at the rites was less mandatory than the attendance of relatives. And a feast it was: three whole, baked, glazed Polish hams; a mountainous mound of potato salad; a twenty-three pound stuffed turkey; a platter of cold sliced roast beef, salami, Swiss cheese and corned beef; two enormous casseroles of baked macaroni and cheese; dozens of seeded rolls; deep earthenware pots of baked beans; cakes enough for ten birthdays—angel food, devil's food, mocha, walnut, apple, caramel, fudge, apricot, marble—coffee bubbling in the rented fifty-cup urn. All crammed onto the Wyczinskis' maple kitchen table in the corner beneath the two windows with the brown and blue café curtains Laura had made herself and which Steve would never see again.

And there was the booze: an unlimited supply of beer, Johnny Walker Red, Seagrams 7 (the most popular item), Jack Daniels; Gilbeys gin, Romanoff vodka. It went fast, appropriately enough; for over and over again the words were said: "Steve woulda been the first one to

102

break out the booze at a time like this." And it was true. For he, in their place, would have felt the unspeakable sadness they felt. He, in their place, would have spoken of the present, of the now of death; would have declared that Jerry or Bosco or Philly or Jimmy would have been the first one to break out the booze at a time like this. And it was true. All of the dead ones would have had they been living and would have been living had they a choice. And so the living imitated the dead and numbed the raw pain of loss as they would have.

It was after five o'clock when Joe and Peg and their children left. They drove Marion Collins home first. Joe was as drunk as he ever seemed to get, and if you didn't know him, you wouldn't have known that he was drunk at all. He drove a little faster than usual, but with as much control as if he'd been sober. He lumbered somewhat when he walked, and he was noticeably aggressive. There was a heightened coarseness in his speech. But you would have to have known him sober to make a comparison.

Helen had gone home directly from the cemetery to relieve the baby-sitter and to fix supper for the family. She greeted them quietly and with averted eyes to demonstrate her grief, then she and Peg went into the kitchen. Joe took a shot and a bottle of beer and sat on the flagstone patio reading the *Hainesdale News*. He heard the door chime through the open windows and studiously ignored it. In a couple of minutes, the back door opened and Peg was saying, "Joe, Harry Boyle's here. Sure you don't want a drink or anything, Harry?"

Harry was a tall, thin, sick-looking man of forty-five. Joe knew him well, for he was the County Inspector of Building Construction.

"No, thanks, Peg," Harry said. "Sure'd like to sit down, though."

"Hey, Harry," Joe said, getting up to greet him. "Come on, have a drink with me."

"Well, maybe a beer."

"Get him a beer, Peg. Sit down here where it's comfortable."

Harry sat on a chaise longue and straightened out his legs as if it were painful for him to do so. "You got a beautiful yard here, Joe."

"Thanks. We don't do much to it, but I like to keep it neat."

Peg returned with a bottle of beer and a glass and gave them to Harry.

"Thanks, Peg. That'll hit the spot."

Peg went back into the house, and the two men were silent for a moment.

"That was an awful thing about Steve Wyczinski. My sympathy goes out to his wife. To you, too. I know you were close."

"Thanks, Harry."

They were quiet for a long, uncertain time.

"Joe, I've known you a long time. In a way, that makes it easier to ask. In a way, it makes it harder, too."

"Ask what?" Joe said, the belligerence in his voice as clear as the tone of a bell.

"I been over to the new school . . . what was the new school." Joe waited. "I saw the specifications over a year ago, but I got a copy in my office. Checked 'em Saturday night." Joe waited out the new pause. "Joe. You . . . you followin' those specifications in that new school building?" Harry knew it was entirely unreasonable for Joe to hit him, but for a long moment he was afraid it was going to happen.

"You better finish your beer, Harry," Joe said quietly, "and get the hell out of here."

"Joe, listen . . ."

Joe was on his feet moving toward Harry Boyle. Harry got up quickly and held out a hand, palm toward Joe. "All right. I'll go. But I'm gonna have to ask you again. I wanted to do it friendly like, but . . ."

"It's one hell of a friendly question. Just go, Harry."

Harry put his beer glass on the table beside the chaise longue. He turned to Joe as if he were going to say something else. Then he left, walking around the house rather than through it. Joe stared at Harry's back, then for a long time at just the emptiness when he had gone.

CHAPTER V

The friendship between the old neighbors and the new ones had flowered with the other growing things of June: the lilacs and violets and wisteria and lilies of the valley and the early roses. And, like the other growing things, the friendship had its aphids and Japanese beetles. Having won too many easy victories, Michael was becoming more and more bored with the cookouts, the mediocre bridge, community politics and deliberate provincialism. Peg, on the other hand, was becoming fed up with Michael's deliberate sophistication. Joe seemed withdrawn from everyone. Ethel had not entirely forgiven Cynthia's detergent rebuff and behaved toward her in what she hoped was a haughty manner. George was impatient with Michael's intolerance, yet felt defensive about him when he sensed Peg's disapproval. Tom was not absolutely certain, but he thought he noticed a new reticence in Cynthia, both sexually and socially. Herb noticed none of these things, for he was fumbling with a problem of his own.

The private considerations did not impede the flow of

invitations and counter-invitations among the neighbors. They played bridge on Wednesdays (they had two tables now), rotating hosts each week. There were dinner parties on Fridays and Saturdays and sometimes brunches on Sundays. In spite of a numbing, overall sameness, each household maintained a style of its own. At the Jablonskis' it was the picnic tables and Gallo and beer in the backyard. At the Radnors' it was individual TV tables and rosé in the garden. At the Parkers' it was the redwood furniture and *sangria* on the patio. At George and Michael's it was the long, white wrought-iron-and-glass table and an expensive white bordeaux on the terrace. There was also Gian-Carlo, who was utterly a servant. He was not a servant and an unmarried relative; not a servant and a colored girl who came in three times a week. He was a servant whose sole apparent function in life was to minister to the needs of his employers, George and Michael. Gian-Carlo—like the family silver, the Porthault table linen, the expensive wine and the terrace itself—lent a distinctive tone to George and Michael's style. But of all these elements, it was only Gian-Carlo who aggravated Herb's problem, aggravated it at this moment because the neighbors were assembled on the terrace on the evening of the third of July, and Gian-Carlo was serving them cold watercress soup. And because Herb's son was there and would soon begin to eat the entrée with his fork in his left hand and his knife in his right, without changing them from hand to hand.

Herb's problem had begun when David had said at the end of a Saturday morning breakfast, "Hey, I'm going over to see Michael. Did you know he's helping me with my writing? I've been fooling around with like short stories, and he said he'd help me. I think that's great."

The simple statements raised so many questions that Herb was stunned into silence. David had bounded from the table and out the kitchen to the front door before he could speak.

"Well, what do you think of *that?*" he asked.

"I agree with David," Cynthia said, clearing the table. "I think it's great."

"Well, I'm not at all sure I do," Herb said.

"What's wrong with it?"

"Don't be ridiculous. You know perfectly well what's wrong with it."

"No, I don't. I'm not even sure I know what you're suggesting."

"I'm suggesting that the man is a homosexual. And I consider homosexuality vile."

"And yet you invite Michael and George to our home?"

"I consider myself sufficiently adult to be able to put sexuality in its place."

"Even though it's vile."

"Cynthia. There's no reason why you should keep up with these things, but as an educator, I have to. An investigating panel of psychiatrists recently said in a report that most—mind you, *most* male homosexuality is caused by early seduction."

"You read that in *The New York Times,* and so did I. And that conclusion was challenged and even repudiated by dozens of other psychiatrists." In the absence of a sexual relationship between them, or perhaps more in the presence of the incestuous restraint which had replaced it, Cynthia and Herb felt required to discuss sex from time to time, however uncomfortable it made them. Only clinical language made such discussions possible. "Personally I think the theory's absurd."

"You don't think a young child is sexually vulnerable?"

Cynthia closed the refrigerator door and turned to him. "I mean that I don't think one seduction or a hundred seductions can turn a heterosexual child into a homosexual child. And I think we're off the subject. I wouldn't want David subjected to a homosexual advance under any circumstances. But I'm dead certain Michael would never make one. Even if I were wrong, I believe the worst that could happen would be . . ." Suddenly Cynthia stopped. For a moment, the alabaster poise seemed

109

to quiver like a monument in an earthquake. "For God's sake, you're not afraid David would . . . would . . . acquiesce or . . . succumb to . . . For God's sake, don't you know anything about your son?"

In his own mind, Herb had not gone beyond the abstract idea of corruption. The actual sexual image seemed to stagger him. He averted his eyes as if looking at Cynthia would cause him unbearable embarrassment. "I . . . I didn't mean to infer . . . It's just that . . . I guess I don't like the idea of it." He glanced at his watch. "Oh, I'm going to be late." He got up from the table and left.

As Gian-Carlo served the watercress soup to Herb, Herb was considering his second encounter with his problem. It had been less than a week ago, and the memory was fresh and vivid and painful.

Since the beginning of June and of David's summer vacation, he and Michael had spent more and more time together. Outwardly, Michael maintained the position of mentor. But since they spoke almost exclusively of each other's private intimacies, an intimacy between them was inevitable. It was, in utterly different ways, a rewarding friendship for both. Michael's rewards were the more ecstatic; David's were the more real.

David had rewritten his short story three times, the third time not at Michael's bidding, but because he himself was dissatisfied with the latest version. They were mutually proud of the final form, although it was too sophisticated for amateur publications and not quite sophisticated enough for professional ones.

David had also read the first sixty pages of Michael's novel and was convinced that it was better than anything he could ever write. Michael pointed out that David was merely impressed by the achievement of sustaining a story beyond twenty pages and that there were parts of his story that were better than anything in the novel.

The essential function of the relationship was to make David reach upward toward higher levels of intellectual and emotional maturity and to make Michael reach

110

downward to meet him. The friendship existed on this happy plateau. David had never before felt so knowledgeably old, and Michael had not for years so carelessly young.

On the morning of Herb's second confrontation with his problem, Michael and David had gone to the hill above the country club. They sat on the seats in the rock, Michael, as always, on one slightly higher than David's. They had agreed that David should abandon his other two stories and start a new one. They talked for a long time about the direction the story was taking. Then there was an uncharacteristic silence between them. The sounds and smells of summer where heavy in the air.

"You know something?" Michael said. "You've never shown me your list."

"What list?" David said. And before Michael could answer, he said, "Oh, *that* list. I just happen to have that list right here in my pocket. I thought you'd never ask." He took a folded piece of notebook paper from his shirt pocket and handed it to Michael. Michael unfolded it and read it.

I LOVE		I LIKE
My mother and father		School
Books		Math
Music		~~Summer~~
June (Cathy)		Grass
Grass		Bobby Geary
Summer		The guitar
Sex		Food! Eating!
Words		Rita Corwin
Peace	God	Basketball
Honesty		Tennis
Writing		Being alone
Being together		Quiet
Loving		J.O.
		Poetry
		Being sloppy

"So?" David said.

"So you played like most people. You faked in the beginning, then got serious about it. 'My mother and father.' "

"You don't think I love them?"

"Of course you do. You're supposed to. And you're supposed to love books and music . . . and the flag and apple pie. Then all of a sudden we get to 'June (Cathy).' And you start playing fair. Oh, I like 'school' and 'math,' too. The All-American Boy. Christ!"

"All right."

"If 'grass' and 'grass' mean what I think, you learn fast. What happened with 'summer'?"

"I decided I love it. I don't have to go to the school I like to study the math I like. I'm free."

"You really are a smart-ass. 'Words,' 'peace' and 'honesty' I'll ignore as being merely pretentious. But . . ."

"You've got a hell of a nerve."

"I know. May I ask what God's doing in the middle?"

" 'Lines on God,' by David Radnor," David said. " 'I'd like to think there is One/ I'd love Him if there were . . .' "

"That's all?"

"What do you want?"

"I don't know. Something like . . . 'I'll find out if there is One/ When they do me inter.' "

"That's awful."

"It rhymes."

"It's still awful."

"Who's teach here?"

"You."

"Okay. I like 'sex' and 'loving' as separate entities."

"I don't mean it that way. But sometimes they are."

"Who are Bobby Geary and Rita Corwin?"

"Friends."

"Of each other?"

"Yeah. And of mine."

"But you don't love them?"

"Not quite. Isn't that what the game's about?"

"Smart-ass. A big, fat smart-ass. Well, you're certainly 'sloppy.' Your writing proves that."

"It's nice of you to say that."

"Just a passing thought. Who's J.O.?"

David grinned and said, "Come on."

"Who's J.O.?"

"Would you believe Jackie Onassis?" Michael looked annoyed and didn't answer. "Come on, Michael." There was still no answer. "J.O. Jerking off. Come on, you knew that."

Michael had not known it. He didn't want to know it. He had found a hundred doorways to David's sexuality and had stopped outside each one. Now the entrance gaped at him again. "You sure it's in the right column?"

"I had to think about it a lot."

Then Michael blundered through the doorway. "How often?"

"What? Oh." David was embarrassed, but he took the responsibility for his embarrassment. "Would you believe daily?"

Michael had stepped into a world in which he could not survive. He did not care how awkward, how clownish his retreat would seem. He simply wanted to get out. "You like being alone, and you love being together. That's pretty schmaltzy. And I think it would be marvelous if you *loved* being quiet."

"When do I get your list?"

"You don't."

"Why not?"

"I'm teach."

"And you talk about playing fair."

"Let's split."

"Nobody says that any more. I mean, if you're trying to do the young bit."

"You are a mean son of a bitch."

"When do I get your list?"

"I told you, you don't."

"Why not?"

Michael had stood up and taken a few steps down the hill. "Let's adjourn the meeting and punt on the lake."

"Why not?"

Michael turned to him with the expressionlessness of a bird. "All right. Let's see how much Master Radnor has grown up. You don't get my list because if *I* made a list for you, you'd be on it."

As they looked at each other, birds made their noises and a dragonfly, looking for the lake, hovered near them.

"Wow!" David said, looking away. "I goofed."

"It's not important."

David looked back and said, "Yeah, I can tell. You think I can say all the other things and not that?"

"Come on. It's punting time."

"I love you, Michael." Michael had turned around, and the words were like cannon fire at his back. "Maybe not the way you want, but I love you. You need a list to know that?"

"No, I don't need a list. You want to punt or not?"

"Yeah, I want to punt."

They rented a rowboat at the country club dock and behaved in it like drunken children. They splashed each other with water and rowed in opposite directions. They shouted and sang and cursed in a vain effort to erase the evidence of their separate and different loving. And in a final moment of buffoonery while returning the boat to the dock, they fell into the lake. They were laughing too hard to make sense to the renter of the boats, but they made enough sense to each other to agree that they would go to Michael's to dry their clothes.

Their arrival, soaking and impenitent, was not taken well by George. But their good humor was infectious, and soon George was part of the comedy. Gian-Carlo, whose job it was to put Michael's and David's clothes into the dryer, was not so easily won over. He stood in the den as intrusively as possible while Michael and David took off their wet clothes and handed them to him. There was

114

one moment when they stood naked together, each swearing silently he would do it no matter what the moment cost.

Michael was laughing from a previous joke as he threw his jockey shorts to Gianni and said, "I'm sorry. I know you have other things to do."

"Gianni, my mother would kill me if I went home wet," David said. Gianni turned and left the room.

"There are some towels in the john," Michael said to David. "Would you get one for me, too?"

"Sure." David went into the bathroom and did not see George's look of accusation. David came out of the bathroom wrapped in a red towel and threw a blue one to Michael. Michael put the towel around him, twisted it at the top and fell into a leather armchair. George and David sat on the sofa. The glass curtained French doors were open onto the terrace. A warm, heavy breeze crept in on them.

"I really thought we were going to drown," Michael said, giggling again.

They told themselves they ought to have heard the bell, but it was too late. Gian-Carlo was already standing in the doorway of the den, ready to announce Herb, who stood beside him.

George said, "Hello, Herb."

Michael started to jump to his feet, but fell back into the chair. "Would you believe it, Herb? We fell into the lake at the club."

"We were in a boat," David said. "I was afraid . . . I was afraid Mother would be upset if I came home wringing wet."

"So Gianni's drying them for us in the laundry. Our clothes. I wouldn't risk Cynthia's displeasure for anything."

Herb stood staring and astonished at his son and his neighbor, sitting in a room together, to his mind, naked. Michael and David stared at him, waiting for the casual laugh of approval that did not come.

"I came to borrow a Phillips screwdriver," Herb said quietly.

"Oh, sure," George said. "I have a couple of them in the garage. Come on." He left the room and led Herb from the scene. Neither Michael nor David could speak in the complex silence that was left. George came back and invited Herb back into the room. Herb stood in the doorway and said, "The screwdriver's fine. I'll see you at home when your clothes are dry." Then he left. George saw him to the door.

Gian-Carlo, smiling, returned the clothes to the den in neat, separate piles. He put them on a table and left. George had gone into the drawing room. Herb had gone home.

Michael and David dressed in silence. David buckled his belt and said, "I don't know what to say."

"Try 'Wow!' " Michael said.

"Okay. Wow! I've got to go home."

As David started from the room, Michael said, "Maybe I'll see you again."

David stopped and turned back to him. "You will."

"Are you sure? I don't think Herb was very happy."

"Yeah. But Herb won't be able to talk about it. I know him. He just can't." After a moment he said, "I'll call you."

David was right. Herb had not mentioned the incident. What, after all, could he have said? How could he have discussed it without suggesting that it had looked as if something sexual had been going on between David and Michael—perhaps even with George involved in some . . . in some way? How could he forbid David to see Michael or even warn him without saying he feared Michael would make a sexual advance toward David? It was difficult to discuss such things even with Cynthia. Discussing them with David was unthinkable.

And so Herb ate the watercress soup, which he didn't like, and watched and listened as the conversation became an elliptical one between David and Michael.

116

David was saying to Cynthia, "Wait till you read Michael's novel. It's really great."

"That's an extravagant compliment," Michael said.

"I was using the word in its colloquial sense," David said.

"Cynthia," Michael said, "your son is being disrespectful."

"Would I be disrespectful to one who sits higher on the rock?" David said.

"Eyebrow," Michael said.

David chuckled, but no one else did.

"Tell us about the novel, Michael," Tom said. "What's it about?"

"That's a professional secret," Michael answered. "Even George hasn't read it."

The faux pas of "even George" was compounded by the fact that although "even George" hadn't read the novel, David had. Everyone but Herb thought of something unsayable to say, and Gian-Carlo reappeared in the silence.

"Excuse me," he said. "There is a telephone call for Mr. Jablonski."

Mr. Jablonski, who had been almost totally silent all evening, rose without a word: no nice but needless explanation that he had left the number with someone and no request to be excused. Gian-Carlo ushered him to the phone in the den and left the room.

"Yeah?" Joe said into the phone.

"Augie."

"I know."

"The *Hainesdale News* is gonna have it Monday."

"You sure?"

"Yeah, I'm sure."

"Holy Christ," Joe said quietly. "You talk to McManus?"

"No. He's away for the long weekend."

"What the hell kind of a lawyer is he? I told the son of a bitch to stick around."

"Well, he ain't here."

"I'll run over to Ridgewood tomorrow. Talk to Robbins."

"You oughta call first. "It's Fourth of July, Joe."

"Yeah. All right. Thanks for callin' me, Augie." Joe returned to the table and sat down.

"Who was it?" Peg asked.

"Just Augie."

"What'd he want?"

"Nothing. Nothing important." It was clear that this was the only explanation Joe was going to offer, even though it was made utterly illogical by the obvious fact that Joe had had to leave George's unlisted number with Augie.

It was an unsuccessful evening. Only Michael and David seemed to be having a good time, which contributed to the failure. The others seemed too preoccupied for any effective social contribution. Even David felt it strongly enough to check his impulse to stay on when his parents announced their departure earlier than usual. Michael had noticed the pall before David had and had begun to drink heavily. All seven guests left at the same time.

When they had gone, George said with excessive enthusiasm, "How about another brandy?"

Michael knew he was drunk, in disfavor and being humored; but as long as he was being humored, he didn't care about the other two. "That's a goddamned good idea," he said, striding toward the drawing room.

Michael took his brandy and went out onto the terrace. George followed. It was a soothing kind of evening, cool for midsummer and quiet.

"Not much of a dinner party, was it?" George said when they were settled.

"The food was delicious, the wine was splendid and I had a very nice time. The company was a pain in the ass."

"Including me?"

118

"Oh, for Christ's sake! No, of course not including you."

"Everybody's entitled to a mood now and then."

"And because Joe Jablonski behaves like a sick bear, everybody's supposed to act like it's a funeral."

"You didn't."

"You're damned right I didn't," Michael said emphatically. "I was having a perfectly good time. Up to a point."

"You *and* David."

Michael looked at him angrily for a moment and said, "Yes."

"That was part of it, you know."

"Part of what?"

"Of what was wrong."

"You're even crazier than I thought you were." George didn't answer. He was looking away toward the rose garden. "Everybody got depressed because David and I were enjoying ourselves?"

"No. Each other."

Is that a grammatical correction?"

"A semantic one."

"I don't think I like it."

"I don't like it when the gardener tells me there are gypsy moths on the trees. But that doesn't remove the gypsy moths—or make the gardener responsible for them."

"Oh, Christ, George, spare me your metaphors!"

"Don't be angry with *me*, Mike. I haven't done anything to deserve it."

"And I haven't done anything to deserve your accusations."

"I'm not accusing you. Michael, please listen to me. I know I shouldn't discuss anything controversial with you when we've been drinking, but . . ."

"A nice touch, George, that 'we've.' "

"But you never seem to want to talk about anything serious anymore when you're sober either. And in a good humor. And I think we've got to talk about this."

"What is 'this'?"

119

"You and David."

"There's nothing to talk about."

"If the relationship between you can affect seven other people at a dinner party, I think there is something to talk about."

"What's the matter, George? Do they think David and I are fucking?"

"No, they don't think that. And neither do I. But I'm sure they wonder why you seem to be a better friend of David's than of theirs."

"You bet your ass I am."

"I'm sure they wonder what a man your age has in common with a boy of David's age."

"If Herb Radnor wonders that, he must be one hell of a teacher."

"We're not talking about a pupil. We're talking about his son."

"Well, his son *is* a pupil—of mine. Who coaches him in basketball, a six-year-old? Who gives him music lessons? Who teaches him history? Children? I'm just teaching him whatever I can about writing."

"He doesn't go for long walks in the woods with his history teacher. He doesn't fall into the lake with his basketball coach."

"Where would you like us to talk about his work, George? In the middle of Jefferson Turnpike so the great big world of New Jersey will know we're not groping each other?"

"Jefferson Turnpike wouldn't be any less appropriate than in the lake. That's the point, Michael. You and David obviously have something much more than a teacher-student relationship. Painfully obviously."

Michael stared at George for a long time. A weak, ill-humored smile spread across Michael's face. "I'll be goddamned! I do think I see the approach of the green-eyed monster."

"Don't be ridiculous."

"Oh, I know, kiddies aren't your bag. But I think you're jealous of the friendship, the intimacy."

"No. But I'm worried about the fact that you don't seem to be able to handle two intimate friendships at the same time."

"What?"

"Do you realize in the last four days, I've seen you only at dinner? After which you get smashed and go to bed. The rest of the time you've either been working or been off somewhere with David." George could see Michael calculating the time in his head and realizing that George was right. "I don't object to your relationship with David, and I certainly don't envy you for it. But I don't like what it seems to be doing to *our* relationship, and I don't like the justifiable suspicions of the neighbors."

"Justifiable? What do they suspect?"

"I think they suspect that when a thirty-eight-year-old man and a fifteen-year-old boy seem to need each other, there is probably something wrong with one or both of them. And that it isn't an especially good idea for them to spend most of their time together."

"Is that what *you* think?"

"I'm trying to make you understand that it doesn't matter what I think. I'm trying to make you understand that it's perfectly natural for the Parkers and the Jablonskis and especially the Radnors to be . . . upset, to wonder about the . . . the common denominator of such a relationship."

"And it doesn't matter whether the relationship is good or bad, right or wrong, moral or immoral?"

"That's right, Michael. It doesn't matter."

"As long as the fuckin' idiot neighbors get their way. As long as I conform to their stupid, middle-class, blind, ignorant, double-standard morality. As long as . . ."

"Now that you've retired from the theater, I'd hoped you'd given up being dramatic."

Michael wanted to throw his brandy glass at George. Instead, he put it on the glass-topped table beside his chair. He looked at George for a long time. And George looked back calmly, as if he were waiting for Michael to tell him what time he wanted to get up in the morning.

"I'll tell you one thing I haven't given up and am not going to give up: my friendship with David Radnor. Certainly not because of something somebody else *thinks* it to be. It's the nicest, cleanest, decentest, most interesting thing that's happened to me in a very long time. And I'm not giving it up for you or them or anybody else."

"Thank you," George said. "For the cooperation and the deeply personal compliment."

"I didn't mean to . . ."

"No. You never do. You never mean to hurt anybody or insult anybody or inconvenience anybody. And by some strange reasoning that has always escaped me, you think saying you don't mean it makes it perfectly acceptable to whoever's getting hurt or insulted or inconvenienced. And on top of that, you expect everybody to think it's all delightfully young and childlike, when in reality it's simply immature . . . and selfish and mean."

"Is that what you think of me?"

"I think you ought to stop seeing David Radnor."

"Well, I'm not going to."

George got up and went into the house.

CHAPTER VI

Augie Sorrentino had been wrong about only one aspect of the information he had given to Joe Jablonski: the *Hainesdale News* was not published on Monday, July fifth, because it was a holiday by extension. For the same reason, Joe was unable to reach any of the people he wanted to reach over the long weekend. But on Tuesday morning at nine-thirty, he was in the office of his attorney, Francis X. McManus, with a pre-publication copy of Tuesday's *News*.

Joe did not like Francis X. McManus, but he respected, if not envied, his status symbols. He was from a family who had been in the "area" for generations. He was rich and prominent in the community. He had gone to Princeton. There was a charisma about the man which Joe admired and distrusted.

Joe had never been able to decide on an answer to the multiple-choice question which popped into his mind at odd times. The question was: Why do I always feel uncomfortable with Frank McManus? The choices were because (1) He deliberately tries to make me feel inferior; (2) I feel inferior to him; (3) I am inferior to him. Joe had wanted the prestige of having Frank McManus representing him, but he also wanted the feeling of having Frank McManus working for him. Somehow he was never able to look on Frank McManus as an employee.

As Joe walked into the private office, Frank McManus stood up to greet him. "Morning, Joe. Have a good weekend?"

"Where the hell were you?" Joe asked.

Frank's cordiality fell away as quickly and easily as it had been assumed. "I went away with my family," he said flatly and sat down.

Joe put the copy of the newspaper on the desk and said, "There. The third column, down about the middle."

Frank looked at Joe for a moment, then put on his horn-rimmed glasses, which, in Joe's opinion, added to his handsomeness and distinction. He read the brief item, while Joe remained standing.

INVESTIGATION COMMENCED

July 6 . . . The County Department of Buildings has announced it will begin an investigation into the collapse two weeks ago of two sections of wall of the new high school being erected in Hainesdale.

Mr. Harry Boyle, an inspector for the Department told the *News* on Thursday that he wanted to satisfy himself that the construction specifications were being met by the Hainesdale Construction Co., Inc., general contractor on the building. An employee of the company, Mr. Stephen Wyczinski, 36, died in the accident.

Frank McManus looked up and said, "Well?"

"Well, what?"

"Joe. Ninety-nine percent of the buildings erected in the United States don't fall down during construction. When one does, it's perfectly natural for people to ask why."

It was things like Frank's changing "collapse" to "fall down" that made Joe wonder.

"As a matter of fact," Frank went on, "a clean bill of health from the Buildings Department would be very helpful in the inevitable lawsuits."

"I never had anything like this happen before," Joe muttered.

"That's very good. Now, when Laura Wyczinski sues you, it will . . ."

"I don't think she will."

"She would if she were *my* client. And I'm not the only good lawyer in the country. When a partially completed building of yours falls down . . ."

"It was one wall."

"And part of another . . . falls down, it is presumed that your corporation has a liability for the consequences. One of those consequences is the expense of putting it up again, for which the county could sue you if you were not willing to assume the expense. Another consequence is Stephen Wyczinski's death, for which his widow can sue you."

"I know that. I don't think she will."

"If lightning had struck the building, that could hardly be said to be your fault. But if something were wrong . . . a neglected safety regulation or . . ." Frank McManus tapped the newspaper with his horn-rimmed glasses. ". . . or sub-specification materials, it could be construed to mean that Mr. Wyczinski's death was due to the negligence of the Hainesdale Construction Company. That's why having the county Building Department say there was no such negligence would be helpful. You see, in a trial, it would be the obligation of the plaintiff to prove that there was. I am assuming the Department would in its investigation find no negligence."

"That's what I want to know. If we can stop the investigation."

"Ah. Did I assume too quickly?"

"It's not that. It's just . . . how's it gonna look for my business to be investigated like that?"

"Perfectly all right, I should think. Unless, of course, I did assume too quickly."

"But what if I couldn't prove it wasn't negligence?"

"As I explained, Joe, you don't have to prove it wasn't; the plaintiff has to prove it was."

"All right. Put it that way: what if they did prove it was?"

Frank looked at him thoughtfully for a moment. "If the Department's investigation found evidence of negligence, the county would almost certainly sue you for whatever they've paid you plus damages and costs."

"Yeah, I know that, too," Joe said impatiently.

"Laura Wyczinski would almost certainly sue you for a vast sum of money. The rest would be up to the District Attorney."

"What do you mean, 'the rest'?"

"We've been talking about civil suits. If you—you, Joseph Jablonski—had ordered, say, a grade of steel inferior to that specified in your contract with the county, and the District Attorney felt that it could be proved by the evidence of the investigation that the building fell down because of the inferior steel, it would then be up to him to decide whether or not to bring against you a charge of criminal negligence."

Joe stared hard at Frank McManus, and it was obvious from his expression that he had not known that.

Frank dropped his elaborate syntax as he had dropped his cordiality. "I'm telling you it means nothing unless you cut the specifications." He resumed it again. "It's an interesting situation, actually. I mean, even if you had cut the specifications, it would still be incumbent on the county to prove that was the reason for the building's having fallen down. If you could prove it fell down for some other reason, even though you admitted cutting the specifications, you would in theory not be guilty. You would simultaneously prove yourself innocent in the crim-

126

inal action and guilty in the civil ones. It's very interesting."

"It doesn't interest me a hell of a lot," Joe said.

"Oh, I'm sorry. I was being academic."

"I asked you if we can stop the investigation."

"*I* can't stop it."

"What am I paying you for?"

"Joe. I am not the mouthpiece in an Edward G. Robinson movie. I will defend you in any of the actions I've described. That's all."

"That's all. You mean, 'So long, Joe.'"

"Not at all. You pay me a quite fitting retainer. I'm perfectly willing to discuss the situation further if you wish. I would make every effort to settle the civil actions out of court. But it is simply not my function as an attorney to try to prevent an investigation of this accident by the Department of Buildings."

"Like I said, 'So long, Joe.'" He got up and went to the door, but before he opened it, he turned back to Frank McManus and said, "You didn't even ask me if I did cut the specifications."

Frank stood up and said, "You don't understand. Whether you're guilty or not, either in a civil or a criminal proceeding, you're entitled to a defense. My job is to supply that defense. Whether you're guilty or not. I don't need to know. It doesn't matter."

"No. I don't understand that at all."

Joe spent the rest of the day in his office, which was unusual for him. Just before he left, he called Jack Schneider, an assistant district attorney, and asked if he could see him that evening. They had been close friends in high school, and, although they did not see each other socially, the closeness had left a permanent bond between them. Jack had said, "Sure, Joe. Want to come over to the house?"

"Why don't I just pick you up? About eight okay?"

"Fine. See you then."

At exactly eight o'clock, Joe stopped his car in front

of Jack Schneider's house and blew his horn. Jack came out immediately and got into the car. They exchanged greetings and Jack said, "You got a problem, Joe?"

"Yeah, sort of. You read about the Building Department's investigation?"

"I heard about it."

"Is there . . . is there any way to stop it?"

"I don't know. It depends."

"On what?"

"A lot of things. Why do you want to stop it?"

"Does that matter?"

"Yeah, it matters. Look, Joe, let's say you're pissed-off at some . . . some building inspector, and you want to show him he can't push you around. That's one thing, but . . ."

"It's something like that."

"On the other hand, maybe it's a more important reason, a more serious reason. Like maybe you want to stop the investigation because it might uncover information you'd rather not have uncovered. That's a very different thing."

"I don't see what's different about it. If you stop it, you stop it. Right?"

"Not right. One is a simple political favor. The other is . . . something else. It could be any one of a lot of things, and as of right now, I don't know what it is. The consequences are . . . could be different."

"You mean if somebody got caught?"

"That's not quite how I'd prefer to put it. Joe, you know I'll do what I can, but you've got to trust me. I've got to know what it is I'm supposed to be doing."

"It's kind of complicated."

"Okay. As long as it's also straight."

"Okay. How long have I been puttin' up buildings? Like since we graduated high school. Right? It'd take a long time, but I could put up that school single-handed. I *know* what makes a building stand up."

"Then you must know what makes one fall down."

"That's the whole point." Joe paused for a moment, noticed the darkening twilight and turned on the headlights. "I didn't strictly stick to the . . . to some of the specifications in the bid. I admit it. But the things I cut back on couldn't possibly make those walls collapse. They just couldn't."

"But in any case, an investigation would reveal the cutbacks."

"Right."

"And you'd certainly lose the contract for the school."

"I'd lose a hell of a lot more than that. As it is, it's gonna cost me plenty to put those goddamned walls back up, because the county sure ain't gonna pay for it. Okay. I'm willing to do that . . . at my own expense. But how many more contracts am I gonna get if it comes out that I cut those specifications? And what if the jury doesn't accept my proof that that couldn't be why they collapsed?"

"You talked to a lawyer?"

"Frank McManus."

"Ah, Francis X. McManus, Esquire. I hope his sense of propriety didn't keep him from telling you there's a possibility, a faint possibility of criminal charges?"

"He told me."

"That's the difference I was talking about," Jack said. "I don't like the word 'fix.' But I also don't know if you're asking me to fix a simple, routine county investigation, or if you're asking me to fix the outcome of a criminal proceeding. Believe me, there is a difference."

"I think I'm askin' you to stop the investigation so there won't be any proceeding." After a long silence, Joe said, "What do you think?"

"I don't know, Joe. I'll do what I can. It might cost you."

"I figured it might."

"I'll do what I can. Home, James."

"Thanks, Jack."

Just before Jack got out of the car in front of his

129

house, he said, "One thing, Joe. Those cutbacks. They really couldn't have made the wall collapse?"

"Honest to God. I swear it."

"Okay. You'll hear from me."

The next night was bridge night for the neighbors, and it was the Radnors' turn to host. During the afternoon, Peg called Cynthia and said that Joe had come home from the office early and wasn't feeling well. They wouldn't be able to make it for cards. Joe really didn't feel well, and he didn't mind at all missing the bridge. He didn't enjoy bridge, but he felt it was good for business for him to know how to play.

Herb's problem—his inability to deal in any way with the relationship between David and Michael—persisted and had quite literally driven him to drink. As he never had before, he drank during the day now as well as in the evening. The combination resulted in a nearly constant alcoholic content in his physical system beyond any discipline Herb had to cope with it. He was already unpleasantly drunk at nine-thirty.

Herb and Ethel were not playing the hand and George was dummy. They sat in a neat triangle in one corner of the room as Cynthia, Tom and Michael played.

"Read about Joe Jablonski?" Herb asked George loudly.

"Read about him?" George asked. "In what?"

"*Hainesdale News*."

Since Herb was virtually shouting, the bridge players could not help hearing the conversation.

"We *get* the *Hainesdale News*," Michael said without looking up from his cards, "but we certainly don't read it."

Herb ignored the interruption. "The county's conducting an investigation to find out if Joe was using substandard material in that school building that fell down. Killed one of the workmen."

George said, "I'd think an investigation would be mandatory."

"No," Herb said, shaking his head emphatically. "No. I checked. Not mandatory at all. There has to be a suspicion of negligence."

"I'm sure it's all just routine . . ." George started to say.

"No. I told you. There has to be suspicion. Cynthia, tell them how many times have I said I suspected Joe Jablonski of . . ."

"Herb, we are trying to play this hand," Cynthia said.

"Just take a minute and tell them how many times I've suspected Joe."

"Herb, I wish you'd stop this and let us play this hand."

"I think it's too important to ignore. I think there might be good reason to suspect Joe Jablonski of using substandard materials."

Tom was still examining his cards. He said, "Come on, Herb. Joe wouldn't do anything like that."

"He has young children of his own," Cynthia said. "He wouldn't . . ."

"Who are Catholics," Herb said. "And who, when the time comes, will go to the high school of Our Lady of Perpetual Help."

The card-playing stopped, and the others stared at him for a long time.

Cynthia said, "What a terrible thing to say."

Michael looked away and played his next card, and they finished in silence. When it was over, no one bothered to put down the score. Cynthia did not offer fresh drinks or suggest a snack. New partnerships were not formed. Things were quiet and awkward.

George said, "Cynthia, would you mind if we made it an early night? I guess I spent too much time in the garden in the sun. I feel absolutely terrible."

Herb saw the Parkers to the door at the same time as Michael and George. He offered no apologies or explanations and seemed in no way reluctant to have the guests leave. When he turned back from the front door, Cynthia was staring at him again.

"What's wrong?" Herb said.

"How could you say that about Joe . . . and in front of everyone?"

"All I said was there was a suspicion."

"But you believe it, don't you?"

"It's only an investigation. He's innocent until proven . . ."

"But you actually believe that Joe would build a school that wasn't safe, as long as his own children weren't going to go to it."

"Yes. I believe he's capable of it."

"Yet you call him a friend."

"Who was it who said, 'We should all have a large graveyard in which to bury the faults of our friends'?"

Cynthia was looking at him with open contempt. "I know what a man has to do to earn your admiration, but what in the name of God does somebody have to do to make you despise him?" She started toward the stairs.

"Where are you going?"

"I'm going to bed."

"Dave's not in yet."

"I stopped waiting up for David two years ago. I'd advise you to do the same." She went up the stairs without turning back to him.

It was exactly one week later that Michael and David went to New York together to go to the theater. A few days earlier, Michael had asked David if he'd ever been to a Broadway play.

"Once," David had said. "My mother took me to see *Sound of Music.*"

"Would you like to go again? There's a play I'd like you to see. There's a subplot in it that's exactly like one of your stories."

"That'd be great," David said enthusiastically. "I mean, I'd love to."

" 'Neat' would be okay with me. David . . . this is one

thing I don't think you should mention to your parents. All right?"

"Sure."

"I can get house seats for this Wednesday's matinée."

"House seats?"

"I know a couple of people in the cast. We can go back and . . . backstage and meet them afterward if you want to."

"Wow!"

"And I guess you deserve to be given lunch since you've been such a good boy all summer."

"Thank you, teach. I'd like that a lot."

"We should really leave by eleven. It that okay? You never know what the traffic's going to be like or how long it'll take to park the car."

"Any time you say."

"It's a deal."

"I'm very excited about it. Thank you, Michael."

David arrived ten minutes early more dressed up than Michael had ever seen him. He was wearing slacks, a striped blazer and a shirt and tie. He had hidden the blazer and tie by the front door, said goodbye to his mother and grabbed the clothes on the way out, putting them on on the way to Michael's.

They got to New York just before noon, parked the car and started to walk.

"I thought of about two hundred restaurants I wanted to take you to," Michael said. "Like Sardi's. But Sardi's on matinée day is like eating at Schrafft's. Anyway, I settled on the Oak Room. At the Plaza. It's an old, old favorite of mine."

They got to the Plaza and went into the Fifty-ninth Street lobby. They were hardly inside when Michael said, "Damn it! I forgot to tell George."

"Tell him what?" David asked.

"About . . . Never mind. But I'll have to call him. I'll only be two minutes. I'll meet you right here." He started off toward the public phone booths.

133

David's eyes were drawn for a moment to the gigantic crystal chandeliers, and when he looked down again, he saw her—or thought he did—for only an instant. He had known when his eyes fell on her that it was his mother, standing before the bank of elevators. But when she disappeared into one of the elevators, he had a moment of shattering doubt, as if his sanity were suddenly in question. He stood staring across the ornate, elegantly bustling lobby, knowing it couldn't have been his mother and knowing it had been.

It was less than a minute later when he saw Tom Parker come through the revolving door and walk to the elevators without looking to either side. In a moment he was gone. David was still staring when he heard Michael from slightly behind him, saying, "Did he see you?"

David was startled. He looked up and back at Michael without speaking for a moment. "No."

Michael smiled and said, "Christ! Tom Parker, in the lobby of the Plaza. The same day we're in the lobby of the Plaza." He shook his head. "Come on. It's this way." As they walked through the corridor toward the Oak Room, Michael said, "The really amazing thing about coincidences is that they don't occur more often. When I lived in town, I used to . . . I'll tell you in a moment."

The maitre d' approached them the instant they walked through the doors of the restaurant. He smiled warmly and said, "Mr. Kaye. It's been too long since we've seen you."

"I'm a country squire now. And I miss the Oak Room."

Even through the massive cloud of his confusion, David was impressed—by Michael's being known, by Michael's manner of easy elegance, and by the restaurant itself; the oak paneling, the nail-studded leather armchairs, the dark heavy aura of a men's club. The impression was disappearing into the cloud by the time they reached the table.

When they sat down, Michael ordered a martini for himself and a Coke for David. Michael wanted David to be impressed, but he would never belittle him by asking him to say he was.

"What I was saying was about a coincidence. I lived in New York, off and on, for almost twenty years. It must have been the first year I was here. I saw a guy on the street. A guy—a *boy*, then, as I was myself—about my age. Very high-class gigolo type. European clothes. Always a quiet, dotted scarf at the throat and a pipe. Sandy hair and a hawky kind of nose. Handsome in an offbeat, almost decadent kind of way. I have seen that man I think on an average of once a month for nearly twenty years. I don't know his name. I've never met him. I don't know anything about him. I'd be willing to bet I know at least one person who knows him, but I've never met him. And I've seen him everywhere. Usually in the East Sixties, walking briskly, deliberately briskly. But I've seen him at the theater, in the Village, at the movies. I almost said hello to him once. Not because I wanted to meet him, but because I'd seen him so often, I suddenly thought he was a friend. I'm glad I checked my impulses. I like a little private mystery in my life. I have to admit that every time I see him, I hurry home to look in a mirror to see if I've aged as much as he has."

David was not looking at him, nor was he looking around the room. He looked down at the table. He had taken the napkin from the serving plate and carefully spread it across his lap, and his hands were folded on top of it under the table. The incessant animation was gone from his face. Michael was astonished; he could not understand the reaction.

"What's wrong?"

David looked up as if he were startled again. There was probably no one else he wanted or would be able to tell. But here and now, in the immediacy of it, with their having almost shared it, he knew he wanted to tell Michael.

"I just saw my mother."

"You wh . . ."

135

"She was in the lobby about a minute before Tom Parker." Michael was staring at him wide-eyed. "She didn't see me. She got into an elevator just before he did." Michael couldn't speak. "I don't think . . . that was a coincidence . . . do you?"

David had had a moment to try to sort things out. Michael was now at least as confused as David had been. "David . . . it couldn't have been. You must have . . ."

"You mean you think I'm going to mistake somebody else for my own mother?"

"Of course not, but . . ." Suddenly, to argue against the implications was to suggest them, and there was no way to do one without doing the other. And there was the momentarily ugly bond of honesty between them. "Well . . . why . . . why not two coincidences . . . instead of one? Is that impossible?"

"Come on, Michael."

"I don't know what you're thinking, but I'm telling you . . ."

"Yes you do. You know what I'm thinking . . . and you're thinking it, too. Or . . . or did you know before?"

"I didn't know anything before, and I don't know anything now."

"And how's that for honesty? Wow!"

"I'm not being dishonest. David, what the hell would I have to be dishonest about?"

"I don't know. Loyalty to my mother, maybe. Or even to Mr. Parker. Wow. The mystic cult of the over-thirties."

"My loyalty in a situation like that would be to you. And I have every right to expect you to know that."

"Yeah. That's why you won't tell me my mother and Mr. Parker are . . . what do you people call it? . . . having an affair."

"I can't tell you what I don't know. But I can tell you a hundred other reasons why they might be in this hotel . . . and together."

David called his bluff. "Like what?"

"Like . . . Tom and Ethel Parker are having trouble . . .

136

Of all leading cigarettes, True is the only one that puts its tar and nicotine numbers right on the front of its pack.

True has nothing to hide.

Latest U.S. Government tests show True is lower in both tar and nicotine than 99% of all other cigarettes sold.

Think about it. Doesn't it all add up to True?

20 CLASS A CIGARETTES

TRUE

FILTER CIGARETTES

LATEST U.S. GOVERNMENT TESTS:
12 MGS. TAR, 0.6 MGS. NICOTINE

Regular: 12 mg. "tar", 0.6 mg. nicotine,
Menthol: 13 mg. "tar", 0.7 mg. nicotine av. per cigarette FTC Report Aug. '71

trouble with their marriage. And Tom wants to talk to somebody . . . somebody who knows them both."

"He's a man. Why wouldn't he talk to my father?"

"Would you?"

David was silent for a moment. "So the only place they can think of to talk is in a hotel room."

"Because they didn't want to be seen."

"In New York? Who's going to see them?"

"*We* did." It was exquisitely unconvincing.

David looked at him squarely. "You really had me fooled, Michael. You had me arguing with kids about maybe adults are straighter than we think. And then you hand me all this bullshit. That's beautiful. That's really beautiful."

Michael turned away after a moment and said, "I'll get a check."

He looked around the room, but before he could find a waiter, David said, "Don't. Please don't, Mike." When Michael looked back, David's face was sad and pleading, as if he might reach across the table and touch Michael's arm. "I goofed. It isn't your fault that . . ."

"It's all right." The waiter appeared with the Coke and the martini. When he had gone, Michael said, "Besides, in a way I wasn't being entirely honest with you. I think what you think, but I didn't want you to think it. Whether it's true or not. And I swear to you, I don't know anything about it."

"Maybe I should have a martini. It isn't every day you find . . ."

"Look. Do you want to just have lunch and skip the play? We can do it another . . ."

"No. I don't want to do that. Anyway, there's nothing I can do about the other thing. Is there?"

"I don't know. It must seem very simple to you. A matter of right or wrong, moral or immoral. But it isn't. Christ, I don't know. Maybe it is that simple."

"You know I don't think I know a hell of a lot. You know I don't think I'm automatically better than people

137

older than me. But kids are saying why do you have to sign a contract to live together. When you want to get out of it, you get out of it anyway. And you don't have to sneak around . . ."

"David. There's just as much sneaking around the un-written commitment as there is in the written one. If you never believe anything else I say, please believe that. I know."

"It's really great to hear that," David said.

"We'd better order," Michael said, signaling for the maitre d'.

There was a measure of bravado about David's be-havior for the rest of the afternoon. His enthusiasms were as blatant as polished brass. He ate ravenously and declared that he would someday write the luncheon menu into a story. He was rapt during the play, and he cheered afterward. He was fascinated by the backstage world, a world more made-up than the one it supports in front of the scenery. He was excited at meeting two young actors he had just seen perform on the Broadway stage.

But between these sustained moments of fiercely man-ufactured joy, there were sudden unguarded moments of sadness. A line of curiosity suddenly abandoned. A sudden inattentiveness that was so complete it was an interrup-tion. And the lingering melancholy in the eyes.

It was painful for Michael to watch, but there was nothing he could do. There was no way he could spare David the agony of the deception without destroying the deception, and he knew there was no way for David to get through the day without it. And beneath the pain, there was Michael's very real joy at knowing that David wanted to get through the day to please him.

On the drive back to New Jersey, David talked almost uninterruptedly about the day. It was like the bright, mindless chatter of very young schoolboys on the way home from an excursion.

As they neared the property, approaching on the road furthest from the Radnors' house, David took off his blazer and tie. He looked at Michael and said, "I hate deceiving my mother, but could I leave them in the car? I'll get them later."

"David . . . Sure. Leave them."

Michael stopped the car three blocks from the property, and David started to get out.

"I'm sorry it happened," Michael said.

"Yeah. Well. At least the part we planned was really great. I hope you believe me, Mike. I had a great time. Really great. Thank you."

"I'm glad and you're welcome. Call me."

"I will."

Cynthia was talking to Mrs. Turner in the dining room. Mrs. Turner disappeared into the kitchen, leaving Cynthia alone for a brief moment. That was how David saw her as he entered the house: standing alone in profile, it seemed to him, just as he had last seen her. He did not notice that she no longer wore the jacket of her suit, or her white gloves nor carried her handbag. She was to him exactly as he had seen her in the lobby of the Plaza. He wondered if he would ever be able to see her any other way. She heard him come in and turned to him.

"Hello, darling," she said. "Wasn't it a *scorcher?*"

"Hi," David said.

"Want a Coke or some iced tea or something?"

"No thanks. I'm going to go upstairs for a few minutes before dinner."

"All right, dear. Don't be long. It's almost ready."

He heard his father's voice from the back garden. "Is that Davey, Cynthia?" he called.

"Yes, Herb."

"Hi, Dave."

"Hello, Dad," David called back.

He turned away from his mother and went upstairs. He closed the door to his room and took off his shoes and slacks and shirt and lay on the bed on his stomach. After a moment, he pushed his face into the pillow to

139

muffle the sound, and he cried. He cried like a much younger and less sophisticated child than, not very long ago, he had thought he was.

CHAPTER VII

On the following Saturday, the Parkers entertained the neighbors, and the dinner was in honor of Tom's visiting mother and father. The elder Mr. and Mrs. Parker had never before been East from Indianapolis. They did not approve of the East. They believed that the best of Early American stock had moved West by the middle of the nineteenth century, and any family that had not moved West was a family of ninnies. It did not matter that the Parker clan had stopped geographically about a third of the way on the great migration. Not having stayed behind was the badge of merit. The only greater sin was to deny the priceless bequest of the move by returning East, a sin which one of their five sons—their favorite one—had committed. They viewed their own temporary return as a compromise with approaching death. It was not an attitude to be desired in the guests of honor at a dinner party in New Jersey.

Tom had fulfilled his parents' direst prophecies by becoming everything they were not. When he had left

141

Indianapolis to attend the Wharton School at the University of Pennsylvania, they felt they had lost him forever. They were right. They predicted that he would lose his religion, Presbyterianism; would go into some fool glamorous line of work; would marry the first pretty, flighty girl who caught his eye; would pretend he liked the East; and would raise his children sparing the rod. And, at least in their view, they were right.

Althea Cooper Parker had heard herself described as being raw-boned, and she liked the description so much she often applied it to herself in a facetiously derogatory way. She had been told so frequently and from such an early age that she was of pioneer stock that she seemed to have taken it upon herself to look like a pioneer. One saw her and thought of log cabins and pitchforks and plows. Her husband looked like a bad photograph of her.

Mrs. Parker had a strong sense of herself, which was manifested in her incessant talking. Although she talked *to* people, she did not want, almost did not allow conversation. She often talked in code. She would say the last syllable of the last word of the punch line of a family joke, and her husband would slap his knee and chuckle. Mrs. Parker then would join him in chuckling as she looked individually into the faces of those present until everyone was smiling appreciatively.

Since Mrs. Parker's arrival in the East, this barrage of words had been directed principally at her daughter-in-law. She did not so much criticize Ethel as pretend not to understand her. "Why do you fill those ice cube trays so full they spill?" "What's little Jonathan doin' out in the backyard on a bicycle he could fall off of?" "Why do you need a cocktail to make you hungry?" "What have you got to keep you so busy you can't bake your own pies?"

Ethel met these questions stoically. She giggled and offered inane responses and left the room on the pretext of some chore. Mrs. Parker would follow her. Secretly, Ethel feared she would lose her mind if Mother Parker

142

and her husband did not go home soon, but in the meantime, to keep her sanity, she kept fleeing from room to room with Mother Parker in pursuit.

The dinner party guests had been asked privately to keep controversy at a minimum by listening as much and talking as little as possible. The guests began to see how difficult this might be when Mother Parker greeted the Radnors with "You're the school teacher," and the Jablonskis with, "You're the Polish couple." When George and Michael arrived, she resorted to her not-understanding technique by whispering loudly to Ethel, "Are they the two men?"

The guests had also been advised to tank up a bit at home, since the cocktail hour was to be curtailed in deference to the guests of honor. This advice panicked the guests into over-compensation, and they all arrived in a fairly advanced state of drunkenness. Then they compounded the error by drinking their first drinks quickly so as to have time for a second. Mother Parker drank Welsch's grape juice, and Mr. Parker drank Hi-C.

It could not be said that the elder Parkers did not do their share. Mother Parker resigned herself to the cocktail hour and told the others, "You people go ahead and drink as much as you want. I guess it's your way." There could hardly be a more viable way of enforcing prohibition.

There could also hardly be a more viable way of ensuring controversy than to forbid it. Like a hypnotically cured neurosis, it would inevitably pop up in some other form.

During the brief, but odious cocktail time, Mother Parker sat in a redwood armchair, moving slowly back and forth as if she were in a rocking chair.

"Dad and me've been havin' a grand visit with Tom and his wife," she was saying. "First time we've seen our grandchildren, you know. Cutest little things, though they do get their own way a lot. Got twelve more back home with the best manners I ever saw. Haven't they got good manners, Dad?" Dad nodded without enthusiasm. "Tom's four brothers all settled down in Indianapolis or suburbs thereof, as we say. Dad and me see them regularly once a week. Each have their own night of the week with Dad and Mother Parker, though sometimes we get 'em all at once for Sunday supper. Those are the times! That means twenty-two of us, you know, with the four boys and their wives and the twelve kids. We do miss Tom, of course, but distance is distance. Ethel keeps a pretty place, don't you think?"

The monologue never really ended. It was interrupted occasionally by a question or a comment of agreement from one of the guests, then it continued. Sometimes there was a separate conversation, conducted as a quiet obbligato to the monologue. But the monologue was Mother Parker's defense against being alive. It was the wall behind which she existed, and every pause was a chink through which life might flood in. When a chink appeared, she stuffed it with words.

Mother Parker had developed a quite remarkable system for eating and talking more or less at the same time without seeming uncouth. One of the techniques of this feat was for Mother Parker to spear a tiny morsel of food, ask a question which could be answered briefly, pop the food into her mouth and attack it savagely with her dentures for the duration of the answer, and begin talking again. With a piece of barbecued lamb on her fork and already on its trip to her mouth, Mother Parker looked at Michael and said, "And what do you do, young man?" The dentures snapped shut on the lamb.

"I'm a writer," Michael said, pulling himself out of the coma Mother Parker's voice had put him in.

Mother Parker stopped chewing suddenly and swallowed visibly. "What of? Of books?"

"Yes. Novels."

"Well. First writer I ever met."

"I'm also an actor," Michael said adventurously. "Played Indianapolis once. Perfectly marvelous town."

"Must've been tame after Eastern cities."

"I loved it. It was . . ."

"We don't live the same way out there. But a taste of the good life never hurt anybody. An actor, you say. Well, Tom, this lamb is delicious."

At first, the guests took Mother Parker's performance with tolerant good humor. But as their boredom grew under the weight of words, alternately snide and vacuous, they began to feel victimized. There was not one among them who would take out his annoyance on a garrulous old woman, particularly the mother of a neighbor, and so a testiness had built up in the group by the time dinner was over. Mother Parker joined the women in clearing the table, sparing the men, at least, for a few moments. But when the table was cleared and, to Mother Parker's horror, a round of after-dinner drinks was served, she reappeared on the patio, rubbing her bare arms with citronella (brought with her from Indianapolis) and talking about the difference in size of Indiana and New Jersey mosquitoes.

No one realized it, but Joe Jablonski had been Mother Parker's principal victim. He had come to the party prepared for a personal celebration and had instead been subjected to a lecture. He had tried more doggedly than any of the others to be heard, but had failed to "get a word in edgewise," as Mother Parker would have put it. Joe wanted to celebrate the phone call he had received that morning from Jack Schneider. Jack had said, "It's okay, Joe."

"You stopped it?" Joe asked eagerly.

"No. It's over. It's just over, and they didn't find anything."

"You mean it's . . ."

"You'll get a letter from the department. We couldn't stop it, but . . . well, it turned out okay."

"Jack, I gotta thank you some way."

"Forget it. But like I said before, it's going to cost you.

145

None of it's for me, but these things cost. It's got to be spread around."

"Sure. How much?"

"Three grand."

Joe sucked in his breath audibly. "That's a hell of a lot of money."

"You'd say the same thing if I said five hundred. Look, don't let me down, Joe. I should have had the money first. I guaranteed this."

"Would I let you down?"

"I hope not. When can I get it?"

"I can't put my hands on it till Monday."

"That'll do. I'll call you Monday morning."

"It's a load off my mind, Jack. I really do thank you."

"Don't mention it. I'll call you."

Now, as Mother Parker's voice droned on across the still night air, Joe decided his time of celebration, if there were to be one, had come. He was sitting next to Herb, and he addressed him in a voice that rivaled Mother Parker's in volume.

"Had some good news today, Herb," Joe said.

"Well, don't keep it to yourself," Herb said.

"I guess you read in the *News* about the investigation. You know, the school."

"Yes. As a matter of fact, I did. I didn't see any point in bringing it up."

"Yeah. I can see that."

"You should see that Kenny in the Little League back home," Mother Parker was saying. "He's my oldest son's boy. They say he's the best little pitcher that's ever come up through the Indiana Leagues."

Joe went on. "It doesn't even matter now, though. Got the good word today. The investigation didn't find one thing wrong . . . like I said they wouldn't."

Herb looked at Joe curiously. "You mean they found nothing wrong with the building?"

"Nothing," Joe said proudly. "Not a thing."

"Then why did it fall down?"

146

"What?" Joe said, pausing with his highball glass on his lips.

"If there was nothing wrong with the building, what made it fall down?"

"You just don't understand these technical things, Herb," Joe said cordially.

"The hell I don't. If you're putting up a wall, and it falls down, there has to be something wrong with the wall, doesn't there?"

"Not necessarily."

"Don't be ridiculous. Of course there does."

One by one the guests had turned their ears from Mother Parker's recitation to the now louder conversation between Joe and Herb.

"Don't tell me I'm ridiculous when you don't know what you're talking about," Joe said.

"I know what *I'm* talking about. What I'm trying to find out is what *you're* talking about. A county building collapses during construction. The county wants to know why it collapsed, so they conduct an investigation. Are you telling me they couldn't find out why it collapsed? Are you telling me they just stood there scratching their heads and saying, 'Now, why the hell did that wall fall down?' "

Joe's words were quiet and measured. "I'm telling you they didn't find anything wrong."

"And I'm telling you, that's ridiculous. There had to be something wrong, and they must know what it was."

"Why don't you keep your mouth shut?"

"Is that what *they're* doing?"

Mother Parker had become quiet.

"I'd be careful if I was you, Herb."

"After all, you've always told me just about anything could be arranged around here if you knew the right people."

Joe stood up. "Listen, you son of a bitch, you make one more accusation, and I'm gonna belt you in the mouth."

Peg was at Joe's side. "Come on, Joe. He's just a little tight."

"Well, what the fuck does he mean, accusin' me?"

"I'm just doing my civic duty."

Joe lunged at Herb with a terrifying suddenness, but Peg was already on his arm, and her weight slowed him. Herb was still sitting down, and Joe towered over him threateningly.

Peg pulled at Joe's arm. "Joe! Joe, don't cause any trouble!"

Joe was staring down at Herb. "If you say anything like that again, to me or anybody else, I'll tear your fuckin' head off." Joe turned away and strode across the patio and into the house. He and Peg left within a few minutes.

On the way home, Joe continuously muttered curses at Herb. Peg remained silent. She had wondered herself about the investigation and had decided she didn't want to know. She had changed her mind in the last fifteen minutes, but knew this was not the time to ask about it.

The rest of the guests saw the evening through intrepidly, if boozily. Mother Parker tried several times to resume her monologue, but it always sputtered out with a shake of her head and, "Land sakes, such language!" or "In front of ladies!" or "Why I never!" When it became clear that Mother Parker was too shaken to continue her performance, Michael had a try at entertaining her with the few repeatable private stories he knew about television entertainers. Only Ed Sullivan and Lorne Greene seemed to revive her from her distress, and even this success was short-lived.

The incident between Herb and Joe was ignored, partly because Herb was still there, and partly because anything more violent than an argument over a bridge bid was unheard of among the neighbors. They didn't know quite how to handle tonight's fracas. Where did loyalties lie? Where did friendship stop and public duty begin? What were the boundaries of privacy? Did they all drink too much?

148

The Radnors and George and Michael left together, only slightly earlier than they would have if the senior Parkers had not been there.

Ethel insisted on leaving the few remaining after-dinner glasses and coffee cups till the morning. Mother Parker insisted on clearing and washing them. She was obviously fully recovered as she and Ethel washed the dishes, for she talked absolutely without respite.

Tom and his father sat in the living room, talking alone for the first time since Mr. and Mrs. Parker had arrived.

"Gee, Dad, I'm sorry about the hassle tonight. I hope it didn't upset Mother too much."

"Wouldn't you think it'd upset her?" Mr. Parker said, nodding his head like a chicken.

"Of course. But I couldn't know it was going to happen. I mean, I wish I could have done something to . . ."

"Wasn't you, of course. Was your friends. I hope it's not true you can tell a man by the company he keeps."

Tom had only two images of his father. One was of the tall, laughing, gaunt, but handsome man he knew as a child. Then there was a blur, a shifting, colorless blur for a long time. And there was this one, now, at this very moment. The first clear image he'd had since that mysterious one so many years ago. It was the image of his mother. His father had become her. He had maintained the outward vestiges of sexual difference——he watched the ball game on television; he had a bedtime shot of whiskey six or eight times a year; he played roughly with the grandchildren; he sat, bent and silent, at the head of the table——but Mother Parker thought for him, felt for him, loved for him; and in exchange for his life gave him her fear of living and the wall of words, her words, to hide behind. He was willing now to let her protect them both.

Tom had found himself introducing them with, "Would you believe they'd been married for *forty-six* years?" And he would feel the uncertain, unwanted sense of embarrassment, because he knew they looked as if they'd been fiercely married every minute of that forty-six years.

They looked welded, blended, mongrelized into each other. They looked like grotesque Siamese twins, one of whom had died. As he sat now looking at his father, he wondered how many other atrocities had been committed in the proud name of marital longevity. And if he was committing one himself.

It did not matter now who had abandoned whom. It did not matter whether his father had made himself inaccessible to Tom by allowing himself to be swallowed up by Mrs. Parker. Or whether Tom had turned his back on them both by choosing an Eastern college. Both sets of steps were irretraceable, and there were no new paths by which any of them could return.

"How about a shot before we turn in, Dad? Help you sleep."

"I guess I seen enough drinkin' around here for one night," Mr. Parker said.

Tom gave up. They sat in a heavy silence which made Tom uncomfortable, but which his father seemed to claim and use as he would have a birch rod.

At last, Mrs. Parker and Ethel came in from the kitchen. Mother Parker did not sit down, but stood in the middle of the room. "Now, I don't want you gettin' upset," she said, "but Dad and me's decided to cut our visit short."

"Oh, Mother!" Ethel said, almost wailing.

"It's just that we're homesick. Too old to be gallavantin' around like this. Too set in our ways."

Mr. Parker, who had not heard a word of this plan before, sat smiling and nodding in his armchair.

"Mother, that's terrible!" Tom said. "You were going to stay at least another ten days. You . . ."

"I know. I know. But like I said, we're just plain homesick."

"I know you well enough to know there's no point in arguing with you." Tom sounded both annoyed and disappointed.

"No point at all. Now, I figured we could leave right

150

after church tomorrow. Matter of fact, you could drive us to the bus station in the city right from church."

"Mother!" Ethel said. "Won't you even come back and have lunch?"

"What for? I always say if you're going to do a thing, do it. If you're going on a trip, get started early. Right, Dad?"

Mr. Parker nodded emphatically.

"If that's the way you want it, Mother. But I'm very disappointed. And Ethel is, too."

"That's sweet of you both, but you'll recover. Well, let's go upstairs, Dad. Big day tomorrow. Get your light there."

Each night of her visit, Mother Parker announced her departure for bed and began turning out the lights—*all* the lights. Now, the downstairs lights out, the four Parkers climbed the stairs to their rooms. Ethel and Tom said good night to the elders, went into their own room and closed the door. For the first time in longer than either could remember, they turned to each other spontaneously and hugged each other in mutual joy.

When the Radnors returned from church the next morning, Herb, as he always did, went upstairs and put on a button-down Oxford shirt and a pair of old gray slacks. But when he came downstairs again, he did not sit in his armchair and start reading *The New York Times*. Instead, he stood in the living room with his hands in his trouser pockets and his head bowed. David had gone to his room, and Cynthia was in the kitchen. She came into the living room, tying on an apron. She looked at Herb strangely.

"Would you hold lunch a little while, Cynthia? I'm going over to the Jablonskis'."

"You're what?" Cynthia said, her hands motionless behind her, her fingers still on the bow of the apron.

"I want to talk to Joe."

"What on earth for?"

Herb hesitated. "I . . . I want to apologize."

"Herb. I understand that. I mean, you were rude. I can't think of a worse place or a worse time or a worse way to say what you said. But you said it, and you believe it. I don't see how you can apologize for one without apologizing for the other. Don't you think it'd be better to let well enough alone?"

"Look. When you come right down to it, what right have I to judge Joe Jablonski in this thing?"

"What right?"

"The County Building Department has conducted an investigation. They've absolutely absolved Joe of any wrongdoing. I think I must accept that."

"In spite of the fact that you think he used influence to have the investigation come out that way?"

"I don't *know* that. Don't you think it'd be generous to give him the benefit of the doubt?"

"I think it'd be . . . admirable if you'd take one position or the other," Cynthia said wearily, "and then stay with it."

"I'm taking a position right now."

"Yes. The easiest one. Do whatever you want." She turned away and went back to the kitchen.

Herb thought for a couple of minutes about what Cynthia had said. Then he left and crossed the lawn toward the Jablonskis'.

Peg answered the door when Herb rang. She managed to look only mildly surprised.

"Good morning, Peg," Herb said.

"Hello, Herb."

"Is Joe in?"

"Yes. He's in the back. Come on." She stepped back and closed the door behind him. She led him through the kitchen and out onto the patio. Joe was sitting in a reclining deck chair reading the newspaper. The children were playing noisily in the yard. They heard the kitchen screen door close and saw Herb. They ran to the patio to say hello to him. He greeted them all as the younger ones tried to climb up his legs.

After a few moments, Joe said, "Okay. That's enough. Go back and play in the yard."

Joe had stood up and was now facing Herb silently as the children reluctantly returned to the yard.

"I won't beat around the bush, Joe," Herb said. "I'm sorry about last night. I made a damned fool of myself. I know saying I was a little tight doesn't excuse it, but that's all it was. I was wrong, and I'm sorry."

So eager were both men to restore the solidarity of the neighborhood that the simple apology sufficed. There was no need for Joe to ask or for Herb to state specifically what he was sorry for or what he was wrong about. They were friends and neighbors again, and that was what was important.

"Forget it, Herb," Joe said. "I guess I've shot my mouth off enough times when I was loaded. And speaking of that, how about a drink before lunch?"

"It's a little early for me, Joe."

"Aw, come on. A hair of the dog. A gin-and-tonic never hurt anybody."

"Well . . . why not?"

"You sit down, Herb. It'll only take me a minute."

He was back with the drinks in almost that short a time. He handed one to Herb and raised the other in a toast. "Let bygones be bygones," he said.

Herb raised his glass and they both drank. And the incident, like the investigation, was officially closed.

At exactly that time, George and Michael were having breakfast and reading *The New York Times* on the terrace, as they did every Sunday morning when rain didn't prevent it. They had spoken very little. George had made several attempts at conversation which Michael did not encourage. Now, except for the occasional turning of newspaper pages and the small noises of Gian-Carlo's clearing the table, there was silence.

153

George lowered his newspaper and said, "Say something, Gianni. I long for the sound of a human voice."

Gianni scowled and said in Italian, "Silence is better than what I would say if I spoke."

"What would you say?" George asked him, also in Italian.

"That this is a terrible place, and I hate it."

"I know," George said. They were still speaking Italian.

When Gianni had left the terrace, Michael said, "You know what? Even I know *that* much Italian."

"Then you know that Gianni hates it here," George said.

"Tough," Michael said without taking his eyes from the newspaper.

After a long moment, George said, "Is there to be no visit from Master David today?" Again his face was hidden behind the newspaper.

Michael looked toward him then, thought for a moment and said, "He's playing an outdoor rock concert somewhere."

"Somewhere?" George said, peeking around the paper. "Come, Michael. Surely you know the place and the time and the seating capacity."

Michael stared at him coolly. "It's at the bandstand in the Mary McCombs Wood Park in Mahwah, which seats fifteen hundred. It starts at noon and is expected to go on well into the evening. David's group is called The Iron Feather, and the names of the other three members are Bobby Geary, Stan Peckman and Jimmy Meeken."

"And you're not attending?"

"Who put the snide in the orange juice?"

"Yes. I am being snide. Because I've tried everything else. I've tried handling the problem by explaining to you that I understand it and asking you to talk to me about it. And you turn away. I've tried being abrasive, but you didn't even feel it. I've tried being sulky and distant, but you're already so distant, you didn't even notice. So now I'm being snide. Yes."

"What 'problem,' George?"

"It's tiresome of you to ask that every time the subject comes up. The problem is your ever-accelerating friendship with David Radnor—which the neighbors suspect is indecent, and which, for you at least, seems to have taken the place of our relationship here in this house."

"It is not taking the place of our relationship and fuck the neighbors."

"That suggestion is also getting to be tiresome." George put the newspaper aside altogether and leaned toward Michael. "Mike, be reasonable. He's too young, and it does look strange. And, even more important to me, in spite of all my suggestions, you won't go to the theater with me; you constantly turn down dinner invitations in New York; you won't go away for a weekend . . . We never do *anything* together. And I mean *anything*. For Christ's sake, you never even talk to me about David."

"Do you want me to?"

"Not particularly."

"That's what I thought."

"Michael. Let's go to Europe for the rest of the summer . . . maybe even the autumn. It's been two years. We could go directly to London for a couple of weeks and stay with Martin. There's no deadline on the novel, and you've written while we traveled in Europe before. We could . . ."

"No."

"Why not?"

"I don't want to."

"Why don't you say it? Why don't you say you don't want to leave David?"

"I don't want to go to Europe."

"Because you don't want to leave David."

"All right! He goes back to school in September. How much will I see of him then?"

"Will you promise to go to Europe with me in September?"

After a brief pause, Michael said, "No."

Gian-Carlo was standing between the open French doors. "Is there anything else you want?" he asked.

"No. No, thank you, Gianni," George said.

Gianni went back into the house, and, for the first time since he'd known them, he listened secretly to their conversation.

"If you're so concerned about appearances, why don't you start there?" Michael said, looking down at his paper again.

"What?" George said, unable to believe Michael meant what he thought he meant.

"*You* be reasonable, George. If I were married and were helping David with his writing, there wouldn't be a whisper, would there? If I were single, but respected in the community as a writer, there wouldn't be a second glance. If I were the writer-friend of country squire George Carr, living in his house while I finished my latest novel, my helping David would be considered an act of charity. But our living together with a slightly faggy, young, Italian houseboy—who hovers around like a guinea butterfly every time the neighbors come to dinner —anything *either* of us does is suspect."

"Michael . . . are you . . . are you saying . . . you want us to get rid of Gianni?"

"I'm saying that if you're so concerned with appearances, there are better places to start than with my friendship with David."

"But you were implying that we should . . ."

"Anything that jeopardizes the success of my living here, I don't want."

"Including Gianni."

"Anything. Why don't you take him to Europe for a month . . . and leave him there?"

"Is it that import . . ." George's graciousness shifted almost imperceptibly, like the gears of a very expensive car, into delicacy. He raised his hand toward his mouth, but it stopped in midair. Then it went on, and his fingertips played across his lower lip. He looked out across the sunlit garden for a moment. He put both hands in his lap and looked back toward Michael. "Mike. He's fifteen years old. You . . . can't think you're in love with him?"

"Why not?"

George nearly sputtered in the shock of it. "Because . . . because . . . whatever you feel for him—and I don't doubt that it might be very deep and good—but whatever it is, you can't call it 'love.' "

"Why not?"

"Because he's fifteen years old, for God's sake!"

"Would you like to explain to me precisely what that has to do with it?"

"Don't be an ass, Michael. You know what it has to do with it. Maybe it's a symptom of your longing for your lost childhood. Maybe it's a desire for the son you're never going to have. Maybe it's just an extraordinarily profound friendship. But if it *is* love you feel, then . . . then it's an aberration."

"It is not an aberration! George, he's bright, he's decent, he's kind, he's . . ."

"For Christ's sake, we don't fall in love with people because we admire them! Tell me what you feel for David is passionate admiration, and we'll break out the champagne."

"Couldn't you say that love is passionate admiration?"

"If you're a complete jackass you could. We continue relationships beyond love, after love because of admiration and respect and mutual interests. But if you're in love with David, you want to kiss him, you want to caress him, you want to have sex with him. You want to share the things he does and is. You want to be a part of his life. And all these things are impossible."

"And because I can't physically fulfill the love, I can't love him."

"Because you can't fulfill the love you *shouldn't* love him. It's unnatural."

"I suppose you think Gianni is middle-aged."

157

"There's a hell of a difference between fifteen and nineteen. And I'm not in love with Gianni. But even if I were, Gianni's a homosexual. At least we'd have some remote chance at making a relationship . . . at being together."

"What do you thing I'm going to do, ask David to quit school and run away with me to . . . to make a relationship?"

"That's not what I'm afraid of."

"What are you afraid of, George? I told you I'd never make a pass at him."

"I know what it's like to be constantly in the presence of somebody you love when you can't express the love in any way. I know the awful desperation that has to come eventually. And then you start . . . misinterpreting things. Every casual glance of understanding is a . . . a look of love. Every innocent gesture of friendship is a token of passion, every accidental touching is a subconscious groping for contact. Until you convince yourself that you're both hiding your love for each other. And you decide that you're going to be the one to break the ice. If it were just the pain of finding out you were wrong, I'd try to spare you. But in this case, the consequences would be a hell of a lot worse than that."

"But we both know I'm not going to do that, don't we?"

"No, we don't. In Roman Catholicism it's called an occasion of sin. Deliberately courting temptation. If you're not around him, it can't happen. Don't risk it, Mike. Please."

"You've got everything backwards, George. You seem to think that because I'm a grown man, the love is dangerous. It's because I'm a grown man that it isn't. I'm in complete control of myself. I know David is straight. I know he doesn't, can't love me that way. I know . . ."

"There's the danger: that way. In your mind, you'll turn 'that way' into the way you want it to be. How many times have you dreamed of how it would be? How many times

158

have you turned your last afternoon with David into a sexual fantasy?"

"George, look. I'm content with what I have. David has two more years of high school here in Hainesdale. All right. I know he'll go away to college then and it's over. But in the meantime . . ."

"You're planning that far ahead."

"Yes, I am. It'll probably take me that long to finish the novel anyway."

"And in the meantime, what happens to us? You live here like a roomer? We don't dare go away for a weekend or, indeed, make any plans that aren't contingent on when you can see David?"

"It won't be quite like that."

"Oh, yes it will. What are you going to do, meet him secretly between a Saturday football game and dinner, when he ought to be with his friends? Are you going to hang around, freezing on some snowy street corner, waiting to grab a few minutes with him when he comes home from a dance or a basketball game? Are you going to surprise him by showing up at the public library when you know he's there studying? Don't you know what it'll do to you?"

George got up and walked to the stone railing of the terrace, turning his back on Michael.

"It's reassuring to know you've been through it, too." George did not answer and did not turn around. "I don't know how to make you understand. I have what I want, and it's not going to hurt you or anybody else. But for the next two years, I intend to hang on to it."

George turned around and said, "What if I refuse to go on living here?"

"I still love you enough to think you wouldn't do that to me."

"But what if I did?"

"You're not going to do it, so let's not talk about it."

"You'd try to find some way to stay on somewhere around here, wouldn't you? Without me."

159

"I don't know. I think so."

"And you expect me to accept that?"

"It isn't going to be that way."

"Don't be too sure."

"George, you've given me a great deal. But I've actually asked you for very little. I'm asking for this."

George stared at him for a long time without even trying to hide his anger. "Before you start taking any serious risks, consider that David's as volatile as any other fifteen-year-old. In six months, you'll probably be no more to him than a relic of the distant past. Before you do anything, look around you. And remember the last eighteen years." George went into the house.

CHAPTER VIII

George Carr had come into sole proprietorship of his own life at an early age. It was not much later when he had met Michael Kaye and decided to share that life with him; and although he shared it faithfully and generously, he never relinquished the iron control of his existence. He often decided on a course of action based largely on Michael's wishes or needs, but *he* decided. He was capable of enduring a less than ideal situation as long as he had authorized that situation. Now, however, he found himself in a status quo which had come about primarily through his own lazy acquiescence.

When he had told Michael weeks ago that if they were going to live in the house while Michael worked on his book, they would have to be friendly with the neighbors, he had not meant bridge every Wednesday and dinners and lunches every Friday, Saturday and Sunday, with random social events claiming many of the uncommitted evenings. He had not meant to become inextricably caught up in their lives. He did not want to know their relatives or their family problems or their private opinions of each other. He did not want to become caught on the flypaper of their social expectations any more than he wanted similarly to trap them. Above all, he did not want to be in every way victimized by Michael's need to win their approval in order to sustain a hopeless fantasy with a fifteen-year-old boy.

George was a cautious man, and he had considered his present circumstances from every conceivable angle. He had played his own devil's advocate, trying to prevent each separate line of reasoning from leading to the same conclusion. The devil's advocate had failed. The facts remained. He was not so much bored with the neighbors as he was resentful of their requiring his presence and participation in their every social function. And his social life outside the neighborhood, whether it was an evening at the theater in New York or a summer in Spain, was being rendered nonexistent by Michael's fruitless preoccupation. It could not be tolerated much longer.

But George was also a subtle man. He was incapable of repaying the neighbors' kindness with an abrupt and unexplained rejection of them. He was incapable of seeing them less either by telling them the truth or by lying to them. And he was incapable of openly insulting them. The plan he devised was in every way worthy of him.

He had begun to execute his plan on a warm and lovely day in August. Michael had spent the afternoon with David and had expected to return to the vague sullenness with which George had begun to treat him on such occasions. Instead, Michael found George in high good humor. George had Gian-Carlo bring them iced tea in the den. He talked volubly of the success of the garden and the joy it brought him. He asked Michael how the book was coming. He told him the afternoon's gossip about their New York friends with a wit and blitheness that made it seem as inconsequential as he knew Michael believed it to be. He talked about doing over a bedroom as a studio for Michael. "A place specifically and inviolably yours," he had called it. "You know, a place for your typewriter, your books, your photographs . . . your Academy Awards. You know."

Michael had laughed at the joke and said, "George, I can work anywhere. It doesn't matter."

"I know that. But it's not as if we were cramped for space. Christ, Mike, why should you have to work in a room designed for something else? We're probably never going to have enough guests to fill the guest rooms. If you'd prefer it, we could use one of the servants' rooms on the third floor. Then we could have a whole houseful of people, and you'd never be disturbed." Michael was smiling in amusement. "I mean it. I really don't think in order to write successfully, you have to have an unheated garrett and a quill pen and gloves and get wrapped up in monk's cloth against the cold and sell your poems on the street to buy candles."

"You know, George," Michael said, "even what you *don't* think is very nineteenth century."

"You're making fun of me."

"No, I'm not. I've been writing since I was about ten years old, and nobody, even in my family, nobody except you has ever really taken the time to read much of it. But when I did a part in my first Bonanza, I heard from relatives I didn't know I had. They took the acting seriously once it got to be on television. But they ignored the writing. So I've never . . . I've never really had a place of my own just to write in. If you'll forgive the reference, I'm beginning to sound like David."

"If you'll forgive my sounding like Scattergood Baines, I don't suppose David is so bad a person to sound like."

Michael shook his head, and said, "You're something else, Uncle George. I'm almost tempted to think you're up to something."

George looked somber. "Why? Is it so unusual for me to behave decently?"

"No. No, it's not unusual at all."

"Go take a nap."

163

"What?"

"We should both take a nap. It's twenty minutes to six. So we miss the news; it might be a very uplifting experience. We'll both take a nap, shower and shave and come down to one of our mutually favorite dinners. And before dinner, I have a surprise for you. Don't get excited. It's nothing earthshaking. It's just a little, tiny, nothing surprise."

"I can't wait."

"I'm taking a nap."

"Me too."

George lay down for fifteen minutes. He wanted to sleep, but, as he expected, could not. For the first time in a long while, he was about to manipulate deliberately the lives of other people, not to their detriment, but to their and to his benefit. Nothing exhilarated George as much.

What had happened to him and to Michael and to the neighbors since last May was the result of various sets of circumstances set in motion by accident. What, hopefully, was to happen to them now would be the result of various sets of circumstances set in motion by George Carr. And guided by him to a pre-ordained conclusion, beneficial to all, though hardly likely to be considered universally so by any of the participants.

His Aunt Janet had unwittingly—or perhaps not—taught him to manipulate. Even as a child, George had watched across the great distance between them as Aunt Janet had caused people to become what she required them to be.

"Tennis is less enervating and just as beneficial," she would say to her weekend guests, "between the hours of nine and twelve as between noon and three. Don't you agree, Dr. Andrews?" Invariably, Dr. Andrews, seeing no reason to fuss, would offer his impeccable medical reputation in support of this observation; and the house guests would be back from tennis at the country club, free for three hours to enjoy the long, leisurely lunches Janet Cartwright favored.

Aunt Janet's favorite anecdote was about her mother, who in extreme old age still presided elegantly over the Georgian silver service, pouring tea for her guests. She would pour a cup of tea, delicately add milk to it and present it to a guest, saying, "I do hope you like milk in your tea; it's so very difficult to get it out." Aunt Janet felt that in a pleasantly facetious way, the story revealed just enough of herself.

But not all of Aunt Janet's manipulations were so benign. Her masterpiece had been the manipulation of George's mother's marriage into a disaster. Janet's sister had died during childbirth, and Janet had raised the daughter she bore. Her brother-in-law had paid less and less attention to his daughter as Janet had become, perhaps unavoidably, more and more the child's mother. He died when the child, Anne, was ten and left his entire estate in trust for her until she was thirty.

Janet had begun her machinations early by carefully instilling in her niece a set of marriage standards which were impossibly high. When Anne committed her one, faint-hearted act of rebellion by marrying an attorney of little reputation and modest means, Aunt Janet had destroyed the marriage by obliquely but systematically reminding Anne how far below their standards Anne's husband was. "When John finds himself," Aunt Janet would tell Anne, "your life will be easier. I've known men who didn't find themselves until forty. Of course, some men never do." "Will you be spending Christmas with John's family in . . . where is it? . . . Scranton? Oh, good! You know I love having you here." "Shall I have gin put on the bar, or has John learned to be satisfied with sherry before dinner?"

The niggling had its effect. At Anne's request, when visiting Aunt Janet, John would content himself with sherry before dinner, but only after having three brought-from-home martinis in his room before appearing downstairs. Anne truly wanted him to do one or the other: to have only sherry or to have his martinis in Aunt Janet's presence. She saw the weakness inherent in her husband's deviousness, as Aunt Janet knew she would. And soon she saw that his lack of pedigree would be a disadvantage, particularly to their expected child, as Aunt Janet had said it would be. She saw that if John did not "find himself," she would have to rely on Aunt Janet to supply the money to raise her child as she wanted to. If John accepted the money, he would sink further into weakness, and she would come to despise him. If he did not, he would have to supply it himself, and Anne became increasingly convinced that he could never do it. It had all happened just as Aunt Janet had predicted, and when George was ten months old, his mother and father were divorced, and Anne and her baby came to live with Aunt Janet. John Carr had never seen his son again, for he knew it would be pointless. He left New York soon after the divorce, and they had never heard of him again.

George had hated Aunt Janet for as long as he could remember. From the beginning, she had stood firmly and deliberately between George and his mother, allowing him only a meager portion of the love Anne wanted to give him. Acts of affection between them became a forbidden ritual, to be performed in secret. As George grew older, they both became embarrassed by the clandestine meetings and the shameful displays of love. They ceased altogether, and the distance between George and his mother became almost as great as the distance between him and Aunt Janet.

Aunt Janet had never made an issue of her personal, periodic inspections of every room of her house, surprise being the best device for detecting negligence on the part of the staff—or even of the other members of the household. On one of these inspection tours, during the summer when George was not quite fifteen, she had quietly opened the door of the third-floor storeroom and found George and a boy of his age completely naked and wrapped in each other's arms on a bare mattress in the middle of the floor. She had waited until her subliminal presence had interrupted their passionate writhing, and they had looked up at her in unimaginable horror. Then she withdrew and closed the door as quietly as she had opened it. She never spoke to George again.

George never knew whether or not Aunt Janet had told his mother of her discovery. She became suddenly indisposed and took her meals in her room. His mother told him a few days later that it had been decided that a military academy was the best possible place for him to finish his high school education. There was no hint of punishment or discipline in the announcement. His mother simply thought it was a fine idea, one that would please him. He did not tell her how much the idea terrified him and filled him with loathing. He knew it would have been senseless to resist.

On the day of his departure, George's mother informed him that Aunt Janet had had a very difficult night and could not possibly see him to say goodbye. And so he left Aunt Janet's house to attend the military academy chosen to reform his unspeakable sexual tendencies. Aunt Janet never knew the magnitude or the absurdity of her error in the choice.

For the next four years, George spent his brief holidays at school, where his mother would visit him. Long holidays and summers he spent at the homes of fellow-students or traveling with his mother. When George went to Princeton, he saw his mother even less frequently. He spent summers in Europe.

After his graduation from Princeton, George's relationship with his mother consisted of monthly letters, rare telephone calls and an occasional lunch at a New York restaurant. On his thirty-second birthday, he received a telephone call from Aunt Janet's attorney, informing him of his mother's death. He was told that his mother's body now rested in the Boyd Funeral Home in Hainesdale, and that he could visit it there if he wished. There was to be no viewing. There would be a service at the Calvary Episcopal Church at two o'clock on Thursday afternoon, then interment in Fairview Cemetery.

George sat apart from the mere handful of people at the church and drove alone in his own car in the procession to the cemetery. Aunt Janet, in a black crepe dress and a large hat with yards of black veiling, sat on a folding chair at the graveside. George stood a few feet from her. Because of the veiling, he could not tell if Aunt Janet ever looked at him. At the end of the burial service, without a word to anyone, she walked directly to her limousine and was driven away. George got into his car and drove back to New York. It was on that day that Mrs. Cartwright had gone into seclusion.

Several days later, George received another phone call from his aunt's and mother's lawyer. He was asked if he could be in the attorney's office for the reading of the will on the following Friday. When he arrived, there was no one in the office but two attorneys and himself. The will was relatively brief and perfectly clear. His mother had left all her assets to George, which made him considerably more than comfortably rich. There was no mention of her personal effects, and George did not ask about them.

It was twelve years before he heard from his mother's attorney again, this time to tell him that his Aunt Janet had died and left everything she possessed to him. He had been utterly stunned. He thought for a brief moment it might have been a posthumous expression of the forgiveness she could never have offered him alive. Then he realized that it was merely that her sense of family had taken precedence over her disapproval of him. There was not another being on earth with Cartwright blood.

Now he was living in this house again, and he felt that it had brought him no more good fortune than it had when he was a child.

George was moving through the den toward the terrace, where Michael was waiting for him. He carried a silver tray with Michael's surprise on it: two mint juleps in fourteen-ounce tumblers, coated a quarter of an inch thick with mottled ice and decorated with sprigs of fresh mint, dusted with powdered sugar. An ounce of cognac floated on the sugar-laced bourbon of each drink.

George came out onto the terrace and, putting the tray on a table, said, "Here you are, Colonel."

Michael was delighted. "George!" he said. "You're wonderful! What the hell do you mean a *little* surprise? Making a proper mint julep is an art and a profession."

"I'm glad you think so, because there are four more in the freezer."

"Wow! Are we going to be smashed!"

"Who cares?" George transferred a drink to the table beside Michael's chair and said, "Don't touch. Melts the ice."

"I know that," Michael said. "Don't talk down to me." He sipped the drink through the straws sticking up through the cluster of mint. He savored it, swallowed and sank back into his chair as if in overwhelming ecstasy. "Nectar of the gods. Nothing less. I thank you from my deepest heart."

For the first time in many weeks, they seemed absolutely contented together. They talked and joked and drank their mint juleps with intense pleasure. By the time they had started their third drink, the sun had gone down, leaving the evening touched with the pink-gray glow that sometimes precedes summer darkness.

George said, "Well, if I can still walk, I'm going to set the table."

"What's the matter with Gianni?" Michael asked.

"Nothing. I just feel like doing it."

"I'd help you, but in my present condition, I'd drop something."

"Stay put. I don't mind at all."

Within minutes, George had finished the table. At both places there were silver and crystal wine glasses and white linen napkins and cigarette jars and small bone china ashtrays. In the center, he but a low cut-glass bowl filled with dahlia blossoms of red and orange and white, flanked by silver and crystal hurricane lamps with white candles. He sat down again and returned to his drink.

"That's beautiful," Michael said. "I've never known anybody who could set a table as beautifully as you."

"Aunt Janet could," George said, looking at the table thoughtfully. "I've often wondered if she could have done it herself. I mean physically done it herself without servants. After all, the servants only did what she had told them to do. But there's a difference. I've often wondered if she could cook, too. She knew one hell of a lot about food. I remember one night at a very formal dinner, I happened to be looking at her just as she tasted the fish course. For an instant, only an instant, there was a murderous look in her eyes, but she went on eating calmly and quietly. I was fascinated. I had to know what caused that look. When the guests had gone, and I was supposed to be in bed, I hid in the hall there just outside the drawing room. I didn't have to wait long. She told the butler to send the cook to her. Now, the cook had long since gone to bed. And she knew it. The butler knew it, too, but he wasn't about to remind Aunt Janet of the fact. After ten minutes or so, the cook appeared in the drawing room. He was a middle-aged Frenchman with a tiny gray moustache. I couldn't see them, but I could hear every word. 'Madame?' he said. Aunt Janet said, 'I ordered the sole poached in white burgundy.' 'Yes, madame.' 'It was poached in white bordeaux.' For a moment there was a very heavy silence. I imagine he was trying to decide whether to admit what he'd done or bluff his way through it. Then he said, 'Madame, there was no burgundy in the kitchen when I began the fish. If I sent to the cellar, it would destroy the timing of the dinner.' There wasn't a pause, there wasn't time for a breath before she said, 'If you find yourself incapable of organizing the kitchen in a fashion which will permit my being served precisely what I order, perhaps we should make other arrangements.' 'I am sorry, madame. It will not happen again.'

'That will be all.' I guess it never happened again, because the cook was still here when I left. But I've often wondered if she just had hypersensitive taste buds or if she knew how to cook. If she did, I can't imagine how she learned. Women of her class in her generation weren't even supposed to know what a kitchen looked like. All of which reminds me, we're having sole for dinner."

"Baked in cream?" Michael asked.

"Of course."

"By our own famous Italian cook, Chef Boyardee?"

"Come on, Michael. Gianni cooks very well."

"He cooks very well what you taught him to cook."

"Don't be testy. Are you ready for dinner?"

"Supremely."

George went to the kitchen to tell Gianni to start serving. He rarely rang for him when he and Michael were alone. He came back to the terrace, lit the candles and he and Michael sat at the table.

The dinner started with madrilène with sour cream and red caviar. Then there was the filet of sole baked in cream, new potatoes with salt, pepper, parsley and garlic, and peas cooked with diced onion and lettuce. There was a well-chilled liebfraumilch. For dessert, there was fresh fruit with kirsch, then coffee.

It was quite dark when they finished eating. A faint breeze had come up and made the candle flames flicker erratically inside the etched Bacarrat crystal chimneys of the hurricane lamps. They sat for a while, smoking in contented silence.

"More coffee?" George asked.

"No, thanks," Michael said. "You know, George, whenever I'm dissatisfied with my lot in life . . . you know, when I start sulking about my lack of talent or my unhappy childhood and all that crap, I should just remember dinners like this."

George smiled. He wanted very much to say, *Yes, and think how you'd miss them if you gave it all up.* For bringing home the realization to Michael was the precise

171

purpose of this particular dinner. But George contented himself with, "I think we live well enough," which was sufficiently oblique not to give away the little plot. Then George started working on the larger one.

"How would you like to give a party?" George said.

"What do you mean?"

"Well, with the exception of Linda and Chris and Gene and Derek, we haven't had anyone out from New York. And a big party would be a change from our intimate little dinners with the neighbors."

"How big a party did you have in mind?"

"Big. As big as we want."

"Like the one in St. Croix?"

"Something like that."

"Stun the natives, huh?"

"Have you ever known me to try to do that?"

"George, you are incapable of ostentation. I know that."

"Thank you. What about the party?"

"I wouldn't mind *having* the party, but I sure as hell don't look forward to making the goddamned preparations."

"You won't have to do anything. You know I thoroughly enjoy that kind of thing once in a while. You just go on with your work."

"If it's going to be the kind of party you enjoy giving once in a while, it's going to be like the Inaugural Ball."

"Now, come on. It's summer, in the country."

"Just a thousand violins playing in the garden."

"As a matter of fact, I had thought about having some musicians."

"Oh, we're pretty far along with this thing, aren't we?"

"You can't think about having a party without having some thoughts about what kind of party you want it to be."

"Okay."

"Remember that string group we hired for the party in Easthampton? It was campy, but they were really rather good."

172

"The Hungarians?"

"Yes. I thought it might be amusing . . . now, this is completely subject to your approval, Mike, but I thought it might be amusing if we hired the Hungarians and alternated them with David's group. What's it called? The Iron Feather?" Michael was totally unprepared for this suggestion, and while he was recovering from his astonishment, George said, "You know. Twenty minutes of Auf Wiedersehen, then twenty minutes of hard rock . . . or whatever it is they play. I think it'd be absolutely marvelous. Of course, the hitch is that David would otherwise be a guest at the party, and I wouldn't dream of making the offer if you thought it would in any way insult him."

"Uncle George, there are times, to use a phrase, when I'm not sure where your head is."

"You think it would be all right to ask him?"

Michael thought for a moment and said, "I think, to use another phrase, it would blow his mind."

"Which I assume means he'd be delighted."

"You really are something else when you start playing games. In addition to its being a great idea, you know goddamned well David would be delighted. You know Cynthia and Herb would be delighted. You know the rest of The Iron Feather would be delighted. You know *I'd* be delighted."

"I had merely hoped."

"You know, the preparations for this party are going to be a hell of a lot more fun than I thought."

George smiled and studied the pattern of the etching on the chimneys of the hurricane lamps. He felt a distinct pang of guilt, for he knew that with a few well-chosen words from someone he trusted, Michael could have been led, eyes wide open, into the Inferno.

They moved away from the table then, and George went inside and got brandy for them. Gian-Carlo came out to clear away the coffee things.

"Hey, Gianni," Michael said. "Why don't you have some cognac with us? Or some strega?"

George noted that it was the first civil thing he'd heard Michael say to Gian-Carlo for a very long time.

"No, thank you," Gianni said, continuing to clear the table.

"Come on, Gianni," Michael said.

"I am very tired." He picked up the tray and said, "If there is nothing else, I will go to bed."

"Nothing, Gianni," George said.

Gianni did not say good night to them. He took the tray and disappeared into the den.

George and Michael sat on the terrace, drinking brandy until nearly midnight. They talked of nothing but the party, and Michael's enthusiasm grew far beyond the bounds George had predicted to himself. They decided to have the party on the Saturday two weeks from the coming weekend.

As they walked through the hall toward the stairs, Michael was laughing loudly at an absurd idea he'd had for the party. George put his finger to his lips and hissed at him. "You'll wake Gianni."

Michael looked down the hall toward the kitchen and hesitated for a moment, all laughter gone and a faint look of indecision in his eyes. Then he turned, smiled at George, and they went up the stairs to their separate beds.

George had a magnificent talent for giving elaborate parties without ostentation, parties which were "the best in ages!" for people of widely varying tastes. Giving either a dull elaborate party or a jazzy ostentatious one was easy. But giving a large, elegant party with enough wit and imagination to make it fun required the special capacities of a George Carr—and required a great deal of work.

George began work on the party the morning after the effective dinner with Michael. Two weeks was not very much time in which to prepare the kind of party George

174

wanted. His first move was to call Gregory Thompson, a homosexual friend of many years, who ran a very exclusive catering service which was among the most elegant in New York. The firm had no other name than Gregory Thompson. To add anything explanatory would have been sacrilege, something like saying George Washington, the President, or Shakespeare, the playwright. If you didn't know who Gregory Thompson was, you probably couldn't afford his services.

"Gregory Thompson," a flute-like male voice said when George dialed the number.

"Is Mr. Thompson there?"

"May I tell him who's calling?"

"George Carr."

"George! It's Henry. I didn't recognize your voice. How are you?"

"Fine, Henry. And you?"

"As well as can be expected for a man of my years. Gregory's right here. Just a minute."

After a moment, Gregory was on the line. "George! My dear boy, how are you? We don't hear a word from you now that you've gone away from us."

"I'm fine, Gregory. How are you?"

"I'm exhausted. These goddamned women couldn't put out a bowl of California dip by themselves. How did they entertain before me? Of course, I'm older than most of them, so they never had to. But they're wearing me to a frazzle."

"I'd think you'd be grateful."

"I am. And, anyway, I love it."

"How'd you like to do a party for me?"

There was a pause and the sound of inhaled breath. "For you? It's like asking an actor how he'd like to play Hamlet. After some of the circuses I've been doing, it'd be like a vacation. When?"

"Two weeks. I know it's not much warning, but . . ."

"On Saturday night, of course."

"From four on."

"Heavenly. You call me at the height of the season, two weeks before the party and expect me to do an all-day job. Heavenly."

"You can't do it."

"I can't, but I will. It will just mean my not personally being at Mrs. Arthur Cavanaugh's party which I'm doing at Southampton and which will be the third biggest social event of the season and for which she'll probably kill me with her bare hands. That's all it means, George."

"Gregory, I don't want you to do that."

"Oh? Now you don't want me at your party. You don't even want me to *do* your party. I offer to ruin my career for you and . . ."

"That's what I don't want. I don't want you to risk . . ."

"What are friends for? All right. That's settled. Now, what kind of thing is it?"

"It's a kind of combination garden party, buffet-dinner-dance, possibly late-evening thing."

"I see. What you're trying to say is that it's *three* parties. How many guests?"

"A hundred to a hundred-fifty. Count on a hundred-fifty."

"I'll count on two hundred, unless you've come to scrimping."

"And a few children at the beginning."

"Ah, George. Who else but you would remember that children will not eat caviar?"

"Now, Gregory, I don't want to have to fight with you about this again, but . . ."

"You aren't? You aren't going to suggest it again?"

"You know goddamned well I am. My food, prepared in my kitchen under my supervision. Just send me three or four people for a couple of days to help me prepare it, and . . ."

"And then send you waiters and bartenders and dishwashers to serve the party. George, I am not running a domestic employment service."

"I know that. It's just that I'm . . ."

"A fastidious old bastard. And you get worse as you get older. And where do you think I make my money? The waiters' salaries are the waiters' salaries. Do you think I take kickbacks from them?"

"No. I think you charge more for them than you pay them."

Gregory ignored this. "I make my money from supplying and preparing food."

"I'll pay you exactly as if you'd done the party from scratch."

"That's not the point. It bruises my ego. Well . . . maybe it is the point. All right. Once again you win. But I can send you only two chefs and an apprentice for Friday and Saturday."

Gregory was so accustomed to playing his customers' games that he couldn't do business any other way. George understood the process completely and, in a way, enjoyed it. And when he hung up, he knew that the essential elements of the party were under control.

Next he called the neighbors, for without them the party would be meaningless.

"Cynthia, it's George," he said into the telephone.

"How are you?"

"I'm fine. I called to ask if you and Herb could come to a party here on the twenty-eighth, two weeks from Saturday."

"Why yes, I think so. The twenty-eighth. Yes, I'm sure of it. Is it dinner?"

"It's rather more than that." There was more than one George Carr, and George had decided to introduce the neighbors to one they had not yet come to know. "You see, we thought it was time we had our New York friends out here. It would take weeks to do it piecemeal, so we've decided to do it more or less all at once. Have them meet you and you meet them. But there are so many of them, and their schedules are so erratic, we've decided to spread the party out. It will be from four o'clock on. You know, a kind of garden party with dancing and a more or less continuous buffet dinner. I think it's the only way to handle more than a hundred people, don't you?"

"Yes. Yes, of course," Cynthia said. "It sounds exciting. And I can see I'm going to have the opportunity of buying a new dress."

"If the party gives you an excuse for buying a new dress, it's already a success. There's one other thing, Cynthia."

"Yes?"

"I didn't want to do anything about it without consulting you. We're going to have a group of very schmaltzy Hungarian violinists, and I thought it would be great fun to have David and his group, too. The Iron Feather? They'd play alternating sets."

"Oh, George, that would be . . ."

"Now, be honest, Cynthia. After all, David would otherwise be a guest at the party, and I don't want him to think . . ."

"George, it's an absolutely marvelous idea. He'll be thrilled. He's not without a sense of humor, you know."

George found it reassuring that Cynthia was beginning to imitate his manner of speaking. "It's really all right with you and Herb?"

"Of course it's all right."

"And, Cynthia, would you do me a small favor? Don't tell David just yet. I'm sure Michael will want to ask him himself."

"Michael? Oh. Yes, of course. They're such good friends."

"That's what *I* thought. I'm delighted you can come."

"I wouldn't miss it for anything."

Ethel and Peg accepted just as readily for their respective families. George spent the next hour locating and hiring the Hungarians. The rest of the day he gave over to calling his most intimate friends and writing invitations to others. Although at five o'clock there were still sixty-five names on the guest list unaccounted for, George felt he'd done a good day's work. At just that hour, Michael returned from his afternoon with David. George, clipboard in hand, met him in the hall and said, "Well, did you sign up The Iron Feather? I got the Hungarians."

Michael looked startled. "No. No, I didn't even mention it. I thought you wanted to do it."

"Me? I am signing no contracts with musicians whose work I don't know. I've heard the Hungarians. *You* sign up The Iron Feather."

Michael smiled for a moment. "Thanks, George."

"For what?"

"For letting me ask him."

George smiled too and said, "You're welcome. And I want you to know that this may be our last conversation for the next two weeks. If you knew how much there is to do. And the first thing I have to do is go into the kitchen and tell Gian-Carlo about the party. Post yourself at the kitchen door, and if I'm not out in five minutes, come in and rescue me."

George didn't wait for an answer. He walked down the hall and into the kitchen. Gian-Carlo was at the sink and looked toward George when he came in.

"Gianni, I have some news for you which you may not like."

Gianni turned back to the sink and said, "I know. I heard you on the telephone."

"You know about the party?"

"Over a hundred people. The dumb little guinea figured it out."

"Gianni, don't . . ."

Gianni turned off the water and turned around, wiping his hands on his butcher's apron. "I will work for the party. I am paid to do that. Yet I want to tell you. I used to feel invited to such a party, even if I worked. Now I am a servant. And that is all right with me if it is what you want."

"It is not what I want," George said. "The guests are just guests. You live here."

"No. Not for a long time."

George knew it was true. It was not only the preoccupation with the neighbors, a pastime which could not include Gianni. It was that as Michael had withdrawn more and more from Gianni, George, in his effort to reach Michael, had withdrawn, too.

"All right. It's true. Things change, Gianni. But they can also change back again. And that's what this party's for: to start things changing back."

"I don't understand that."

"No, and I'm not going to explain it. Trust me, Gianni, and help me. I can't do it without you."

Gianni smiled and said, "Yes you could. But I will help you."

Through Cynthia's Mrs. Turner, George hired two local women to do a major housecleaning job. At first they were resentful at having Gian-Carlo as their supervisor. But he soon charmed them into complete cooperation. Together they went through the house from top to bottom, washing and dusting and waxing and vacuuming. They rubbed the old wood of the furniture until its patina glowed, and the floors looked as if some subtle inner light showed through them.

George joined them then in what he called The Great Search. He knew there was enough matching silver, china and crystal in the house to serve an authentic banquet; but he didn't know where it all was. In the butler's pantry they found one hundred complete place settings of Royal Derby. George insisted there was service for at least two hundred, but further search of the kitchen and pantry failed to turn it up. They found crystal goblets and wine glasses ample for the party. All the silver—flatware, trays, serving dishes, candlesticks—were in one small room off the pantry. Over the vocal doubts of the others, George was insisting that the rest of the china was somewhere in the house, when he realized exactly where it was. It was in the third-floor storeroom.

He felt a faint pang of fear. He felt for an instant that he could not go into that room where he had not been

180

for nearly thirty years, since the day Aunt Janet had discovered him there with another boy. Then he smiled and said, "I know exactly where it is. Come on."

As they climbed the stairs to the third floor, Gianni and the women chattered excitedly. The women had become so much a part of the household, they had almost dispelled Gianni's loneliness. They were making bets on whether or not the rest of the china was where Mr. Carr said it was.

George was having quite different thoughts. He was about to violate a place that Aunt Janet had tried to make inviolable by memory. But Aunt Janet was dead and he was alive. That was a triumph of some kind. She could no longer reach out and intrude on his existence. Here he was, everything Aunt Janet had loathed and despised, living in her house, searching for her china on which to serve guests, most of whom she would have held in bitter contempt. Yet it was an empty victory, for Aunt Janet, through pride and misplaced loyalty to family lineage, had defeated herself. George could never have done it himself. She had left him the property and the luxury. She had invented the irony. She may even have done it knowingly.

George unlocked and opened the door to the storeroom to a wave of intense heat and intense shock for in his mind he felt again the warm dampness of the other boy's flesh; the mixed flood of innocence and excitement he had felt that day; the immeasurable gratification and its instant destruction. He saw the dusty packing crates and steamer trunks and bridge lamps and vases, all relics of enthusiasms and involvements long since dead, and he was sure they stood just where they had before when he and James Richard Henderson III had lain, surrounded by them, in passion and in each other's arms.

George scanned the room for a moment to let the excitement of his memories fade. "Nobody offered *me* a bet," he said. "But I will bet two dollars, even money, that those wooden boxes on the top shelves contain the rest of the Royal Derby."

No one took the bet, and the Royal Derby was in the boxes. And in similar boxes they discovered fifty hurricane lamps, identical with the ones downstairs, including the crystal chimneys.

At nine-thirty on Friday morning Gregory Thompson's three cooks arrived, and the culinary preparations began. The buffet was to be built around six whole salmon poached in court bouillon: six whole filets of beef, sliced and served *en gelée;* six baked hams glazed with brown sugar and fresh pineapple juice; and six roast turkeys stuffed with wild rice and chestnuts and basted with champagne and honey. This was Friday's schedule for the chefs.

On Saturday, they roasted guinea hens, baked French bread, and made crab and lobster soufflés and spinach mousses. They prepared salads of twelve different kinds of greens and a score of salad dressings. There were crème brulées, key lime pies, punch bowls full of fresh fruit *au* kirsch. And at a given moment of the party, the waiters were to rush to the tables, flaming cherries jubilee and one monumental baked Alaska. Even at the risk of vulgarity, George wanted a culinary orgy—as long as its separate elements were impeccable.

At noon, Gregory, the fifty waiters and the dozen extra kitchen help arrived. Gregory inspected the kitchen and beamed as if he had done it all himself. Then suddenly losing his benign countenance, he turned his bullwhip tongue on the poor waiters and set about trying to transform George's garden into the nineteenth-century park of an English palace. At one point, he paused amid the chaos, put his folded fingers to his lips and said, "Oh, George! If only we could get some small deer to roam in and out!"

By three-forty-five it was done. There were forty round tables set up in the garden, each with a white damask cloth, ashtrays, a cigarette dish, a bowl of freshly cut flowers, a hurricane lamp and four chairs. Twenty-five of them were on the open lawn, and the rest were nestled in the shade of maple and elm and oak trees. There were three long, white-clothed serving tables in the garden already set with crystal and china and silver, which caught and glowed with the afternoon sunlight. At the end of each serving table was a smaller table which served as a bar, each one stocked as if to defy exotic drink orders. And behind these were earthenware crocks filled with ice and the wines which needed chilling: liebfraumilch, piesporter, montrachet, white bordeaux, champagne. The red wines were in shade under the tables on silver trays. At each "station" there were four waiters and two bartenders in spotless, starched white jackets. They stood not quite at attention, smiling and radiating eagerness as Gregory Thompson had taught them to do. In a far corner of the garden was a charcoal barbeque, attended by two waiters who cooked hamburgers and hot dogs to order and served Cokes and 7-Ups and Fresca for the children.

The small terrace at the north end of the house was, like the garden, set with tables. Most of the large terrace at the back of the house overlooking the garden, was reserved for dancing. At one end of it were the fourth serving table and bar, and at the other was a small area at which the two alternating groups of musicians were to play. The three pairs of French doors stood open invitingly, giving access to the downstairs rooms of the house for those who preferred to be indoors.

At exactly four o'clock, the first violin strains of a Strauss waltz floated through the summer air. It was so alien a sound to the natives who heard it that it sounded like a symphonic concert. Ethel Parker, who had been sitting, duly dressed for the party, at a living room window since three-thirty, widened her eyes and cocked her ear to be sure she was hearing what she seemed to be hearing. She ran to the foot of the stairs and called to Tom. From the bedroom, he answered, "I hear it. I hear it." He went back to tying his tie.

Peg was sitting at her dressing table, putting on make-up. She held her lipstick motionless against her lips for a moment and turned her head toward the sound of the music. Joe had just finished his shower and came into the bedroom.

"Joe. Is that music?" Peg said.

"What'd you think it was, a cement mixer?"

"But I mean it doesn't sound like a record player or anything."

"No. It sounds like live music, because that's what it is. I guess they really splurged on this wing-ding, huh?"

The Radnors' was the only one of the neighbors' houses with even a partial view of George's garden. They knew about the live musicians, of course, since David was to be one of them. But Cynthia had gone to the window intermittently throughout the day to watch in fascination as waiters swarmed over George's property like bees in a hive, creating a transformation much more elaborate than any Cynthia had imagined. Herb came downstairs and found her watching.

"For God's sake, Cynthia, you're going to be there in a little while. Do you have to gape out the window like . . . like Ethel Parker?"

"Have you seen what they've done? It's amazing."

"I've seen. And I can imagine how much it must have cost. I hope George is as generous in September when I ask him for a contribution to the Hainesdale Community Fund."

"I'll bet he'll surprise you."

"The only way he can surprise me is by giving me a large check."

Cynthia had been holding aside a panel of the glass curtains. She let it fall back into place and said, "For the honorary head of a charity, you're being pretty uncharitable."

"I know these people. I've known them all my life."

Cynthia arched one eyebrow slightly and said, "Oh, have you? I didn't know."

"George Carr isn't the only rich man I've ever met. They're very magnanimous when it comes to their own pleasure, but when it's a matter of the public good, they're stingy as hell."

"I hope you won't let the expense spoil the party for you. You sound as if you're about to grab a pitchfork and lead the peasants against Versailles."

"Don't be sarcastic with me, because if . . ."

"Oh, God, Herb! Just because George is giving a large party, you . . ."

"George and Michael."

"What is that supposed to mean?"

"Maybe you're willing to talk about Ethel and Tom and Peg and Joe and then throw in George and Michael as if it didn't connote something quite different. I am not."

". . . he said as he dressed to go to George and Michael's party."

He looked at her sourly and said, "Maybe I just won't go."

"Oh, you'll go. Yes." She started for the stairs. I'm going to fix my hair."

George came out onto the terrace and found Gregory Thompson standing at the railing looking out over the garden like a captain on the bridge of his ship.

"Everything under control?" George asked.

Gregory turned. "Completely." He studied George frankly from head to foot. "You look ravishing."

George was wearing white slacks with thin blue stripes, a double-breasted blazer of dark blue linen, and a white shirt with a blue and white dotted silk ascot. His face and hands were nicely tanned from working in the garden, and the tan made his graying hair seem whiter. Gregory's look of inspection gave way to one of admiration. Standing in the afternoon sun, relaxed and smiling, George belonged to this house, to this terrace, to this party; and just as clearly, they belonged to him, and it seemed altogether fitting.

Michael appeared behind George. He was wearing a red

and white striped blazer and white ribbed cotton slacks. His shirt was also of red and white stripes, and he wore a red workman's handkerchief casually knotted at his neck.

Gregory clasped his hands before him, sucked in his breath and said, "Beautiful! Utterly, utterly beautiful!"

"Thank you, Gregory," Michael said. "Time for a drink."

"Champagne, of course, to start things off," Gregory said.

"Of course," George said.

Gregory raised his hand toward the terrace bartenders without turning toward them, flicked his wrist almost imperceptibly and said, "Champagne."

In seconds, both the white-jacketed young bartenders appeared, one carrying a tray with three iced champagne glasses and the other with a bottle of vintage Bollinger. When the wine was poured, Gregory took a glass, lifted it and said, "To a smashing success."

"Thanks to you," George said, "I don't see how it could fail to be."

They drank then and looked out over the garden. The tablecloths and the jackets of the thirty waiters stationed strategically around the garden gleamed immaculately white against the dark, rich green of the lawn. There had been no color used in the décor of the party. The garden itself and the flowers on the tables supplied all that was needed. There were red, pink, yellow and white roses. There was blue-red celosia and yellow phlox; pink dianthus and salmon-colored day lilies. There were marigolds and Zinnias and snapdragons and dahlias. There was blood-red salvia and cat's paw like purple velvet. It was all vibrant and fragrant with life.

George turned at the sound of voices in the drawing room. Then Kate Mulligan, a staple of network television game and interview shows and an old friend of George's, came through the French doors with her producer husband, Kenneth Greene.

She said, "George. Michael." She embraced them both. "The house is beautiful. And the garden!"

The men shook hands and Kate's husband said, "I understand now why you left the city."

"I know we're early, but I have a show at nine o'clock," Kate said.

"I'm trying to remember," George said, "if we've ever had an uninterrupted evening together."

"If I can't have one," Kenneth said, "I don't see why you should have."

"That's a point," George said. "I'm not complaining. I think it's wonderful of you to come all the way out here when you have to go back and work."

"Do you think we'd miss a party of yours?" Kate said.

"Drinks. Drinks," Michael said.

"I shouldn't," Kate said, "but I guess one glass of champagne isn't going to incapacitate me."

"Well, I should," Kenneth said. "Scotch and water?"

A waiter was already hovering near the group. He went to the bar and got the drinks.

"You know Gregory Thompson," George said. Gregory, for all his flamboyance, was discreet as a bishop when he was doing a party. He had moved off a few feet as soon as Kate and Kenneth had arrived and left it to George to acknowledge him or not, even though he knew both guests well.

"Gregory," Kate said. "You've done it again! Look at all this," she said, gesturing toward the garden.

Gregory looked haughty and said, "George did the garden, of course." Over their laughter, he added, "I say it extremely reluctantly, but George did virtually everything else as well."

"Not true," George said.

"Yes, it is. George is the only client I allow to reduce me to the status of a caterer."

"Gregory," Michael said, "there is only one word for you, and it isn't 'caterer.' You are an impressario."

187

"And you are a man of perception and taste," Gregory said with a little bow.

By this time, other guests had begun to arrive. As automobiles pulled into the driveway and their occupants got out, three attendants drove the cars away and parked them in a field a half block away. Ethel had seen the first car, Kate Mulligan's limousine, arrive and was so consumed with curiosity, she immediately began prodding Tom. Tom did not want to arrive early and did not want to be the first of the neighbors to arrive, but Ethel's nagging insistence won out. They gathered up their carefully scrubbed and outfitted children and started for George's house.

The first person Ethel saw when she stepped out onto the terrace was a red-haired woman, standing with her back toward the French doors. Ethel was not so harebrained as to lose *all* composure on meeting a celebrity, but when the red-haired woman turned around, it was the suddenness with which Ethel stood face-to-face with Kate Mulligan, her favorite television star, which unnerved her.

"Hello," Kate said, extending a hand. "I'm Kate Mulligan."

Ethel caught her breath for an instant, then bent toward her ten-year-old son and said, "Look, Jonathan! It's Kate Mulligan!"

Kate laughed and said, "Hi, Jonathan."

"Oh, excuse me!" Ethel said, dreadfully embarrassed. She extended her hand belatedly and said, "It's just that . . . I had no idea it was you. I mean, I didn't expect . . . you see, you're kind of our family favorite."

"Thank you, and I do understand," Kate said. "It was very sudden."

"This is my husband, Tom." She paused for a moment, then remembered. "Oh! And I'm Ethel. Ethel Parker. And this is Jonathan and Susie."

"They're beautiful," Kate said. "Not you, Jonathan. You're handsome." She turned back to Ethel and Tom. "And this is *my* husband, Ken Greene."

As Tom shook hands with Ken, he said, "Strange as it may seem, we have a common bond."

"We have?" Ken said.

"Our agency handles Milgonite, who sponsors your show."

"Which I produce," Ken said. "Well, we're brothers under the skin."

"Isn't that amazing?" Ethel said.

"Absolutely," Kate said. "How about a drink? There's an absolute army of waiters. You don't have to move a muscle."

That, of course, was George's intent. He wanted it to be possible for a guest to come in, sit at a garden table, have as many drinks as he wanted, have hors d'oeuvres, dinner with wine, dessert, coffee and cognac without ever having to leave the table. Certainly no one would do that, but for George it was like wearing a gold collar button: one knew oneself it was there.

The guests arrived in a continuous stream now and had begun to flow into the garden from the terrace. The downstairs hall of the house became so crowded that arriving guests began to walk around the house, so that they were soon coming from all directions.

It was soon insistently apparent that the guest list was eclectic. There was a light sprinkling of socialites, who went largely unnoticed except by each other. In addition to Kate Mulligan, there was a night club comedian, familiar to almost everyone through television variety shows; a rising female star of the legitimate theater; several slightly lesser known actors and performers on television quiz shows. There were also directors, scriptwriters, costume designers, set designers, two choreographers and two extremely well known and controversial novelists. There were painters, musicians, and a poet. There was a contingent of dancers from a New York ballet company who stayed in a group as if they were at a rehearsal. Another group of eight male, homosexual chorus boys arrived and immediately split up and mingled with everybody. There were many people from less "glamorous" professions: law, medicine, advertising, the market. The most momentous arrival was that of a Hollywood superstar, biblical and heroic, with his beautiful wife. He and Michael had done a play together before the star's first motion picture, and they had become great friends. It could not honestly be said that the longevity of the friendship depended upon George's and Michael's social or financial position; but those positions made an active social relationship considerably more convenient.

As the superstar made his way through the now crowded garden, Michael noticed, as he had many times before in many similar situations, that the show business people, in their own secretive way, were more impressed by him than the laity.

There was also a sartorial eclecticism among the guests. Many of the men wore blazers and slacks or slacks with bright-colored shirts. And many of the women wore short-sleeved or sleeveless dresses of crisp cotton in white or lovely pastel colors. But from there, the styles spread out in an incredible range. There were a few genuine hippies in threadbare, tie-dyed jeans, leather sandals, fringed suede vests, headbands, hammered metal peace symbols and unattended hair. There were many more stylized hippies, both male and female, who wore elaborate and expensive versions of basic hippie attire: heavily embroidered jeans, see-through shirts and blouses, custom-made shorts. There was an aging lady theatrical agent in a printed chiffon garden dress and a wide-brimmed straw hat. There were authentic, venerable eccentrics who wore the same style clothes they had been wearing for thirty years. It was a colorful collection of people in all respects.

There was one other prominent characteristic of the group: there were a great many more men than women.

Herb Radnor and Joe Jablonski, standing with their wives in a corner of the garden, were sharing this observation. Joe, with a cigarette in one hand and a vodka and tonic in the other, was saying to Herb, "Think most of them are fags?"

"Did you see the group of young men that came in about twenty minutes ago?" Herb asked.

"Yeah. I heard somebody say they were dancers. You know, from Broadway shows."

"Dancers among other things," Herb said.

Ethel and Tom approached with the children running interference. "Hi," Tom said. "Did you just get here?"

"A little while ago," Herb said.

"It's a big party. Where are the kids, Joe?"

"Over there at the barbeque. They just started the hot dogs and hamburgers."

"Looks like George thought of everything," Tom said. "Come on, kiddies," he said to the children. "Let's get some hot dogs."

As he herded the children off toward the barbeque, Ethel said, "Cynthia, have you met Kate Mulligan? She's absolutely the sweetest woman. She's right over there. Come on, I'll introduce you to her. Come on, Peg."

"Ethel," Cynthia said, "I'm sure we'll meet her eventually. We don't have to . . ."

"You'd better do it now. She has to go back to New York to do her TV show. As soon as we came in, Tom and I . . ."

George interrupted her. "Oh, there you are. I've been looking for you everywhere. How did you all get in without my seeing you? Never mind. First of all, do you all have drinks? Good. Now, you are not going to stand around in a group like our good friends from the ballet over there. They have an excuse: they can't talk about anything but dancing. But *you* have got to meet some of our friends. Herb, Charles Aaron is here. You've got to meet him. And tell him you want him to come out to the school in the fall and give a lecture on the State of the American Novel—for free."

"I met Kate Mulligan," Ethel told George.

"I know you did. Ken Greene told me Tom's agency

handles the sponsor of their show. We're just one big, happy family." George turned to a dark, well-groomed man who was passing by. "Marvin. I want you to meet our neighbors. Marvin Hoffman, these are the Radnors, Cynthia and Tom; Peg and Joe Jablonski; Ethel Parker . . . Where's Tom?"

"With the kids at . . . Oh, here he is."

Tom came into the group and said, "I parked the kids at the picnic tables in the capable hands of the waiters. Hello, George."

"Hello Tom," George said. "I want you to meet Marvin Hoffman. Tom Parker."

As they shook hands, Marvin Hoffman said, "You live near here? You all live here?"

"Just across the lawn," Ethel said.

"I should never have come here. I hate all of you. Did you ever try to raise two kids in a New York apartment?"

"Buy a house out here and commute," Tom said. "I do it, and it really isn't bad."

"I'd do it in a minute. My wife would do it in ten seconds. And when you meet her, don't mention it. I'm an agent. I go to the theater at least four times a week. If I have dinner at home twice a week, I'm lucky. What would I do if I lived out here? I'd never get home till two o'clock in the morning. 'It's criminal to raise kids in this filthy city,' my wife keeps telling me. I don't know that? But I've got to be in New York. I'd have a very hungry family if I weren't." He looked up and around sadly. "But look at the trees . . . and the sky. I even heard birds a little while ago." When he looked down again, he said, "Oh, God! Here she comes. Pretend you hate it out here, huh? Hey, Ruth!" A dark, handsome, stern-looking woman joined them, and Marvin said, "This is my wife, Ruth. Cynthia and Herb Radnor, Ethel and Tom Parker and Peg and Joe Jablonski."

Ruth smiled and said, "Hello."

"That's fantastic," Joe said. "You got every one of our names right. I mean, you just met us."

"I'm an agent, Joe. I couldn't tell you the street number of my office building, but names. That's my business. Ruth, don't start with me. These are George's neighbors."

Ruth looked at them as if she had just met the tenants of some exotic Eden. "You *live* out here?"

"Just across the lawn," Ethel said.

Ruth looked profoundly pathetic and said, "Oh, how I envy you!"

"Excuse me," George said. "I'm going to try to find Charlie Aaron. I'll be back in a minute."

George found Charles Aaron, whose last novel had sold 300,000 copies in hard cover, berating the ballet dancers for their isolationism. He interrupted and said, "May I drag you away?"

One of the dancers said, "Please."

As he led him through the crowd, George said, "I wouldn't want you to give up your caustic self-image, but would you be polite to my neighbors? One of them's a local high school principal, and . . ."

"Have you ever seen me be deliberately rude to anyone?" Charles Aaron asked.

"Well . . . never mind. In one way, the party's *for* the neighbors, and I don't want them standing around in a group not meeting anybody."

"Like those goddamned dancers."

"Exactly. So would you . . ."

"I have the picture."

They had reached the neighbors by then. Ruth Hoffman had insisted that Ethel show her her house, and they had gone off across the lawn, leaving the others still in a group.

George introduced Charlie and added, "Herb is principal of the local high school, and I particularly wanted you to meet."

"I've always wanted to be a teacher," Charlie said, "but I don't think I have the guts."

"You certainly have the knowledge," Herb said. "I

think I've read all of your work. I may have missed the first novel."

"That's the only compliment you have to pay a novelist," Charles Aaron said. "I don't care whether you liked them or not, as long as you've read them. Come on. Let's get ourselves another drink and talk about my work for a while."

They moved off toward the nearest bar, but were interrupted by a waiter who offered to get their drinks for them. "You can't get service like this in the best hotels in Europe," Charlie said. "May I tell you what I think is wrong with my last book?"

"Please do," Herb said.

George was saying, "Marvin, your glass is empty. Let me . . ."

Marvin held up his hand to silence him. He cocked an ear toward the terrace for a moment and said, "I knew something was getting to me. Who's that rock group playing now? They're very good."

George said, "I swear to God I didn't tell him, Cynthia. They're a local group called The Iron Feather."

"Local?" Marvin said.

"Yes. Cynthia's son, David, is the lead guitarist. Why don't you sign them?"

"I don't handle musicians. But if I did . . . Let me listen a while. Maybe I could put Jerry Hellman on to them. They're really very good."

George continued to be dogged about the enforced conviviality. He took Cynthia and Tom and the Jablonskis to the terrace and introduced them to the superstar and to Kate Mulligan and Ken Greene. The violinists had returned, and superstar immediately asked Cynthia to waltz. All Cynthia could think of as they danced was that if Ethel returned now through the French doors, she would probably faint dead away with envy. Tom and Ken Greene were deep in conversation about networks, agencies and sponsors. George snagged Monty Martin, the comedian, and introduced him to Peg and Joe. After a few

194

moments, Monty confessed that he had been born in Newark and, as a child, had been taken on picnic excursions to Hainesdale, which was then mostly forest and open fields. They were delighted with each other.

When The Iron Feather returned to the terrace to replace the Hungarians again, the ballroom dancers retreated to the garden. They were replaced by the chorus boys and the relatively few younger women at the party. Their dancing soon became more of a performance than a pastime. The dancing was professionally frenzied and of nearly the same quality one would have seen in a Broadway musical. The enthusiasm and skill of the dancers pushed The Iron Feather to new peaks of achievement, and the better they played, the better the dancers danced. Spectators gathered to watch from the garden, from the French doors and from every available space on the terrace that didn't interfere with the exhibition. The party was in full swing.

George and Gregory decided simultaneously that with so many of the guests preoccupied and in one place, it was an excellent time to start serving the food. It could be brought out directly from the kitchen and into the garden without crossing the terrace while the traffic was at a minimum. By the time The Iron Feather had finished its set (extended beyond its normal time by the waves of applause and cries of, "More! More!"), most of the food was on the serving tables. It seemed to many of the guests to have got there by magic. Even the most jaded of them were impressed by the sumptuousness of the banquet and the attention to detail. The seemingly endless bowls of fresh caviar were set in larger crystal bowls of crushed ice. Each whole salmon was decorated with lemon and parsley and capers. The glazed turkeys rested on beds of fresh asparagus. There was an aura of elegance about the food which raised it from the level of a well-catered garden party to a gourmet feast.

The appearance of the food was not meant to be taken as a signal that the meal had begun, for the serving of food was obviously going to go on for hours. There were still guests arriving who presumably would not begin to eat for some time. The eating was intended to be leisurely—perhaps a plate of hors d'ouevres first with a cocktail, then as long a pause as one wished before the next course. Some of the chorus boys, presumably unemployed ones, ate immediately and like field hands, rather as if there was some uncertainty as to when they would eat again. Ethel was among the first to eat because Kate Mulligan, who had to leave early, invited her to eat with her and Ken. Tom joined Herb and Charles Aaron at a table where the literary discussion and the drinking took precedence over food. The superstar and his wife ate because he had to return to New York to tape a late-night talk show. Cynthia sat with them, drinking champagne, but not eating. Monty Martin, who had a reputation for heavy drinking, proceeded to live up to it. He and Peg and Joe stood close to the terrace bar, still swapping New Jersey stories.

Although the neighbors were relatively provincial, they were not overwhelmed either by the celebrities or the luxury. But their attitude toward the party was quite different from the attitudes of most of the other guests. Even the stars were not accustomed to such near perfection in parties in private homes, but they were also likely to have attended White House dinners. The literary lions appeared on the kind of programs the television celebrities hosted. The attorneys and agents handled "stables" of illustrious clients and were quite at home with both affluence and fame. Even the chorus boys had worked with the brightest stars on Broadway; had seen them in rehearsal clothes, with hangovers, in tantrums. However impressed they were with someone's stardom, they were first keenly aware of his human frailty.

To the neighbors, on the other hand, there was nothing familiar in the elements of the party. It could not be denied that all six of them were having a perfectly wonderful time. But the lavishness was financially and psychologically beyond them or anyone they knew except George Carr. It did not matter that neither they nor anyone they knew, other than George, would particularly *want* to give such a party. What mattered was that they couldn't have. They could not relax completely in the presence of celebrities they had previously known only as half-deified images on their television screens. And they could not help feeling patronized by them. It did not matter that they neither wanted nor needed celebrities as intimate friends. What mattered was that such relationships were impossible for them. They were not out of their depth; they were simply out of their element.

To the neighbors, the other guests seemed to behave with either casual grace or comfortable familiarity. If the neighbors achieved either, it was through conscious effort. Joe searched through the spectacularly laden table for some kind of food he knew and knew he liked, rather than risk taking something he would be unable to eat. But inside himself, he tried to pretend to be rejecting the same old caviar and cold fish with avocado mayonnaise, and spinach mousse. Even with Kate Mulligan's genuine and subtle assistance, Ethel had to *try* not to behave like a fan. Tom, as an advertising agency assistant account executive, was thoroughly accustomed to playing games. But being treated as an equal by the second most successful television producer in the business made him painfully aware of the vast difference in their positions and made him play the game with an exhausting expenditure of energy. Similarly, Charles Aaron's interest in Herb's thoughts on the underlying psychological themes of certain contemporary novels served less to compliment Herb than to underline the insignificance of his thoughts. Although he tried to forget it for the moment, he was a smalltown English teacher, politely enduring the courteous attentions of a man who was generally acknowledged to be one of America's most important living novelists. Cynthia, who was certainly the most socially confident of the neighbors, was fully aware that she was on an excursion into a holiday country of existence. Her effort was at squelching any evidence of her envy and her renewed awareness of disappointment with her life. Only Peg, more alien than any of the other neighbors in this milieu, was unscathed. She was exactly the woman she had expected to become when she was a child, no more, no less. Margaret Kelly Jablonski would have been Margaret Kelly Jablonski at a fire, a flood, the second coming of Christ or at George Carr's party.

The neighbors did not realize that the attitudes of the guests were just as much poses as their own attitudes, but had been assumed so many times that the effort had gone out of it.

As George and Michael went about the business of hosting, they seemed to the neighbors to lose their Hainesdale identity. The neighbors could not avoid seeing the party in two groups: their own and the other guests. George and Michael seemed to be distinctly a part of the latter. They had agreed that there was something studied— a reserve, a decorousness—about the George and Michael of Wednesday night bridge and Saturday night dinners. That quality was gone now, displaced by an easy joviality they had never seen in them before. They seemed younger, more carefree, more comfortable. Soon the neighbors began to see a parallel: the George and Michael at Wednesday night bridge were, like the neighbors at this party, making an effort. The neighbors at Wednesday night bridge were, like George and Michael at this party, where they belonged. This was what George wanted them to see.

The drawing room and den were now filled with guests, and Michael was completing an inspection tour, making certain there were enough waiters to accommodate the guests who chose to be inside. He was thoroughly caught up now in the success of what had previously been George's party. He found that the ashtrays were being emptied regularly, the cigarette boxes filled, drinks replenished with the same quiet efficiency as in the garden.

He came out onto the terrace and saw David talking with Derek Jones, a ballet dancer turned chorus boy and an old friend. In his incipient drunkenness, he felt an instant of savage jealousy and rage. He told himself no phony English gypsy was going to put the make on *his* David Radnor. And as he started toward them, he added, *Not if I can't do it myself.* Immediately, he saw how funny this was, and he approached David and Derek laughing.

"You're in high good humor, Michael," Derek said.

"It's just because it's turned out to be such a 'swell' party, baby," Michael said.

"I hate to admit it," Derek told him, "but it's the best party I've been to in my four years in America. Which is what I was just saying to David."

"I'll bet," Michael said.

"Don't be bitchy. I'm going to get some champagne, but I'll be right back."

As Derek made his way to the bar, David said, "Wow! The way those kids dance!"

"Derek stopped being a 'kid' about the time you were born."

David ignored this. "I've never seen anything like it!"

"Wow! The way The Iron Feather plays!"

"Something happened, Mike. We've never played better. The wilder they got, the wilder we got. It was really great."

"It must have been artistic symbiosis. I thought for a minute it was grass."

"Grass? Here?"

"David, if the chorus of all Broadway shows stopped smoking grass for a month, the bottom would fall out of the marijuana market. Don't be surprised if that sweet, pungent odor begins to waft across the summer air. And don't be tempted."

"What do you think I'd do, rush up to Herb with a joint and offer him a hit?"

"No. I'm afraid Herb would rush up to you and offer you a hit—right in the mouth. Spoil the party."

"I'll be careful."

"I didn't ask you to be careful. I asked you not to smoke. Not here." David frowned. "Are you holding?"

"No."

"But Bobby Geary is."

"I don't know. Probably."

"Listen to me . . ."

"All right. I'm not going to smoke."

"All right. And tell Geary that if he is, he should get his ass into a car between sets and get at least two miles away from here."

"I'll tell him, Michael. But I have no control over Bobby."

"Would he do it if *his* mother and father were here?"

"I guess not."

"Then he'd be pretty much of a prick to do it with yours here."

"Yeah. He would."

"You mean he is."

"I don't know."

Michael was suddenly terrified. "David, I'm very serious about this. For Christ's sake, don't you know what could happen if somebody caught one of you kids smoking at our party? Don't you realize . . . Look. If I don't get a promise from you right now that none of you is going to smoke grass at this party, you can just pack up and get the hell out. And I mean even if other people are smoking openly all over the place."

"You mean Derek can smoke himself into a coma, but we can't even light up a single joint?"

"That's exactly what I mean. Derek is twenty-eight years old, and his mother and father are in merrie England."

"You don't think that's a double standard?"

"You're sixteen, and your mother and father are friends of mine."

200

"Yeah. And you're beginning to sound just like them." Michael was shocked and deeply hurt, and he could keep neither feeling from showing almost pitifully. "I'm sorry."

"David, if you want to go to your parents and say, 'Bobby Geary has some grass. Do you mind if I smoke?', that's perfectly okay with me. But without that permission don't start sharing joints with the boys in the band."

"What do you mean, 'the boys in the band'?"

"You know exactly what I mean. David, why the hell are we fighting? You know you can't smoke with Herb and Cynthia here . . . and the Parkers and the Jablonskis. You *know* you can't."

"All right. I know. It's just that it's such a great party. Everybody's so free and happy. I'll bet you nobody else but my parents and the Parkers and the Jablonskis would give a shit whether we smoked or not."

"You're absolutely wrong. There are a lot of people here with sixteen-year-old kids of their own. They'd be down on you like . . . No. They'd be down on George and me like a herd of buffalo. David, I'm asking you. For me. Please don't do it."

"Okay. Okay. I won't do it." They were looking at each other without wavering. "What's the matter, Michael? Don't you trust me?"

"No. Not at this minute. Not right now. No."

"I'm sorry about that. We're going to play again now."

David walked away toward the part of the terrace that was reserved for the musicians. Michael saw him, and it seemed to him that David was walking out of his life and back into his own. This was what George wanted him to see.

Michael's first impulse was to run to David, to take him away to the dark, wooded hill at the country club, to hold him in his arms and beg him not to change things, to stay with him forever. But he knew with the certainty and sadness of panic that any word or gesture of persuasion would drive David further away. And he knew that if he did nothing, David would merely drift away from him on some tide of inevitability that had already begun to flow.

He stood staring at David, no more than twenty feet away, as David picked up his guitar, smiled at Bobby Geary, brushed away a strand of hair that had fallen over his forehead. He saw the detail of him: the strong, beautiful hands; the young, firm jawline; the straight, broad nose; and the eyes, the lovely, unloving eyes, devoid now of any emotion except a nameless, trivial pleasure at the prospect of making music. And Michael felt he had never loved or wanted anyone so much. And he had never felt so helpless, so useless, so unwanted, so alone, so old.

He saw, too, the gap between them, the now widening, unbridgeable gap of circumstance that made David young and beginning and made Michael middle-aged and soon finished. And in a silent, insane debate, he told himself he wanted merely to be with David for whatever was left of his own life, to guide, to share, to belong. He heard his internal voice demand his qualifications for the guidance, the sharing, the belonging. What monumental achievement, what talent, what unique spiritual condition certified him fit to rise above convention and tradition and morality? Where could he guide David except into the same terminal void of confusion in which he found himself? A void in which every tomorrow served only to end yesterday and to advance one more step the journey into death. He felt suddenly that the purest demonstration of his love would be to retreat into his own life, back into George's party, as he knew David had just done. This was what George wanted him to feel.

Looking longer at David became unbearable, and he turned away. He turned only away, not toward anything except the voracious vacuum of his being. And he bumped into Ethel Parker's extended, champagne-wielding hand, spilling wine on his striped blazer. Ethel was very drunk.

"Oh, Michael!" she said, unaware of the spilled wine. "This is the most wonderful party I've ever been at. The food! The people!" She giggled and added, "The *drinks!* All I want to know is how are *we* ever going to entertain you and *George* again. I mean, after *this*." She stumbled away toward the drawing room, champagne slopping over the rim of her glass.

In that instant, Michael saw it—or thought he did. In a stunning, paralyzing vision, he thought he saw George's plan. Had it not been for the intervening and sobering minutes it took for him to find George, he might have killed him.

George was talking to Cynthia and Joe and Monty Martin when Michael interrupted them and said, "George, I want to talk to you." Only George felt the pressure and the urgency of Michael's grip on his arm. He looked at Michael and said, "Certainly." He turned to the others, smiled and said, "Excuse me."

Michael turned without another word and started through the crowded garden. George followed him. With guests stopping them every few feet, it took them several minutes to reach the house and several more to get through the den and the hall to the foot of the stairs. Each time they stopped, Michael was pale and silent, making no attempt at geniality. George cut people off as politely as possible. Michael led the way up the stairs and to their room. He stepped inside, waited for George to come in and closed the door behind them.

They stood two feet apart, facing each other. Michael said, "I know why you gave the party."

George looked at him expressionlessly for a moment and said, "Are you sure?"

"Yes."

"Then tell me."

"You thought you could embarrass the neighbors by showing them how rich you are. You thought you could show them that our *real* friends are a bunch of fags and freaks and two-bit television performers. You wanted to show them we live in a different world from them, because if you could alienate them that way, you could keep me away from David. But you're wrong."

There was still no expression on George's face. He said, "Am I?"

Michael lunged at him, screaming, "You son of a bitch!"

He grabbed George by the throat. George was prepared for the violence. He hit Michael's arms hard and sharply from underneath and broke the grip. Then he hit him on the chest with both hands and knocked him across the room. For a moment, Michael was spread-eagled against the wall. Before he could struggle forward and lunge again, George shouted at him, "Mike! Stop it!"

Michael hesitated for a moment. He was panting, and the damp stain of the wine made a dark blotch on his jacket.

"Michael, listen to me for five minutes. You can do anything you want to do after that, but listen to me first. I gave this party for *you*. I wasn't trying to embarrass the neighbors. Christ, they're having the time of their lives. But I did want them to see—and that includes David—what our life *should* be like. What matters is that *you* see it, that *you* know that those people down there—call them freaks and fags if you want—are indeed our real friends. We're part of them, and they're part of us. And we are and always will be different from the neighbors. It took almost thirty years for me to understand the difference. Thirty years of loathing myself. Because even though I hated her, I admired Janet Cartwright more than anybody I've ever known, and she despised me. So I despised myself. But I had to know why. It wasn't until she left me this house that I knew. She considered me a moral leper, but she left me this house because I was family. That's the word, Michael, and that's the difference. They . . . the neighbors and ninety percent of the human race procreate. And it doesn't matter whether it's out of pride or lust or family duty. They continue and sustain. Generations of them dedicate themselves to their own immortality by having children. It only takes one of us to send them to the grave knowing there won't be anybody to trek out to the cemetery on Mother's Day to put flowers on Grandmother's grave. We are to them a terminal disease. We're the wall between them and eternal life. Oh, they're delighted that you're witty or clever or accomplished. They think it's marvelous that you play the piano or speak three languages or have famous friends. But where, oh, for the sweet love of Christ, *where* are your children? And they can turn it around. You can be a drunk or a bum or a thief or a pimp. As long as they have your children as reparation, they can forgive you. Childlessness is the sin. If you're lucky, you have brothers and sisters who continue the line, and they can point to you as the 'bright one' with a certain amount of reluctant pride. But no achievement is as great as the simple act of productive fucking. You're an only child, and so am I. There's no forgiveness for us. I'm resigned to it, and I thought you were. But now you want David Radnor. Whether you admit it or not, what you really want to do is to steal one of their sons like some . . . some mythical dwarf that comes in the night. No. Worse. You want to *convert* one of their sons to your childless life. They'd kill you for that, Michael, as soon as look at you. So I gave the party. To show the neighbors we live in a different world. To show them we're satisfied with that world. To remind you how good that world can be and that David can never be part of it. And to remind you that I love you . . . and that that ought to be enough."

They had not stopped looking into each other's eyes, had not even blinked. The staring went on for a longer time, as if Michael were trying to understand what George had said.

"Get out, George," Michael said finally. "Just get out."

George looked into Michael's eyes for another moment and said, "I would like to point out that you are telling me to get out of my bedroom, in my house, on my property. And that you have every right to do so only because I love you." Then George left the room and closed the door quietly.

It was dark when George got back to the garden. The candles flickered in the hurricane lamps on the tables, and violin music floated through the air like a gentle breeze. There were still people everywhere, dancing and eating and talking and laughing. The sudden air of festivity seemed for a moment inappropriate to George after the somber moments with Michael. As he made his way through the crowded garden, he began to realize that there was a difference in the party now, a difference beyond the synthetic comparison he had just made. It took him several minutes more to figure out what it was, to be sure he wasn't imagining it. Most of the guests who had been at the party since its beginning were now drunk, and the later arrivals seemed to be trying to catch up with them. Earlier, the atmosphere had been gay and carefree; now it was rowdy. Gestures were too large, voices too loud and laughter too raucous. There was a group at the piano in the drawing room, and their singing mixed discordantly with the violins. People were dancing on the lawn.

As he made the rounds of the party, he began to feel apprehensive and helpless. There was certainly no justification for asking the guests to leave, but the revelry was moving in an obvious upward spiral. He encountered Joe on his way to one of the bars in the garden and asked him where Peg was. She had taken the children home and would be right back. George smiled his insincere approval and turned toward the terrace, where he saw a half dozen new guests arriving. People were moving around the entire property now, no longer feeling restricted to George's garden and house. Tom had taken a group of guests to his house to show them the landscaping. He fixed drinks for them while they were there. Others, seeing what seemed to be an extension of the original party, wandered over to join it. Any kind of private conversation was difficult in the din of voices and laughter and music, and those who felt the need of such privacy simply moved over the unmarked perimeter of George's garden and into the Radnors' yard. This was an offense to George's sense of style, and he felt that, just as the party was spilling over the bounds of his property, it was spilling over the bounds of his control.

Those guests who smoked marijuana with any regularity would simply have lit up at a New York party, but here, in New Jersey at a party of this size, it would have been indiscreet. The easy move into the darkness of the rest of the property facilitated smoking with discretion; and within an hour of George's return, "that sweet, pungent odor" was wafting through the summer air as Michael had predicted. It was dissipated by the gentle evening breeze so that the nonsmokers were unaware of it.

George's unease was heightened by Michael's return to the party. From a distance, he saw him come out onto the terrace and go directly to the bar. He could not hear the conversation, but he saw the bartender smile broadly and begin to mix what he presumed, correctly, to be a stinger, the combination of brandy and crème de menthe nearly lethal even to heavy social drinkers. Michael took the drink and started toward the garden, waving a cheerful, nonchalant greeting to David. That was what troubled George: Michael was *too* cheerful. His exchange with the bartender, his greeting to David, and now the camaraderie with which he threw his arm around Derek's shoulder were all too cheerful for the Michael he had left in the bedroom an hour ago. He watched as they talked and laughed with what seemed to be a forced joviality. Then they started to walk toward the edge of the crowd and disappeared into the Radnors' backyard. George decided to follow them.

As he approached them, he could see the orange glow of a tiny cigarette being passed back and forth between them, and he knew they were smoking marijuana. Then he smelled the unmistakable acrid aroma.

Michael saw him coming toward them and said, "Hello, George. I'm back."

"I'm glad."

"This is one of the best parties you've ever given, and

I didn't want to miss it. I didn't want to spoil it, either. I really didn't George."

"It wouldn't be any kind of party at all for me unless you enjoyed it."

"I believe that. I honestly believe that. I'm sorry about before. But I am what I am, and I can't help that. I can't help it that I'm emotionally immature. I can't help that I'm very selfish. I can't help that I'm in love. I am what I am. And one of the things I am is a little bit drunk."

"In love, are you?" Derek said. "With someone other than George? Tell me, Michael, tell me. I can dine out on that for a week."

"It's none of your goddamned business, sweet old Derek."

"Listen, sweet old Michael, I had my first lover when I was sixteen. An older man from the motor trade, as the Beatles have so nicely put it. In the ensuing twelve years, I've had at least fifteen more. Not tricks, mind you—I couldn't count them—but honest-to-God, let's-play-house lovers. My taking a new one has all the stunning effect on my friends of my ordering orange juice for breakfast. But you and George have been together for decades. If you have a lover, you owe it to your public to let them know. I don't believe a word of it, of course, but I can dine out more successfully on an exciting lie than on a dull truth."

"Michael, don't you think it would be a good idea if we didn't smoke until later?" George said.

"Later? You mean when the neighbors go home?"

"No, I don't mean that. I mean . . ."

"I would think you'd be delighted at anything that would alienate them further." He sucked on the joint, held the smoke in his lungs, and passed the joint to Derek.

"I mean when the four teenagers in The Iron Feather go home."

"Oh, don't worry about them. They're pot veterans. Tiny little potheads, they are."

"That's great. If they know other people are smoking,

208

they'll probably start themselves. Cynthia and Herb would love . . ."

"Never happen. I have forbidden it."

"What?"

"I laid down the law, Uncle George—which is about the only thing I've laid for a long time."

"I knew it wasn't true," Derek said.

"Shut up," Michael said. "I told David if any of them smoked, I'd kick them all out."

"And you think it's perfectly fair under those circumstances for you to smoke?"

"I'm over twenty-one, unfortunately. I can do a lot of things they can't. It's not me, George. It's the system."

"Mike, please don't argue with me about this. If one of those kids lights up and gets caught, that's his problem. But if there are adults smoking all over the place at the same time—particularly either of us—it could be very ugly."

"That's more or less what I told David."

"Then please stop."

"All right, all right. One last hit and I'll wait till the kiddies go home. One isn't allowed to do *anything* with the kiddies, is one, Uncle George?"

As Michael took the joint from Derek, George put his hand on Michael's shoulder, smiled and said, "There's no such thing as a bad boy. I'll see you later."

George's preventive tactics had come too late. While George was talking with Michael and Derek, Cynthia and Herb and Tom were sitting at a table in the garden, drinking champagne. They were making an effort at staying on the general level of abandon the party had reached, and were considerably aided by the alcohol they had consumed. Tom had been telling a joke when he saw Herb squinting and peering over Tom's shoulder. Tom turned, saw nothing but people and turned back to Herb.

"You're not listening," Tom said.

"What . . . what's going on over there?" Herb said, leaning to one side for a better view.

"Over where?" Tom asked.

"There. Those two guys. They're . . . I'll be goddamned! They're smoking marijuana." Tom turned to look and heard Herb saying, "They're passing a . . . a joint back and forth between them!"

"Don't tell me you're shocked," Tom said. "Christ, they smoke in the mail room of the agency every day."

"I don't give a goddamn what they do in the mail room . . ."

"Come on Herb. Calm down. Practically every . . ."

"My son is right up there, not twenty feet away!"

"All right. As long as *he* isn't smoking, I don't see . . ."

"Well, I don't care whether you see or not. If supposedly responsible adults are going to smoke marijuana right out in the open in front of those young people as if there were nothing at all wrong with it, how long is it going to be before . . ."

"Take it easy. Don't you know how many . . ."

"You can take this as lightly as you want, but I am not going to stand by and let *anybody* smoke marijuana in the presence of my son and those other kids up there. Doing nothing is tantamount to approval, and I do not approve!"

Herb was on his feet and moving toward the two young men before Tom could stop him. As quickly as they could, Cynthia and Tom followed him.

"What are you two doing?" Herb said when he had reached them.

The two men made no attempt to conceal the joint, but they were obviously startled.

"What . . . what do you mean, what are we . . ." one of them said.

"You're smoking marijuana, aren't you?"

"Oh, yeah." They truly thought Herb must be objecting to something else, for they lived in a world where smoking grass at a private party could not possibly be construed as an offense. "A wee taste of the weed. Want a hit?"

"Don't you realize there are teenage kids here? You can just get the hell out of . . ."

"Just a minute, friend," the other young man said. "I don't know who you are, but unless George has made some pretty kinky arrangements I don't know about, you don't live here and this isn't your house or your party. So I don't quite understand why you're throwing people out."

"Well, I'll make you understand in about thirty seconds why I'm throwing you out. I'm the father of one of those kids up there, and I will not have him subjected to . . ."

The first young man was very stoned and certainly did not realize the intensity of Herb's anger or the seriousness of the situation. He said, "The group? The way they play, man, it's eight-to-five they know more about grass than we do."

"Listen, you young punk . . ."

"We're not subjecting anybody to anything," the second young man said. "Look, I see your point. But if you and your son are guests at a party you don't approve of, don't you think it'd be simpler if you just left? I mean, instead of trying to throw other people out?"

Although the music and the noise of the party continued, the immediate area around Herb and the two young men had become quiet and attentive to the argument.

"*I'm* not committing any offense," Herb said. "*I'm* not breaking the law. It's you who . . ."

George had reached them by this time and said, "Herb, what's the matter?"

"You can see what's the matter," Herb said. "These two . . . people are smoking marijuana! They're just standing here smoking it as if it were perfectly all right! Look. He's still got the lit cigarette right in his hand!"

"And this obnoxious gentleman has just asked us to leave," the first young man said.

The quiet was spreading through the crowd like ripples on a pond. "Herb," George said, "why don't you let me handle this? If you'd just . . ."

"Sure. I'll let you handle it. As long as by handling it you mean stopping these people from doing what they're doing."

"I asked you to let me . . ."

Cynthia said, "Come back to the table, Herb, and . . ."

"Who the hell *is* he?" the first young man asked.

"Herb," George said, "why don't you go back to the table with Cynthia and . . ."

"Are you telling us you approve of their smoking marijuana?"

"I'm asking you to remember that you're a guest here, and so are Arthur and Bob. I'm asking you to give me the . . ."

"And my son is here! And I won't have him attending a party where the use of drugs is open and condoned!"

"I'm afraid grass is as much a personal choice as alcohol. I can't very well . . ."

"And it's illegal!" Herb said. "I could have the police on them in minutes. I . . ."

"Herb," Tom said, "will you come back to the table?"

"You don't seem to realize, George, that there's already a drug problem among the young people of this community. And as a member of this community, as a teacher, as a high school principal, I have an obligation to do everything in my power to clean it up."

George simply wanted the participants to separate, but he couldn't avoid being drawn into the argument. "I'm sorry, but I fail to see how some people from New York who are here for one evening at a private party are contributing to a local drug problem."

"The answer to that is right up there on that terrace," Herb said, pointing dramatically with an outstretched arm. "And if you don't see, it's because you don't want to. Are you going to stop this smoking or aren't you?"

"I'll do my best to see that the kids are in no way influenced by . . ."

"That's not good enough, George." He waited for a brief moment, then added, "You leave me no other choice.

I'm going to send the kids home. And I'm certainly going home myself." He started to turn away toward the terrace.

"Herb," George said quietly. Herb turned back to him. "Why didn't you just quietly go and do that *before* you made a spectacle of yourself?"

Herb stood there for a moment speechless and looking as if his mouth might literally drop open. Then he turned again and pushed his way through the silent crowd. George followed him.

The Iron Feather had just finished a song and were trying to figure out what had caused the silence in the garden. Herb approached them and said, "David, I want you and the boys to pack your things and get out of here. Now."

David was stunned. "What . . . what do you mean?"

"Just what I said. I want you all out of here immediately."

"Maybe you'd better do as he says, David," George said quietly.

Herb turned to him and said sharply, "I don't need your assistance in this. I have authority here."

"Herb, it's still my party."

"And Dave is still my son." He turned back to the boys. "Now go on."

David, still filled with the fun and the glory of the evening, could not understand why his father was trying to destroy it all. "But what's wrong? What've we done?" He was pleading.

"You haven't done anything, Dave," Herb said. "I just don't want you here any longer."

"Dad, you can't expect us to just get up and leave without knowing why . . . without any explanation."

"I can and do expect you to do what I tell you."

"But tell me why. We haven't finished playing, and . . ."

"We'll discuss it at home . . . as we always discuss things."

David turned his pleading look toward George, but

213

George nodded in obviously reluctant agreement with Herb. David saw that it was hopeless.

"All right," he said. "But you can't throw Bobby and the others out. Maybe you're *my* father, but you're not . . ."

Herb was outraged at such insolence. His eyes narrowed and he spoke slowly and deliberately. "I told you—all of you to leave."

Bobby Geary said, "What the hell? We can't play anyway without a lead guitar." And the boys got up and began to pack up their instruments.

The violinists had come out onto the terrace to see what was happening, and George signaled them to play.

Herb turned to George again and said, "I find it hard to believe you've taken the attitude you have. Cynthia and I will be leaving now. I suppose I should tell you I feel very strongly that I should let the police know what's going on here." He turned and walked down the terrace steps into the crowded garden to the strains of a Viennese waltz.

Michael had missed the whole event. He had come back to the garden from the Radnors' yard when it was already finished. The difference in the atmosphere of the party was unmistakable. He saw George on the terrace and hurried to him.

"What the hell happened?" he asked George.

"Just what I was afraid would happen," George said wearily. "Herb saw Bob and Arthur smoking and behaved like a senile old woman. When I refused to guarantee that nobody would smoke, he made the kids go home."

"David? He sent David home?"

"He also threatened to call the police."

"The stupid, pompous son of a bitch! I'd like to . . ."

"Forget it. There's been enough unpleasantness."

"But why should he fuck up the whole party?"

"Maybe it's just as well. It's getting late."

Michael put his hand on George's arm and said, "I'm terribly sorry, George."

"So am I, really."

"Do you think he *will* call the police?"

"I don't know. He can be a very spiteful man. I think we'd better quietly warn people of the possibility."

"That's always great for a party. I guess I'd better stash our own grass somewhere. Or maybe even give it to somebody to take back to town."

"No, don't do that. I'm sure I could talk them out of a search . . . with no warrant and all that. But I think people ought to know about it so they can decide for themselves."

Michael went to the people he knew or suspected were holding grass and explained the situation. They all knew that local police were notoriously hostile toward outsiders who brought marijuana into their communities. They knew that if they were apprehended even simply for possession, they could expect no mercy, the worst possible treatment and the severest possible punishment—if not outright brutality and injustice. There was no panic in their departure. They simply left as quickly and quietly as they could.

While Michael was doing this, Tom came to George and said, "What can I say?"

"You don't have to say anything, Tom. It wasn't your fault."

"Herb's a pain in the ass when he gets like that. I tried, but I couldn't do anything with him. I don't think he'd really do anything about the police, but . . . well, I'll go over there now and see what I can do."

"Thank you, Tom. I'd appreciate it."

"You should thank me? I haven't had such a good time in years. I'm not putting you on about that. It was a great, great party. I thank you for Ethel, too. I don't even know where she is. If she's had any more to drink since I last saw her, she's probably under a table somewhere."

George grinned and said, "I'm delighted you had a good time. Good night."

The party never really recovered from the effects of the incident. It had a psychological dulling effect even on those who neither smoked nor were in possession of marijuana. From the time the violins started playing again, there was a slow, steady exodus until there were only Gregory's staff and no more than twenty-five guests. Those who had decided to stay and had grass gave it to Michael for safekeeping.

An hour later, George stood on the terrace watching as the last of the garden tables was carried away. The waiters had been so efficient throughout the afternoon and evening that there was now no saddening physical aftermath of the party. But the sadness was already there inside George, a sadness at the ignominious end of a brilliant party. Extension cords had been run from the house, and in the harsh glare of the bare bulbs which supplied the light for the cleaning-up, the garden looked grotesque.

Michael came up quietly behind George, a glass of champagne in each hand. He held one out to George, and they drank a silent toast.

"Hey, Georgie," Michael said, "we still have a very good group here. Why don't we have our own party? What the hell?"

George smiled at him and said, "What the hell?"

They went into the drawing room together. There was already a party in progress. There were a dozen young men in the room who were in no apparent way saddened by the end of the other party. Two couples were dancing to the music on the stereo, and the others, all with drinks, were comfortably ensconced in the chairs and sofas.

Arthur was among them, and when George and Michael came in, he lifted his glass and said, "To George and Michael for a sensational party."

As the others toasted, Michael said, "The party, dear boy, is just beginning."

Gregory was standing in the drawing room doorway, surveying the room. George went to him and said, "Gregory, everything, but everything was super. How can I thank you?"

"By paying your enormous bill quickly."

"I'll give you a check right now."

"Oh, heavens, no! It'll take me days to figure it out.

In all truth, George, I enjoy doing your parties so much, I always feel guilty charging you. I don't mean that I'm *not* going to charge you," he added hastily, "but I feel guilty nevertheless."

George laughed and said, "I promise I'll put a check in the mail the instant I get your bill."

"You can see how worried I am," Gregory said, sipping his champagne.

"Why don't you stay on, overnight if you want. I think we're still having a party."

"I'd love to, but I really must get all this stuff back to town. I'll just gather up my kiddies and run. Thank you anyway."

Michael joined them and said, "Gregory, it was splendid as always. You're not leaving?"

"Yes. A woman's work is never done. But first I must check the kitchen."

"To hell with the kitchen," George said. "What isn't done now can be done tomorrow. I have a couple of women who come in."

"I never leave a party without . . ."

"You've done all you're going to do," George insisted. "Far more than anyone else would have done. Stay as long as you like, and when you're ready, just take off."

"Well . . . I *am* tempted to stay. But I mustn't." He drained his champagne glass and handed it to George. "You may take that away, my good man."

"Anything to be of service," George said.

"George, go and sit down," Michael said. "I'll see Gregory to the door. Now, go on. I haven't seen you sit down all evening."

"That's only because I haven't sat down all evening. Good night, Gregory."

"Good night, my darling."

Gregory and Michael started through the hall together. Michael took Gregory's arm and said quietly, "Gregory, there's one of your people, a blond boy. He was tending bar on the terrace."

217

"I've been waiting since four o'clock for you to ask."

"He's very beautiful."

"Have I ever hired an ugly waiter?"

"No, but you have to admit, they're not all up to *that* standard."

"Oh, would that they were."

"Tell me about him."

"His name's Kevin Andrews and—big surprise—he's an actor. I mean, he wants to be an actor."

"How original. Do you think he'd stay on?"

"Probably. He'd be a fool if he didn't. Shall I ask him?"

"Yes."

"Anybody else?"

"Anybody who isn't going to be competition."

"I know three boys who'd be delighted to stay. One has already asked me about Derek. Shall I ask them, too?"

"Sure. But ask Kevin first. Incidentally, how old is he?"

"Nineteen."

Michael sighed and said, "Now, isn't that a nice age?" Gregory executed a little shudder of delight. "I'll kind of be in the doorway, waving goodbye."

"You devil!"

Michael opened the front door and Gregory, assuming his air of generalship, strode out into the driveway. He disappeared behind one of his Volkswagen buses. After a moment, Kevin Andrews came around the other end of the bus and started toward Michael. He stopped, still in the driveway, a step lower than Michael and looked up at him. "Gregory tells me I'm invited to stay."

"Yes," Michael said.

Kevin looked faintly embarrassed. "By you?"

"Yes."

"Then I'll stay."

"Come on in."

Kevin didn't move. "It won't mean trouble, will it?"

"You mean with George?"

"Yes."

"No trouble."

"You're sure?"

"Yes. Or I wouldn't ask you to stay. Trust me."

Kevin smiled then, as he had when he'd mixed Michael's stinger. "Wow!"

Michael thought for a second that the word had stopped his heart from beating. "What's the matter?"

"I thought it couldn't happen. I'd been hoping all night. I was just getting into the Volks to go home when Gregory asked me."

"When the wagons go and the buses stop running, there may not be any way home."

"I know."

"Beautiful. You don't play games. *You're* beautiful, too."

"So are you."

"Come on in."

Michael stepped aside and Kevin went in and stood in the hall. Michael closed the door behind them and stood for a moment looking into Kevin's eyes. Then, without otherwise touching him, Michael kissed him softly and gently. Michael ended the kiss and said, "Come and have a drink."

Just as they started toward the drawing room, the doorbell rang. Michael opened the door, and three boys stood on the doorstep, smiling. They were all in their very early twenties and extremely good looking.

"Hi," Michael said. "Come on in."

They came in rather self-consciously, but relaxed immediately upon seeing Kevin.

Kevin said, "Well, look who's here. Michael, this is Jerry, Earl and Billy."

They shook hands with Michael, and all five of them proceeded to the drawing room. Derek said, "Well, things are looking up," and everyone laughed. Michael introduced the four new guests and took them to the bar. He smiled at Kevin and said, "Turnabout is fair play. What'll you have?"

"Scotch, please."

When Michael had given Kevin his drink, he said, "Would you excuse me for a minute? There's something I have to do. It'll only take a minute."

"Sure. Don't worry. I'll wait."

"Oh, I know you'll wait. I'm worried about what you'll do while you're waiting."

"I have a one-track mind."

Michael ran his hand down the back of Kevin's head, then started across the room. He had taken only a few steps when he encountered George.

"Hello, there," George said.

"Hello. I guess you know I've asked Kevin to stay."

"I assumed you had."

"It's all right?"

"Of course."

"I suppose you're wondering about my faithfulness to my one true love?"

"Did I say I was wondering that?"

"Well, you are. I've decided to be faithful to David as he is faithful to me: intellectually. I find celibacy a pain in the ass. And I know what you said upstairs is true. I mean, I know it in my head, but that doesn't change what I know emotionally. Understand?" George nodded. "I saw David pull away from me tonight for the first time. I'm not going to do anything to . . . to bring him back that one step. Maybe not doing that is doing something."

"I think asking Kevin to stay is doing something."

"Yeah. Very pleasant penance."

"That's the best kind."

"I was just going over to talk to Gianni. Have a good time."

Gianni had just left a group of people and was moving toward the bar. He stopped only because Michael was directly in his path. Gianni's expression was cool, but somehow expectant.

Michael said, "Gianni, I'm sorry about what's been going on lately."

"Yes." Gianni started to move away, but Michael stopped him.

"It's been totally my fault, and I'm sorry. But things are going to be the way they used to be. I promise. Come on. Be nice to me. Please."

Gian-Carlo smiled and said, "It is always easy to be nice to you." Gianni started toward the bar again, but was pulled down onto the sofa where Bob and Arthur were sitting next to Derek and Earl. They squeezed him into the middle.

What followed can be made to occur in many ways: by design, by mutual lust or mutual desire, by alcohol, by grass—even by accident. The most successful orgies are spontaneous, as this one was. Derek was interested in Earl, and Earl responded to the interest favorably. Bob was also interested in Earl and was sitting next to him on the sofa. Arthur had been waiting for two years for an opportunity to have sex with Gian-Carlo, and the waiting had only enhanced his desire. Now he was sitting next to him on the sofa. In the middle of one of Earl's sentences, Derek put his drink on the end table and kissed him. When the kiss ended, Earl put his drink on the coffee table, put his arms around Derek and kissed him. Bob put one hand on Derek's arm and the other on the back of Earl's head and said, "Is this thing strictly private?"

Earl turned to him, smiled and kissed him. Derek said quietly, "I guess not." He put his hand on Earl's thigh and kissed the back of his neck. It had begun.

Had Derek and Earl gone off to a bedroom together, it would not have happened. But when Bob joined their love-making, it ceased, by most standards, to be love-making, and all need for restraint was gone.

Orgy is by nature infectious. The desire to see fosters the desire to be seen. For those who wish merely to be seen, privacy can remain intact. For those who wish merely to see, privacy enhances the seeing. Sometimes both wishes overlap, as they did now. The desire to pair

221

off, to become couples, became subordinate to the desire to participate.

Soon the people on the sofa were undressing each other. On another sofa, George and Jerry were in each other's arms. In a chair near them, a boy was being kissed by another boy standing behind the chair and caressed by a third boy who knelt before the chair. In a corner near the bar, Michael and Kevin were kissing, their bodies pushed together.

"Want to help me with a chore?" Michael whispered, confident now that parting for a moment could not separate them.

"Sure," Kevin said.

"We'll light the candles and turn off the lights."

Kevin nodded. By the time the chore was finished, the people on the sofa were naked. They touched and kissed and caressed each other. When one of the group was momentarily excluded by his immediate neighbors, he simply moved to another couple, where he was invariably assimilated with an eager, tender passion until one of that couple moved on.

Michael and Kevin returned to their corner. Michael took off Kevin's shirt, and the candlelight glistened on his hairless chest. Michael looked at him and, in his mind, reduced him in age to fifteen. It was easy, because his body was the body of a muscular child. But when he tried to transform his identity, something inside him resisted. Michael put his hand on both sides of Kevin's body and said, "What do you want to do? You want to split?"

"I think so. But you don't." Michael didn't answer. "Do you?"

"I don't know."

"Michael, it's all right if you want to stay."

"Look. I want you very much. But I want you in front of them . . . with them, even. As long as it's still you and me . . . anytime we want it to be." Michael did not realize it, but in his mind, orgy was closer to celibacy than the

222

intimacies of conventional coupling. Somehow it did less violence to his fantasized faithfulness to David.

"All right," Kevin said.

Michael took Kevin's hand and started to lead him toward the others, but Kevin did not move. "Mike. Let's take our clothes off here."

They undressed each other quickly and held each other for a long time. They stood away from each other, and Kevin said, "You want to make the move?"

"Are you sure?"

"Yes."

"Do you have a preference?"

"Want me to have?"

"Yes."

"Okay. Him." Kevin nodded toward Gian-Carlo, who, completely naked, was crossing the room. They intercepted him before he had reached anyone else.

Michael whispered, "Hey, Gianni."

Gianni smiled at them both, then put his arms around Kevin and kissed him. Kevin grabbed him around the waist and pulled Gianni's body close to him. Michael put his arms around them both. They stood together in the candlelight, and everybody in the room was naked. Someone nudged Michael and handed him a lit joint. He took it, smoked and passed it to Kevin and Gianni.

Tom had taken Ethel home, put her to bed fully dressed, paid the baby-sitter an extra five dollars to stay longer and gone over to the Radnors'. He went into the house without waiting for an answer to his knock. Both Cynthia and Herb looked at him, but they did not stop talking.

"David and the other kids are gone, Herb," Cynthia was saying. "What difference does it make now what they do over there. It's their own business."

"They are using dope," Herb said. "Two hundred yards from here. That should be a concern of every member of this community. And in my position in this community, I believe it to be criminal for me to stand by and do nothing."

"Why don't you sit down and have a gin and tonic or something," Tom said. "You know you're not going to call the cops on George and Michael. Get him a drink, Cynthia."

"Why shouldn't I call the police?" Herb asked Tom.

"Oh, sit down, Herb," Tom said. Cynthia went to get a drink for Herb.

"Give me one good reason."

Tom sat in an armchair and said, "Cynthia, could I have one, too? Will you sit down, Herb?" Herb didn't. "I can give you a hundred reasons. George and Michael are friends of yours. Nobody wants a scandal. You'd only be causing needless trouble for George and Michael and a bunch of people from New York. You'd get David and his friends involved. Take your pick. Just stay off the phone. Besides, if you really want to do something about the 'problem,' you could probably find more pot in the lockers at your high school than there ever was at that party. You only want to look where you want to look."

"You needn't have come over here to insult Cynthia and me, and to . . ."

"Herb. There's a telephone on that table, ten feet away from you. If you're going to call the police, why don't you just do it? If you're not, for God's sake sit down."

"You have a hell of a nerve."

Cynthia arrived with a tray of drinks. She said, "I hope you've been listening to Tom."

Before Herb could speak, the door opened again and Peg came into the room. "I saw Tom come over, and I thought there might be something wrong," she said.

"There's nothing wrong," Tom said. "Have a drink. But first, call Joe and tell him to come over. Maybe we can talk some sense into Herb."

"My sister's leaving," Peg said. "There'll be nobody with the . . ."

"Tell Joe to tell her to stay," Tom said. "Unless you'd

like Herb to get the cops crawling all over the property."

Peg looked alarmed. Cynthia motioned her to the kitchen, and from there Peg called Joe.

"Your kids are young," Herb said to Tom. "They're not in danger from this thing."

"According to statistics," Tom said, "Jonathan will be eligible for an overdose in about three years. I don't happen to think it will be administered, encouraged or caused by George Carr."

"But you don't know."

"No. And you don't either. Would you just shut up till Joe gets here? Then we'll talk it over."

Herb did not shut up. He talked incessantly about his responsibility as a citizen and a high school principal and a parent of a fifteen-year-old boy. Tom leaned his head in his hand and tried not to listen. Cynthia and Peg talked quietly.

Joe burst into the room and said, "What's the matter?"

"Nothing's the matter yet," Tom told him. "Herb wants to sic the cops on George and Michael for smoking grass, and I'm trying to talk him out of it. I hoped you'd help me."

"Well," Joe said.

"That's a great contribution, Joe," Tom said. "Do you think Herb should call the cops or not?"

"Well, that depends. Where's Davey?"

"We don't know," Cynthia said. "He's probably gone off with his friends. He didn't come home from the party."

"Then what's the problem?" Joe said.

"They're still smoking grass over there," Herb said emphatically.

"How do you know?" Tom asked.

"Well . . . did George stop them when I demanded it of him?" Tom looked away in disgust. Herb said to Joe, "Do you approve of that?"

"No. No, I don't approve of it," Joe said. "But as long as there aren't kids around, I figure it's their business."

"Certainly smoking in front of kids is a heinous crime.

225

But you both insist on forgetting that smoking marijuana *at all* is a crime. If we just let this whole thing go by the board, the problem will only get worse."

"What problem?" Tom asked.

"How are you going to feel when they start bringing it to bridge nights and smoking it right in your own house?"

"Hey!" Tom said, brightening for a moment. "That's not a bad idea. I think I'd like to give it a try."

"And that's how serious you think this is," Herb said disgustedly.

Tom said, "That's exactly how serious I think it is. Herb, don't you read the papers? Virtually all reliable research indicates that marijuana is probably less harmful than alcohol."

"By no means does all research indicate that. And the research hasn't been going on long enough to be conclusive. They know nothing about the long-range effects."

"But we know the long-range effects of alcohol: cirrhosis, eroded stomach linings, brain damage. But that's okay because it's legal. And don't forget there are a lot of sane, responsible people who think grass should be legalized."

"And there are more of the same who are unalterably opposed to it."

"Look," Tom said wearily. "I didn't come over here to debate the marijuana issue. I came to try to stop you from doing something very silly that would have unpleasant consequences for everybody. So why don't you just say you're not going to call the cops, and we'll all relax and have another drink."

"Please, Herb," Cynthia said.

"All right," Herb said angrily. "But I guarantee you it's not going to happen again without my doing something about it."

"Hallelujah!" Tom said. "How about the drink? Come on, Herb. I'll help you." When the drinks were made and served, Tom said, "Well, you've got to admit that up until the pot-smoking, it was some party."

"It was brilliant!" Cynthia said. "What did you think of Charles Aaron, Herb? I never did get a chance to talk to him."

"He's a brilliant man," Herb said. "Cynical as hell, but a fine mind."

Peg said, "I think Kate Mulligan looks better in person than she does on TV."

They went on for a long time, rehashing the party as if it hadn't ended so unpleasantly. It obviously meant less to them than to George, who would never be able to remember it with anything but unpleasantness. Talking about it seemed to get the neighbors back into a party mood. They had several more drinks, and Cynthia and Peg prepared an elaborate snack.

It was well after midnight when Tom said, "I'd better go home and take care of Ethel." He laughed and said, "I put her to bed in her clothes. She's going to have a monumental hangover."

"Poor Ethel," Cynthia said. "Drinking really isn't her long suit."

Tom got up and said, "Herb, thanks for not calling the cops. I really think we did the right thing."

"I can't say I think that," Herb said. "But maybe you're right."

Herb saw Tom to the door. When he came back, Peg was draining her glass. "Well, Joe, what do you say we head home? Sis'll be wanting to get home herself."

"She can stay over," Joe said. "I'm just getting my second wind."

"Come on, Joe. Early Mass tomorrow. Besides, Cynthia and Herb want to turn in."

"Hey, I'm sorry. I guess I always think everybody else feels like I do." He picked up his glass and started to finish his drink.

"Don't be silly," Herb said. "You want another drink, we'll have another drink. It's not five o'clock in the morning, after all."

"No, no. Peg's right. That early Mass is *early*. We ought to go on home."

There were more offers of another drink and more refusals. Five minutes later, Peg and Joe were crossing the lawn. They could hear clearly the music coming from George's house. They were both looking toward it when Joe said, "Looks like their party is still going on."

"They don't go to early Mass," Peg said. "Or any other one."

After a few more steps, Joe stopped and said, "Hey! I wonder if anybody bothered to tell them Herb didn't call the cops."

"Who cares? Besides, they must have figured it out by this time."

"Not necessarily. Hell, they must be kind of nervous about it. Wouldn't you be?"

"How do I know?"

"Well, I would. Look, Peggy, I'm gonna just go over and let 'em know it's okay."

"You just want to join the party."

"Maybe I'll have a drink. So what? You go on home. Fifteen minutes. I won't be more than fifteen minutes."

"Christ, Joe, you're just like some kid. You never want to see a party end."

"So I have one more drink. You go on. I'll be right back over."

As Joe started for the house, he could see the strangely faint light coming through the French doors, and he could see that the doors were open. Since the music was coming from there, and the rest of the house was dark, he reasoned that the party was in the drawing room. He didn't want to make a fuss about the whole thing by ringing the doorbell. Besides, they'd probably think it *was* the cops. He just wanted to slip into the party for a minute, have a quiet word with George and maybe another gin and tonic. He decided to go up the terrace steps and into the house through the French doors.

At the moment Joe made this decision, Gian-Carlo

got up from his place on the floor in front of the sofa and went to the armoire to get the cigarette box full of joints. In the circumstances of sexual preoccupation, people smoked erratically. If the grass was to have any significant effect, at least three joints had to be circulating all the time. In spite of his own preoccupation, Gian-Carlo was aware of the lack and felt it was his obligation to fill it. At the armoire, he looked out through one of the French doors and thought he saw a movement in the darkness of the garden. He thought for a moment it might be the police, and his hand tightened on the leather box. He moved his eyes away from the focal point and got a clearer view. It was one man coming across the lawn toward the house. He waited for a moment and saw that it was Joe. He turned briefly toward the others, all clearly candlelit and naked. Then he went and lay down again before the sofa and lit a joint.

Joe climbed the terrace steps with a rehearsed smile. He saw that the terrace doors opened outward and thought he might tap on one to introduce himself. He had already raised his hand to do so when he looked inside the room.

Joe had no frame of reference in which to consider what he saw. A heterosexual orgy of the same size would have at once enticed him and repelled him. But the sight of nineteen naked men—it seemed to him to be dozens—their bodies entwined, their throats issuing fragmented but somehow universal moans of passion, the muscles of their bodies contracting and relaxing in the commonplace, compulsive movements of sex, defamed every concept of decency he had ever been taught to hold—and in a strange way, terrified him.

Utterly without wanting to, he was able to identify some of the participants. He saw George and Michael and one of the bartenders from the party. Then he saw Gian-Carlo, and he thought for a moment that Gian-Carlo saw him. He was lying on the floor with his head on the abdomen of another man. His arm was extended above

229

him as he passed a joint to someone on the sofa. But Gian-Carlo's eyes seemed to be looking into his. That could not be so, of course, because Gian-Carlo, doing what he was doing, could not have looked into Joe's eyes without some sense of guilt and emergency. Joe did not wait to figure out this puzzle. He turned and went back down the terrace stairs.

When Joe reached the lawn, he was almost running, fleeing a scene of unimaginable vileness. He could not think, but his mind was filled, like a brimming cesspool, with images of what he had seen. For an instant, it seemed impossible that he *could* have seen it, and his mind went blank. But the candlelight and the coils of smoke and the naked, writhing bodies and the hideous baritone grunting burst back into his brain as vividly as when he had seen and heard them. He leaned against one of Janet Cartwright's thick and ancient maple trees and vomited his disgust onto the lawn.

There were still lights on at the Radnors', and he stumbled across the lawn toward their house. He turned the knob of the front door, pushed the door open and came into the room like a helplessly enraged animal. Herb stood staring at him in the living room. Cynthia was behind him in the dining room, holding plates in both hands.

"Herb . . . could I . . . have a shot? I got to talk to you," Joe said.

"What's wrong?" Herb said. "Wait. I'll get you a drink." He poured about two ounces of whiskey into a tumbler and gave it to Joe. "What's the matter? What's happened?"

Joe drank the whiskey in one gulp and said, "When me and Peg left, we . . . we saw lights on . . . at George's and heard music comin' from the record player. You know me. One more drink, what the hell? So . . . I . . . I sent Peg home and went over there. I thought it'd be a good idea to tell 'em you weren't gonna call the cops. So I . . .

I went over there." He shook his head as if to clear it. "I ain't gonna say this in front of Cynthia."

Cynthia put the plates on the dining room table and said, "You're not going to say it any other way. I want to hear."

"Okay. You want to hear it. I started to go in, then I saw the room was full of guys . . . just guys. I swear to God, they was . . . they was makin' love . . . if that's what you can call it. They was bare-ass, everyone of 'em, and they was suckin' each . . . I am not gonna say this in front of Cynthia."

"Cynthia go upstairs," Herb said.

"No."

"All right," Herb said. "It's at your own risk. You mean just a few minutes ago you saw this?"

"Use your head, Herb," Joe said. "How long does it take me to walk across the fuckin' lawn?"

Herb turned to Cynthia and said, "I really want you to go upstairs now, Cynthia. I want to talk to Joe about something that would unnecessarily distress you."

"You're an ass, Herb. I'm not leaving this room."

"Suit yourself. Another drink, Joe?"

"Yeah, I could use one."

Herb got the drink for Joe and one for himself and came back into the room ponderously. He handed the glass to Joe, paused for a moment and said, "I've kept this from you, Cynthia. Unwisely. Just as I unwisely allowed myself to be talked out of calling the police tonight." He looked at Joe somberly and said, "I went over to that house a few weeks ago and found my son David sitting in the den with Michael. They were both stark naked except for bath towels wrapped around them."

"And you didn't do anything about it?" Joe said.

"Oh, there was some cock-and-bull story about falling into the lake at the club. All very innocent. I wonder if it was so innocent. I wonder now what this nice Michael has done to my son over the course of this summer. The

231

long walks in the woods. The afternoon's in that house. I haven't been unaware. I wonder what's been done."

Joe put down his glass. "I think we oughta go over there and find out."

"Yes. It's about time."

"You're not going over there," Cynthia said. "It's none of your business."

"Davey's none of my business?"

"David isn't over there! He's . . ."

"Isn't he, Cynthia? I'd just like to make very sure of that."

Cynthia stared at him, icily calm. "You know he isn't. That isn't why you're going. Don't pretend it is."

"Go to bed. Joe and I will handle this."

They left the house and Cynthia immediately telephoned Tom. She explained the situation as briefly and with as much urgency as she could. Tom was not yet in bed, and he said, "I'll go over right now." When he left to go to George's, Ethel, still in her now rumpled party dress, checked on the children and went to be with Cynthia.

Herb and Joe marched silently across the lawn prepared to invade George's house. They were denied that opportunity, when, just as they crossed the unmarked boundary of George's property, they saw two half-naked men, walking together in the darkness of the garden. As they paused, they saw that one was Michael, shoeless and shirtless and wearing only a pair of jeans. The other person, a very young blond boy, was wearing only white slacks. Michael's arm was around the boy's bare waist, and the boy's arm was around Michael's bare shoulders. Each of them carried a drink, and they walked across the lawn like wraiths.

"Hey! You!" Joe shouted.

Michael turned immediately at the sound of Joe's voice. He felt an immediate sense of panic without knowing why. He saw Joe and Herb and felt Kevin beside him and knew it should not be that way. The panic heightened, and he knew he had to try to be himself again.

232

"Hey, Joe! Herb! Come back for a nightcap?" He had not yet made a complete adjustment between the state of walking in the garden with Kevin and the state of confronting Herb and Joe. In his effort to stall, to wait for some inner moment of clarity, he did contradictory things. "Kevin, go on back to the house. Tell George we have new guests. Go on." He hit Kevin on the ass to prod him. He realized he should not have done that.

He heard Herb's voice. "Is that the kind of relationship you've been trying to have with my son all summer?"

"I know what's goin' on in that house," Joe said. "I walked in ten minutes ago. But nobody saw me."

"Look," Michael said, drawing the one syllable out into a kind of hum. "Herb. Joe. I thought you both came over for a drink. I don't even know what you're talking about. Everybody slow down a minute. I'll get you . . ."

"You son of a bitch!" Joe said, moving toward Michael threateningly.

Herb reached out gently and restrained Joe, as a second might have restrained a duelist who was about to fire too soon. Herb said, "I have every intention of doing something legally about you and your friend George. But I want to know right now what you've been doing to my son."

After a moment, Michael said, "I've been helping him with his writing."

"Yeah?" Joe said. "And what else've you been doin'?"

Michael was staring at Herb. "Nothing. Why don't you ask David?"

"How do you know I haven't?" Herb said.

"Because if you had, you wouldn't be here."

"I wouldn't suggest such filth to him. Besides, you certainly wouldn't expect him to admit it?"

"But obviously you would expect him to participate in it. You don't know him very well, do you?"

"I know that he's fifteen years old!" Herb was shouting now. "And that you're a pervert! A queer!"

Quietly, Michael said, "Get off this property. Both of you."

"And I know you've been alone with him much too often in isolated places where you could do things you certainly couldn't do in public!"

Michael wanted simply to walk away, but he couldn't risk their going back to the house. "I told you to get off this property."

"What does a grown man of your age want with the constant company of a fifteen-year-old boy? Teaching him, indeed! My *profession* is teaching the English language! Why wouldn't he have come to me?"

"If I were you, Herb, I'd ask myself that question very seriously. Now, get . . ."

"You seduced him! With your bragging and your phony sophistication! And I believe you seduced him sexually . . . or tried to!"

"You don't know what you're talking about."

Joe spoke then, and his words had the snarling sound of deep disgust. "You think you can come around here with your drugs and your sick sex and pass 'em off on our kids. You ever lay a hand on one of my kids, an' I'll . . ."

"I assure you I wouldn't want to," Michael said.

It was then that Joe hit him the first time. He hit him on the mouth with all his incredible bullish strength. Michael felt the impact, the terrible pain as front teeth pulled away from bone, then the dizzying imbalance as he fell backward. There was a moment of merciful unconsciousness before he felt himself being lifted as Joe picked him up by the throat with one hand and hit him again in the face with the other. He heard and felt the crunching at the right side of his face, then the dizziness again and the blackness. Joe picked him up again by the shoulders and held him upright until he knew Michael was standing under his own power. Michael regained full consciousness for a moment, then Joe hit him twice, once on the eye and once in the middle of the forehead. He picked Michael up two more times, and each time hit him not just with the force of his cocked arm, but with the strength and weight of his whole body. He had moved Michael's body forty feet across the lawn. For a very brief time, lying on the cool grass, Michael was aware of pain greater than he had ever imagined possible; of an excessive, warm dampness and unattached teeth in his mouth; of being unable to see when he opened his eyes; and, somehow, of being covered with blood. Then there was nothing.

He did not hear the others—George and Gianni and Arthur and Derek and, from another direction, Tom— shouting as they ran across the lawn toward him.

Tom went to Joe and held him by the arms, restraining him unnecessarily, since he had finished with Michael. George knelt at Michael's side saying over and over, "Oh, Christ! Oh, Christ! I think they killed him!" Michael's face was completely covered with blood, and his chest and arms were blotched and streaked with it. Sickening lumps and depressions were visible about his face and head. Occasionally he moaned, and his whole body shuddered.

Tom knelt on the other side of Michael, looked up and said, "Somebody call an ambulance!"

Both Derek and Arthur started for the house at a run as still others emerged from the house and, running through the dark garden, converged on the spot. Suddenly, Cynthia was there, kneeling next to George. Lights were being turned on in the house, and in their dim spill, Cynthia could see Michael. She got up quickly and hurried away a few steps before she began to be sick. Tom stood up and said to Joe and Herb, "What in the name of God did you think you were doing?" Neither of them answered.

From the hideous physical evidence of the beating, George was genuinely afraid that Michael might be near death. Only his shallow breathing and the occasional spasm that ran through Michael's body convinced him that Michael was not already dead. Whatever anger or need for revenge he felt was blotted out now by grief

235

and panic and helpless sadness at what Michael had suffered and was still to suffer. Ethel arrived and was kept from seeing Michael. Everyone hovered about in a dazed listlessness. In an unsuccessful effort to be helpful, Arthur and Bob ran an extension cord with a bright, bare bulb from the house to within five feet of the spot where Michael lay. George seemed incapable of responding to the further wet, red horror exposed by the new light, but Ethel shrieked, and others turned away muttering, "Holy Christ!" and "Oh, my God!"

In the fifteen minutes it took for the ambulance to arrive, George did not get up from Michael's side. Most of the others milled about in a frustrating combination of anxiety and helplessness. Even Herb and Joe remained nearby, as if fleeing the scene would somehow incriminate them. The time was too early and too intimate for questions or accusations.

There had been no need to call the police; they arrived automatically with the ambulance. While one uniformed officer stood by, another officer and two white-suited interns bent over Michael.

"Let's get him out of here," one of the doctors said. "He could be hemorrhaging."

As the stretcher was brought from the ambulance, the stark light of the bare bulb and the red and yellow flashes from the emergency vehicles made everything seem unreal to everyone but the officials. As the stretcher was carried away toward the ambulance, George began to follow it. One of the policemen touched him gently on the arm and said, "Are you George Carr?"

George seemed startled. "Yes," he said.

"There are some questions," the officer said.

"I'm going with the ambulance," George told him simply.

The officer had a pad and pencil in hand. With the tip of the pencil, he touched the visor of his cap, pushing it back on his head. "Look. I understand how you feel.

But he's unconscious. He's not gonna know whether you're there or not. And . . ."

"I'm going with the ambulance," George said again.

". . . and you're not gonna find out anything till they finish examining him. I mean it'll take a while. So why don't we get this over with? Just routine. You got a car?"

"Yes, but . . ."

"Why don't we get the questions over with, then you can drive to the hospital. Or we'll drive you. Save time all around."

"But he's badly hurt, and . . ."

"You really can't do him any good. I'm gonna have to insist."

George seemed dazed. He said, "All right," and his voice was without any of its usual tone or resonance or color.

"What's his name?" the officer said. "The victim."

"Michael Kaye," George said.

"Is he a friend of yours? A guest, or . . ."

"He lives here."

The officer wrote in his notebook. "You want to tell me what happened?"

George was having difficulty speaking. "I . . . I . . . I don't know. I was . . . inside."

"You don't know who hit him?"

"I hit him," Joe said.

The officer turned and looked at Joe. It was not, but seemed to be the first time he had done so. The others looked around then, too, as if to see what he was seeing. Most of them did not really share the officer's impression. He saw Joe Jablonski, whom he had known for many years, and, behind him just entering the area of light, his wife Peg. He saw the principal of the local high school standing next to Joe, wearing a stern, almost challenging expression. He saw the principal's wife, looking pale and frightened with Ethel Parker clinging to her as if to prevent her own hysterical collapse. He saw Tom Parker, whom he knew well enough to wave at when their cars passed on a local street. He saw George Carr, whom he knew only by sight, and from whom every vestige of poise seemed to have drained away, wearing only slacks and a shirt with the tail out. He also saw twelve unidentified young men in varying degrees of nakedness.

As he looked around, the officer tried to put to use two basic rules of his profession. One was to be alert enough to be able to size up a situation immediately from its external appearances. The other was not to jump to conclusions.

His eyes came full circle back to Joe, and he said, "You want to tell me what happened, Joe?"

"Yeah, I'll tell you what happened. That fag son of a bitch was . . ."

"Hold it! Hold it!" the officer said, holding up his hand. He looked at his notebook for a moment, then went to Joe and motioned for him to follow. They walked a few steps more, out of earshot of the crowd. "I think we better keep this thing as simple as possible."

"It's simple, all right. That fag was foolin' around all summer with Herb Radnor's fifteen-year-old boy. Foolin' around sexually. Just look at 'em all! Don' that tell you? I went in that house about a half an hour ago, and all them guys was layin' around on the floor suckin' each other . . ."

"Joe. Listen a minute," the officer said quietly. "I think maybe you hurt this guy pretty bad. The blood always makes it look worse, but he could be hurt bad. If he is, maybe you're gonna need all this . . . extra information. But let's say you just busted his nose. Maybe you both call it a drunken fight and forget about it. But once you start all this other stuff, you can't just . . . well, it's just askin' for a lot of trouble all the way around."

"What're you sayin', Jimmy? You think we should let him get away with it?"

"You see him foolin' around with the kid?"

"No, but . . ."

"What's the kid say? He want to make a complaint?"

"I don't know."

"You see, Joe. If you're gonna tell the magistrate what you're tryin' to tell me, you better be able to prove it. On the other hand, like I said, maybe in the morning, sober, and what have you, maybe everybody'd like to forget about it."

"Yeah? What would you do if it was your kid?"

"If it was my kid and I *knew* somebody did it, I'd kill the son of a bitch. But you don't know for sure."

"What would you do if you knew and couldn't prove it?"

"Oh, I'd handle it."

"What do you want me to do?"

The officer said, "Just keep your mouth shut. Let me take care of it, and I think we won't even have to book anybody."

Joe and the officer walked back to the others, and the officer said, "Mr. Carr, you're free to go to the hospital if you want."

George looked at him as if he didn't understand. He looked at Joe and at Herb. Then he said, "Yes. I think he's hurt badly. I want to go." He looked around dumbly for a moment. "Gianni, stay here and look after things. Arthur, would you . . . drive?" There was no confidence in anything George did or said.

"Shall I get you some other clothes first?" Arthur asked.

"No. No, there's not time. We've got to go immediately."

"George, it might be better if . . ." Arthur started to say.

George didn't seem to hear him. "I'll get the car keys from the house." He looked at Joe and at the policeman once more. Then he turned around and walked toward the house.

"Okay," the officer said. "You can go home, everybody." He started walking toward his partner, who stood by the patrol car listening to the droning police radio.

"Go home?" Joe said incredulously. "I told you, they're the guys that was . . ."

"Joe," the officer said. "I want to talk to you." He went to Joe again and, with a new note of exasperation in his voice said, "You really want to go down to the station? You want me to book you? You want to make a complaint against them? It's gonna be hard to do without bringin' up the assault charge. Or do you want to shut up for a while?" When Joe did not answer, he said, "Go home."

The group dispersed lethargically. The two policemen got into their car and drove off. George's remaining guests went back to the house, made a round of drinks and decided to wait to hear about Michael. The neighbors went back to the Radnors' house.

They entered the living room in heavy, awkward silence. Cynthia and Ethel sat down immediately. The others stood around uncomfortably.

"What the hell did you do it for, Joe?" Peg said, much more loudly than she had intended.

It was extraordinary for Peg to ask Joe such a question publicly, and he ignored it.

"Could I have a drink, Herb?" Joe said.

"Oh. Yes. Sure, I'll get some drinks," Herb said.

"Before you get one for me," Tom said, "would you tell me what happened?"

"Oh, I'll tell you!" Joe said.

"I don't want to hear it again," Cynthia said. "Not from you."

Joe did not entirely understand what Cynthia said, but he was hurt by it. Ethel made a sound of confusion.

"You didn't see what I saw, Cynthia," Joe said. "There were all . . ."

"Then why didn't you try to kill all of them?" Cynthia asked loudly, looking up for the first time and staring at Joe with tears in her eyes. "Why just Michael?"

"You know perfectly well," Herb said.

"No! No, I don't! And neither do you! You're both despicable!" She said the word with superb bitterness, putting the accent on the first syllable.

Herb took a step toward her and said, "Cynthia, I know you're upset, but . . ."

"I'm a great deal more than upset. For God's sake, Herb, haven't you ever experienced anything like a thought process? I mean a continuous series of ideas that leads to a conclusion? I don't think you even have thoughts. You just get a single, stupid idea in your head, and it stays there. Either you think your son is a homosexual and has been having a homosexual affair with Michael all summer—which even you should know is beyond the realm of possibility. Or you think Michael makes passes at David, and David just submits to it and goes on seeing him—which is also beyond the realm of possibility. But on the basis of one of those assumptions, you and this . . . this half-witted clown go over there and beat Michael half to death! And now you stand here like a pompous little rooster, trying to justify it!"

Herb took a deep breath before he spoke, which was always a sign that he was going to be patient. "Cynthia, we've had this discussion before. I know that for some mysterious reason, you think that Dave, indeed, that all fifteen-year-old boys are incorruptible. You seem to think they have the sophistication and experience to withstand the sinister and subtle wiles of an experienced seducer like Michael Kaye. You seem to think that adolescents are towers of strength. I deal with them, Cynthia. My professional life . . ."

Suddenly, Cynthia stood up. "Oh, you are . . . you are so full of shit!" It somehow wasn't nearly enough. She picked up a glass from the table before her and threw the dregs of a gin-and-tonic into Herb's face.

There was not enough in the glass to produce any drama lasting beyond the act itself. Herb wasn't drowned in a lateral Niagara. Instead, he stood with tiny drops of tepid liquid clinging to his face like spittle. Yet the very ineffectualness of the gesture made Herb seem pathetic and ridiculous. He waited for Cynthia to run across the room and up the stairs, still angry, but too embarrassed by her outburst to remain in the company of the witnesses. Instead, she merely sat down again.

"I suppose you think that accomplished something," Herb said, wiping his face with a handkerchief.

"Yes, I do!" Cynthia said. "It gave me a great deal of pleasure, and it didn't put anyone in the hospital."

"Is somebody going to tell me what happened?" Tom asked.

"Joe went back to George Carr's house after he left here," Herb began.

"Why, for Christ's sake?" Tom asked.

"To tell 'em Herb decided not to call the cops," Joe explained.

"How thoughtful of you," Tom said. "You mean, so they could break out the grass again without fear of a raid."

"In any event," Herb continued, "he found the entire remaining company of men, including George and Michael, engaged in a naked, writhing orgy."

To Herb's genuine astonishment, Tom began to laugh. Through the laughter he managed to say, "Usually . . . known . . . I believe . . . as a gang-bang. Wow! That must have popped your Polish eyes, Joe!"

"You think it's funny?" Joe asked sullenly.

"Very."

"Well, fortunately our sense of humor has not yet become so depraved," Herb told him.

"What's so fortunate about it?" Tom said. "If you'd seen the humor in it, you wouldn't have committed assault and battery."

"You mean, it's perfectly all right with you if a homosexual orgy is going on in a house virtually next door to you and your family," Herb said.

"As long as it's *in* the house, and neither my family nor I is forced to participate."

"Well, when we went over there again . . ." Herb went on.

"Why in the hell did you do that?"

"I confess I'm not really sure now," Herb said thoughtfully. "I guess I was just so enraged at the thought of Michael Kaye doing such things to my son . . ."

"Oh, now, hold it just a minute, Herb," Tom said very seriously. "You *know* that Michael had something to do with David . . . something sexual?"

"No, he doesn't know it," Cynthia said. "He hasn't even a valid reason for suspecting it."

"Well, that orgy gave me valid reason! And I *was* enraged . . . as any normal father would be."

"So you went over to poke Michael in the mouth," Tom said.

"I wish you'd stop thinking it's so funny," Herb said.

"Oh, I don't think *that's* funny. And if I were you or Joe, I really wouldn't think it was funny. I only saw the last couple of punches, but I saw Michael on the ground close up, and it looked to me like Joe might have killed him. Even with what *you* think was provocation, that sounds to me like at least manslaughter. If he's only permanently disabled, he could tie up both your incomes for the rest of your lives. If he's just beaten up, he can still sue you for assault. And if I know George Carr, you'll get sued for something."

There was silence for a moment before Joe said, "Jimmy Rausch told me he thought it'd be okay if we just kept quiet. Like it was just a couple of neighbors with too much to drink, and one takes a poke at the other one. The next morning, sober, everybody just lets it ride."

"Now, *that's* funny," Tom said. "Our high school principal in very questionable collusion with the police to save his own skin. I also think it's pretty funny that you can describe what you did to Michael as taking a poke at him."

"It may interest you to know," Herb said, "that the orgy was no longer confined to the house. Michael and a young boy were walking around the garden in each other's arms."

"Sounds hard to do, unless they were dancing. But I'll take your word for it."

"They had their arms around each other's waists and shoulders. They were half naked, right out there in that garden," Herb said, pointing to it illustratively.

"In the pitch dark with not a star or the moon in the sky," Tom reminded him. "If you hadn't gone over there, you couldn't possibly have seen them. I doubt if you could have seen them ten feet away."

"If all you intend to do, Tom, is make excuses for their vicious, immoral behavior, you might just as well leave," Herb said.

"Oh, no," Tom said. "I wouldn't miss this for the world."

"You think maybe I ought to call my lawyer?" Joe said. "Frank McManus?"

Herb thought for a moment. "I . . . Yes. I think it would be a good idea. Why don't you use the phone in our bedroom?"

Joe nodded and went upstairs.

"Well," Tom said. "How about the drinks?"

"I'll get them," Herb said.

"Want some help?"

"No. I'll do it myself."

Joe was gone for a long time. The McManuses had gone to bed more than an hour before, and Frank McManus was reluctant to believe the situation was an emergency. It was a full ten minutes before he even began to listen to the specifics, and then his advice came with the slow caution typical of his profession. In the grave silence downstairs, Tom's witticisms also began to come more slowly and finally stopped altogether.

Joe came down the stairs glumly and stood for a moment without speaking, as if he were deep in thought.

"What'd he say?" Herb said.

"Pretty much what Tom said," Joe told him. "He said you could be tried as an accessory if it was manslaughter. And he said . . . I think I got it right . . . the commission

244

of a crime on their part didn't necessarily justify the commission of a crime by us. He said we could immediately bring charges against them . . . lewd and disorderly conduct, I think he called it. And then the dope thing, too. But his best advice was not to do anything till we found out what condition Michael was in. Like Jimmy Rausch said, maybe it'll blow over." Joe's tone of voice did not seem to indicate that he thought it would blow over.

"Then we just wait," Herb said.

"Yeah, I guess so," Joe agreed. "But there's one other thing he said was important. He said he didn't think there was a jury in any county in New Jersey that would bring in a guilty verdict—even in manslaughter—if the minor involved testified he was molested by the plaintiff. I think that's the way he put it."

Now there was not even the clink of an ice cube against a glass or the hiss of exhaled cigarette smoke. There was utter silence.

"You mean if little Davey could prove Michael made sexual advances toward him?" Herb said.

"I don't think he meant 'prove' it," Joe said. "I think he meant if Dave said it happened, it happened."

"If he testified to it," Herb said.

"Yeah. If he testified. Or said he would testify."

"What?"

Joe looked uncomfortable. "I wanted to write it all down, but there wasn't anything to write on. I think I got it right. He said a man would have to be an idiot and have an idiot for a lawyer to take a father and his friend to court on an assault charge—or even a manslaughter charge—if he knew a fifteen-year-old boy was gonna testify that his father and the friend beat the guy up because he molested the kid. That's about what he said. He's comin' over to my house tomorrow."

There was another silence. "Well, I guess that settles that," Herb said. "I'll just wait up and talk to Dave."

"Like hell you will," Cynthia said.

"Cynthia, stay out of this," Herb said. "It's become . . ." He stopped because Cynthia was looking over his shoulder. The lights of a car had splashed against the window and into the room for a brief moment. It was undoubtedly George's Mercedes.

"I'm going over there," Cynthia said, starting for the kitchen door.

"I want you to stay in this house!" Herb shouted.

"Don't you even care what you've done to Michael?" she asked him as if she couldn't believe that he didn't.

"Let her go, Herb," Joe said. "She could ask him what he's gonna do."

Cynthia did not stop walking toward the kitchen door, but she heard what Joe said. She saw the glow of the headlights in the driveway, and she began running. She didn't want George to go inside so that she'd have to ring the bell. She rounded the corner of the house as George was on the doorstep. They heard her footsteps on the gravel, and both George and Arthur turned toward them. When they saw that it was Cynthia, Arthur opened the door and went into the house. George stood on the step, looking at her.

"Oh, George! How is he?"

Although his composure seemed to have returned, he stared at her with the same glazed look he'd had before in the garden.

"He's all right," he said. "His nose and his jaw are broken, he has a mild concussion, and seven of his teeth were knocked out. But he's alive, so I guess he's all right." George moved toward the door as if he were just going to go inside. But he turned back to Cynthia and said, "He's also had sixty-two stitches in his face. In his face. I don't expect you to know what that means to Michael."

"George, I'm so sorry. And I'm so ashamed."

"You didn't do it. Good night."

Before he could move through the doorway, Cynthia said, "What are you going to do?" She had barely spoken the words before she began to say inside her head, *For David. For David. For David.*

With one foot in the doorway, George turned just his head toward her. "Did they send you over here to ask that?"

"I came because I wanted to."

"But you had to ask, didn't you? All right, I'll tell you. I have a great deal of money, and I'm willing to spend every penny of it to put Joe Jablonski in jail—and your husband, too, if I can do it. And I'm going to see to it that Michael sues them for every penny it takes to restore him to health, including the most expensive plastic surgery we can find. And I'm going to do everything in my power to take away Herb's job and to see to it that he never works again in any public or private educational institution in this country. I'm going to try to make a janitor of your husband. Then I'm going to get out of this terrible place. Tell them that. Good night, Cynthia." He went inside and closed the door.

Cynthia did not want to go home. She wanted to walk freely among grass and trees and flowers and in the aloneness such things produced. But there was nowhere to walk. She realized then how urban the property was, how compressed and bordered and crowded, without even the anonymity the city offered. There was no place else to go, and so she went back to the house.

The others were waiting for her so evidently that they appeared to be doing nothing else, not drinking or smoking or talking. They just waited.

When she walked into the room, Joe said, "You talk to him?"

"Cynthia," Herb said, "I know you're upset, but this is important."

"Yes, I spoke to George."

"Did you . . ." Joe stopped and scratched his face. He lowered the pitch and volume of his voice and said, "Herb, ask her if she asked him."

"I asked him," Cynthia said. "He's going to do everything you were afraid he'd do and more if he can. He's going to try to put you in jail," she said to Joe, "and he's going to try to keep you from ever working again as a teacher." She had turned toward Herb. "And I want him to succeed. I keep wandering around in that empty place I call my mind, and I keep stumbling over the fact that you're my husband. And if this man succeeds in keeping you from ever teaching again . . . you shouldn't teach, Herbert; you are not morally equipped to teach . . . if George succeeds in it . . . whatever it was I said . . . my life will be even less than it is now. My son's life will be less. And I don't want that. And I don't know what to do. I don't know which way to turn."

It was a long time before Herb said, "Cynthia, I want you to let me handle this."

She smiled at him and said, "How I wish I could."

"Don't you think it'd be a good idea," Tom said, "if nobody handled anything until you've talked to Frank McManus tomorrow?"

At this point in their conversation, David got out of Bobby Geary's car on Walton Lane at the side of the house. He was surprised to see the downstairs of the house so brightly lit. His surprise was greater when he came in through the kitchen door and realized there were a number of people in the living room. He did not want to see any of these people. He was still angry and embarrassed at Herb's behavior at the party, and he didn't feel like being nice to guests. He went into the living room and, without any emotion, said, "The party still going on?"

"Dave, there's been some trouble," Herb said gravely.

"I think it would be a good idea if you all went home now," Cynthia said.

Joe looked startled, then fearful. "Herb! I think I oughta be . . ."

"I don't think I'm being rude if I insist on it," Cynthia said.

248

"Of course we should go," Tom said, standing up. He put out his hand for Ethel to take. "Come on, Ethel."

"It's probably best," Herb said now that the decision had been made.

The four neighbors said good night and left the house. David was still standing in the doorway between the living room and the dining room. He looked deeply concerned. "What's the matter?" he asked with a mixture of curiosity and suspicion.

"It's about Michael," Cynthia said.

David looked at his father. "You didn't get him busted for the grass?"

"No," Herb said. "We had a conference and decided . . ."

"A *conference?*" David said.

"Yes. The neighbors persuaded me that calling the police would cause more problems than it would solve."

David thought of a number of unpleasant things to say, but decided on, "I'm glad of that."

"That wasn't the end of it," Herb said. "Now, I'm going to have to tell you some things, some vile things, that I hate having to say to you. The reason there are communities like ours is to prevent young people from exposure to such vileness until they're prepared to handle it, to be aware of its existence without the knowledge doing them harm. But sometimes outside influences invade such a . . ."

"Holy God, Herb, will you tell him what happened?" Cynthia said.

"I am telling him."

"No, you're not! You're spouting a lot of drivel! Just tell him!"

"Your mother is understandably upset. What has happened and what I have to tell you is very ugly. The worst kind of . . ."

"All right," Cynthia said calmly. "I want you to shut up, Herb. I'm going to tell David what happened."

"I won't have you saying such things in front of . . ."

"Somehow it's less obscene if I tell him. Just be quiet. Could we sit down, David?"

"Oh, Christ!" David said. "Yes, Mother. If you want me to sit down, I'll sit down." He sat on the edge of the sofa.

"George and Michael's party broke up shortly after you left."

"Yeah, I'm sure it did."

"I don't approve of your being made to leave."

"I know that."

"I won't have this, Cynthia," Herb said. "I will not . . ."

"Dad, I just want to know what happened," David said. "Let her tell me. Please."

Herb felt somehow deprived, but he resigned himself to it and leaned back in his chair with a sigh.

"We came back . . . the Jablonskis and the Parkers came back here with us. Not Ethel, but . . . Oh, all that doesn't matter! We came back here, and Tom talked your father out of calling the police." David shook his head sadly. "Then . . . maybe it was a sense of relief . . . we just started talking about the party, the people and the food and . . . And before we knew it, it was quite late. We were drinking, of course. I'm sure that's part of it. The others went home . . . or started to go. For some insane reason, Joe Jablonski decided to go back to George's. He says it was to tell them your father hadn't called the police. He just went in through one of the terrace doors. He found them . . . all the people who had stayed on . . . all men . . . having sex together . . . all there . . . together in the living room."

"Cynthia, I think . . ." Although no one interrupted him, Herb didn't go any further. He simply stopped.

"Like nobody knew before they were queer," David said.

"Of course, we knew," Cynthia said.

"So what they do is their business," David said.

"Yes. It ought to be."

"David, where did you learn such . . ."

"Herb, please!"

"Mother, please tell me what happened."

"Yes. Joe came back here and told your father what he'd seen. They decided that Michael had probably done something improper with you. And they . . ."

"Wait a minute," David said in absolute confusion. "I don't understand what . . ."

"They went back to George's together . . . and found Michael in the garden. They . . . I don't know what was said. Your father will have to tell you that. But they . . . Joe hit Michael. He beat him . . . very badly. He's . . . he's in the hospital."

"Michael?" David said in a strained, high-pitched voice.

"He's all right. I mean, he's badly hurt, but he's going to be all right," Cynthia said. She looked away from David for a moment. "I talked to George when he came back from the hospital."

"Oh, wait!" David said. "Wait, wait. Joe Jablonski beat Michael up . . . be . . ."

"Yes," Cynthia said.

". . . because . . ." He turned to Herb. "Because *you* thought . . . something to do with sex . . . was happening between me and Michael?"

"He's a known pervert. I had every reason to . . ."

"What about me? Do you . . . do you think . . . I'm gay or something?"

"Of course not. But you're fifteen, and he's . . ."

"Then how could I . . . how could I be friends with him? I mean, if you thought he was trying to do something to me . . . why would I go on . . . being friends?"

"I don't know," Herb said. "I thought it was something . . . you wouldn't be able to . . . to come to me about . . . would be too embarrassed . . ."

"Oh, man, are you ever right about that! But there wasn't anything to come to you about. Why didn't you ask me?"

"I failed you there, I admit it. Frankly, I would have been embarrassed, too."

251

"Wait! Wait a minute! You were . . . Oh, Christ, what about Michael? Can I call the hos . . ."

"I told you, he's all right."

"Then why is he in the hospital? Mother?"

Cynthia was very selective when she answered. "He has a broken jaw and . . . and a mild concussion. And . . . some minor things."

David stared at Cynthia for a moment, then turned to Herb, looking at them both as if they had suddenly and monstrously sprung up before him. "You stood there and let Joe do that to . . ."

"I couldn't have stopped it. It was too quick."

"Did you try?"

Herb stood up. "All right. All right, young man, that's enough. I've suffered all the insults and accusations I'm going to . . . from everybody. This is my house. You are my family. And now I'm going to have my say. But first, I want to remind you, David, that we live where we live and how we live because of you. I want to remind you that there isn't one aspect of our life that hasn't been chosen for your benefit. Your mother is bored to death with her life, but we decided when you were born that we owed you two complete parents, and she should not work until you were grown. I had other job offers, but we chose Hainesdale because it was at once far enough and near enough to New York to be beneficial to *you*. Your mother wanted another child, but we decided against it because we wanted beyond all doubt to be able to give you everything you needed. When my father died, my mother wanted to come to live with us, and we said no, because we thought it would be bad for you. You are not nearly so much a reflection of us as we are a reflection of you. All right. Members of your generation don't seem to feel that having somebody else live his life for you incurs any kind of obligation on your part. I happen to think it does. I happen to think it creates a very collectible debt. A debt of respect and obedience and loyalty. You are fifteen years old, and I am your father; and you are now going to accept without question my moral judgments. And until you're old enough to get out of this house, you'll con . . ."

"I wish I were old enough right now."

Herb was stunned by David's response. He believed he had been irreversibly persuasive. He believed that his case was unquestionably, unchallengeably clear. And in that belief, he pressed on. "What was done tonight, like almost everything else in your fortunate life, was done for you."

"For *me?*"

"Yes. To protect you against something we thought you couldn't protect yourself against."

"Holy Christ, you think I can't say 'no' if a guy makes a pass at me?"

Herb paced the room for a moment, then turned to David and said, "You think you're very sophisticated, don't you? Well, I'm going to give you a very sophisticated problem. I'm going to give you the solution to the problem, too, and you're going to accept it without one word of argument. Joe Jablonski attacked Michael Kaye tonight on . . ."

"Joe and you," David said.

". . . on your behalf," Herb went on. "However rash, however ill-advised, it was perpetrated on your behalf."

"Shit," David said.

Herb could conceive of no rational response to this comment. He just went on. "Listen to me. George and Michael are going to bring criminal charges against Joe and me. And they . . ."

"Because you committed a crime."

"And they are going to try to put Joe . . . *and me* . . . in jail. They are going to try to so blacken my reputation that I will be employable in the teaching profession." Herb was incapable in the most intimate situations, even in sex, of anything but rhetoric. "They are going to try through the courts to turn an act of justifiable retribution into a crime. They are going to try, out of sheer vindictiveness, to ruin my life. George Carr told this to your mother."

Cynthia knew before Herb, but Herb knew, too, before he finished speaking, that David was going to cry. They saw him fighting it and knew he was going to lose. The tears came to his eyes and ran down his face.

"I'm going to soften this for you, Dave," Herb said. "We can bring charges of lewd and disorderly conduct against George and Michael. We can bring narcotics charges against them. I don't want to do this. And they can bring an assault charge against Mr. Jablonski and me. Obviously, I don't want that, either. There's a way to settle the whole thing out of court."

"George told me they're going away, David," Cynthia said. "They're leaving the neighborhood as soon as possible."

"This is a hard, pragmatic solution, Dave. You know what pragmatic means." Herb paused then to pretend that what he was about to suggest was honorable, to muster the confidence to say it in such a way that his son would be similarly convinced or at least deceived. "If you will testify . . . No, that's not right. If you will *say* you'll testify that Michael made improper advances to you, the whole thing will never come to trial. And that's what I want you to do."

The tears were coming openly now. "But he didn't do it. I know he wanted to, but he didn't do it."

"You will never publicly have to say he did. We are only trying to prevent a public trial which will hurt everybody."

"I don't understand."

"We have it on good legal advice that if George and Michael know you will say in court that Michael made improper advances toward you, it will not *come* to court. And in the long run, no one will be hurt."

"You son of a bitch," David said quietly.

"I will not have you . . ."

David stood up and took a flattened, polyethelyne bag

from a pocket of his slacks. He threw it on the cocktail table and said, "That's two dimes' worth of grass. I bought it from Bobby Geary. You want to call the cops? I can get fifteen years for possession. Bobby could get life for pushing it. You want me to dial the magic number? You want me to call the fuckin' cops for you? I'll . . ."

"You will not say one more obscene word in front of your mother. Now, give me that bag of . . ."

"My mother knows about fucking. And don't reach for that bag. I've never hated anybody before. I am bombed out of my mind right now on grass. So call the police. Or shut up."

Herb got up and moved toward David. He had taken only two steps when David said, "Mother, tell him. You know. Tell him if he lays one hand on me, I'll get out. I couldn't hit him back, but I'd go."

"Do you really think I'd turn you in to the police?" Herb said.

"No. Because it wouldn't be convenient for you. The only time you do anything you think is honest is when it's convenient. Well, it's not convenient for me to testify against Michael. It's not convenient for me to lie when you tell me to just to save your neck."

"I'm not asking you to testify. I'm asking you to *say* you'll do it. But you won't have to."

"Oh, man! Wow! You're not asking me to lie, you're only asking me to *say* I'll lie. Wow!"

"You don't know anything about philosophy," Herb said. "It can be argued that lying is not inherently wrong. The use to which a lie is put can determine its morality."

"I'm not going to do it, but what if I say I'll testify, and they go to court anyway?"

"They won't."

"But what if they do? What do I do then?"

"I think I can give you legal authority they won't."

"You really are a son of a bitch. I won't do it. You can stop asking me."

"I'm not asking you. I'm telling you."

"What's the punishment for refusal? On pain of death?"

"There is no punishment, because there is no alternative."

David picked up the bag of grass and said, "You'd better start thinking of a punishment." He went upstairs and into his room.

Herb sat down again and said, "He's got to be made to understand."

Cynthia said, "You mean he's got to be made to agree. He already understands."

Herb looked at her blankly and said, "Is there going to be even more of it? After George and Tom and David, am I going to hear more from you about what a nothing I am?" Cynthia's old and sour contempt turned suddenly to pity. "I'm a teacher who isn't morally equipped to be one. I'm a husband who is, to all intents and purposes, impotent. I'm the father of one child who hates me. And now, when somebody threatens to try to destroy me, I'm the plaintiff in a trial in which everybody seems to think I ought to be the defendant. Am I really some kind of . . . of cripple or something?"

Cynthia was uncomfortable without her contempt, so she reached out like an angry housekeeper and gathered it up. "You're disabled like everybody else. What difference does it make which disease you have?" She put out her cigarette and said, "I'll try to get him to do it. I don't think I can, but I'll try." She stood up and said, "Will you clean up the glasses? It'll be better if you're down here."

She went upstairs and knocked on David's bedroom door. "May I come in?"

"Sure," David said. Cynthia waited for him to open the door for her, but he didn't. She opened it herself and went in. David was standing with his back to the door at the raw-wood desk she had stained and sanded and varnished for him.

"Your father uses too many words. I'll make it as simple as possible. Will you do it for me?"

"No."

256

"Have you looked at it both ways, David?"

"I think so."

"I'd like to make sure. If you say you'll testify, that will be the end of it. I know you'll lose Michael as a friend, but Michael is going away now in any event. Even if he didn't, you'd be going away to school in two years. Things don't last, David. You mustn't expect them to. I know that seems a very high price to pay. But look at it the other way. If Michael sues Mr. Jablonski and your father, everything will come out. The homosexuality, the marijuana, the drunkenness, the beating. Everybody—you, me, your father, George and Michael, their friends, our friends—will have to go into court. They'll all have to lie or tell the truth as they see fit. I don't know what George can do to your father. I only know he can't do anything if you'll say you'll testify."

"You want me to do it, don't you?" David said without turning to her.

"Yes. I don't expect you to believe me, but I wouldn't ask you to do anything that would hurt Michael. I'm asking you to do something that I really believe would keep Michael from hurting himself."

David turned to her then. "What about me? What about what I think of myself if I lie and say that Michael tried to blow me or . . ."

"David . . ."

"What about what Michael would think of me? Do you know how much he's done for me? And I repay him by accusing him of *that*? And what about what I am? I mean, what I would be if I did it?"

"You'd be what you are."

"You're not a liar till you lie."

"You lied to me about marijuana. I asked you two years ago if you'd ever smoked it. You said no. That was a lie, wasn't it?"

"Yes."

"And you told me all those children's lies about seeing the other kids doing it, and it was around, but you'd never think of it. When I was a child, David, we lied about the cookie jar. Your lies are about drugs and sex."

"Does it make so much difference what a lie's about?"

"Yes. All the difference in the world. I would lie to a man who is dying of cancer."

"Or to Herb about your afternoons at the Plaza Hotel."

Suddenly, Cynthia felt she was in a vacuum, in a soundless, weightless, impossible place. "What did you say?"

"I know about it."

"How . . . how did . . ."

"I know about it, that's all."

Cynthia sat on the edge of David's bed. "I . . . I don't know what to say. I just don't know anything at all to say to you."

"Why don't you lie to me about it?"

She thought for a moment. "Oh, I would. Except for one reason: you can't have made this up or merely suspect it. If you say you know, you know. I couldn't convince you otherwise with a lie."

"Anyway, it's nice that you want to."

There was a long silence. "Do you want me to try to explain?" Cynthia said softly.

"No, I don't think so."

"Will you tell me what you feel about it? About me?"

"Does it make any difference?"

"Yes, a great deal."

"I'm sorry. I know it does. I'll try, but it's complicated. I don't want to feel what I feel. In a way, I don't want it to matter."

"But it does."

"Yes. I don't have any respect for marriage. I mean, I don't think people should have to get married to be together. But if you *are* married, you . . . You know, it really doesn't matter what I think."

"I didn't ask you what you think. I asked you what you felt."

"That doesn't make any difference, either."

"I wish you'd tell me."

"I'd rather not."

"Please."

"Okay." He took the bag of grass from his pocket again and threw it on the desk. "Here I am, your average fifteen-year-old, grass-smoking, fornicating rock musician . . . liberated from the tyranny of the establishment, as I once wrote somewhere. And like your average All-American Boy, I'm shocked, ashamed . . . I guess I'm disgusted. They're the things I don't want to feel."

"Disgust is like love. It isn't something we choose." She got up from the bed. "I am so terribly sorry, David."

She started out of the room. David said, "Mother. I . . . I'll say I'll testify against Michael. It . . . seems to make the most sense."

"I want to discourage you, but I can't."

"Then I guess you don't really want to."

"No. I suppose the appropriate expression is, 'Welcome to the club.' "

"What are you . . ."

"Going to do about it . . .? Stop. Your knowing makes it impossible."

"I wish I was sorry about that. I mean it. But I'm not."

"Good. Good night, David."

When Cynthia reached the bottom of the stairs, she realized that dawn was beginning to come. The lamps were still lit in the living room, but the gray light of day creeping through the house made them pale and incongruous. Herb had finished cleaning up and was sitting in his armchair.

"What did he say?" he asked immediately.

"He'll do it. He'll say he'll testify."

"And if he has to testify?"

"I didn't ask him that. You said it wouldn't be necessary."

"I suppose it won't. It would just be nice to know he'd carry it through. I know I must sound almost . . . indecently pragmatic about this, but I really believe it's the only moral, reasonable, intelligent thing to do."

"Yes, I'm sure you do." She started turning out the lights, and the early daylight seemed brighter. "Why don't you go to bed, Herb?"

"What are you going to do?"

"I'm going to have a drink. I'd be getting up in three hours, anyway."

"I don't think that's a good idea, but under the circumstances, I wouldn't stop you."

"Couldn't stop me, Herb."

Ignoring this, Herb got up with a sudden eagerness. "Well, I'm not going to bed, either. I'm going to shower and shave and talk to George Carr before church."

"Why, in the name of God, are you going to do that?" she asked. "It's Sunday morning, and there hasn't been time . . ."

"He's still up and about. I saw him outside a few minutes ago."

"Cleaning the blood off the lawn?" Cynthia began to laugh. "Isn't it funny how things change? The lawn is no longer 'grass,' and 'grass' is something altogether different. Even though 'cleaning the blood off the grass' is a much nicer phrase. Don't you think so?"

"You're talking gibberish."

"Maybe I'm speaking in tongues. How would you know?"

Herb got back to the subject at hand. "There is little doubt that George Carr has a lawyer. And I'd be willing to bet he's been in touch with him already."

"You have a lawyer, too. Why don't you just let Frank McManus handle it?"

"As I remember my law . . ."

"My God!"

". . . Frank McManus wouldn't be able to approach George except in a pre-trial examination. And we don't want any of that if we can avoid it. I want to get this settled, Cynthia. I want it out of the way at the first possible minute."

"So you can go to church and pray with your mind at ease? You are a terrible man. You know, I think I'd like to divorce you when David goes away to school. Oh, I won't. But I think I'd like to. I hope you'll remember that every minute for the rest of our life together. I've just begun to realize lately how much time I spend doing things I don't want to do and not doing things I do want to do."

"Cynthia, you're drunk."

"A little. Oh, don't worry about that, Herb. I'm not going to become a drunk. It's too untidy for me. I'm not going to become a divorcee, either. I'm not going to become anything. I've simply stopped."

Cynthia went into the kitchen to make her drink, and Herb went upstairs. He showered and shaved with a curious exhilaration. An hour ago, he had felt weak and victimized. Now, such a short time later, he felt a sense of control and power and well-being. He dressed in the suit he would wear to church, looked up Frank McManus's number and called him from the extension in the bedroom.

Mr. McManus was in an even less happy frame of mind than he had been earlier. He answered the telephone with, "What? What is it?"

"Mr. McManus," Herb said, "this is Herbert Radnor."

"For Christ's sake, it's six o'clock in the morning! If the police aren't knocking at your door, there's no excuse for this call! Waking a man up at . . ."

"Unless I miss my guess," Herb said confidently, "this will save everyone time later on."

"Oh, Jesus! What is it?"

"I believe you told Joseph Jablonski last night that if my son would testify in this case to having been sexually molested by the victim of last night's accident, the case would never come to court."

"Do me a favor, Mr. Radnor. Don't ever paraphrase

261

an attorney. What I said was that a plaintiff would have to be an idiot to go into court knowing the defense could bring such a charge. There are obviously a lot of idiots around."

"The plaintiff in this case is not an idiot."

"So?"

"My son has agreed to testify that he was sexually approached repeatedly by this man."

"Repeatedly? Suggest to him that he say once. Repeatedly sounds as if he were enjoying it."

"Mr. McManus, I'm trying to be objective. If I go to this man and tell him of my son's intention, it might deter him from making any further move. Isn't that right?"

"Yes. And it would also save you a fee."

"That doesn't matter to me. My concern is that . . ."

"All right, all right. Will they let you into the hospital to see this man? Do we even know what condition he's in?"

"He's all right. He has some minor fractures, but the prognosis is . . ."

"At least he's alive. No permanent injury?"

"Apparently not. I wasn't planning on going to him, anyway. I was planning on going to George Carr, his . . . his friend."

"Oh, yes. Mrs. Cartwright's nephew. Yes, it comes back to me. As I understand the situation, he'd be involved in whatever action was taken. All right. Go to him and tell him that your son has told you that this Michael . . . somethin-or-other . . ."

"Michael Kaye."

"Yes. That Michael Kaye made a specific homosexual proposal to your son, and that your son is willing to say so in court. Nothing more. Don't say anything else. From what little I know of him, George Carr is a wealthy and intelligent man. He undoubtedly has an attorney, who will tell him to forget it. That is not a guarantee. It is simply my best advice. And I may not be quoted."

"That's exactly what I was planning to do."

"All right, do it. But please don't call me again. I'm supposed to see Joe Jablonski some time this afternoon. I assume you'll be there." He hung up.

Herb went downstairs and found Cynthia in the living room, sitting in a chair, holding her drink and looking out the window. She turned and looked at him wryly. "You'll be happy to hear that George is still 'up and about.' "

"Yes, I am happy to hear that."

Herb went to the telephone in the kitchen and dialed George's number. Gian-Carlo answered the phone.

"Is Mr. Carr there?" Herb asked.

"I will see," Gian-Carlo said.

Cynthia watched as Gian-Carlo came out onto the terrace and spoke to George. She saw George get up and go into the house. Then she heard Herb's voice from the kitchen.

"George, it's Herbert Radnor. I . . ."

In spite of his righteous ardor, Herb heard the tiredness in George's voice. "I don't want to talk to you."

"I think it would be to your benefit—and to Michael's —in fact, to everyone's if you'd see me for a few minutes. If you wish, we could . . ."

"The only thing I wish is that you were dead. If you're able to come here knowing that, I'll see you."

"I'll be there in five minutes. I would prefer not to talk to any of your guests."

"And for your own safety, I would suggest that you didn't try." He hung up.

In fact, everything that Herb had presumed and predicted was true. The ruthless pragmatism he had so recently criticized in himself had triumphed. George had been in touch with not one, but two attorneys: his own and one of the best trial lawyers in the country. He had been asked in the same no-bones-about-it manner employed by Frank McManus if Michael had or even probably had made a pass at the boy. When George had told the lawyer that such a thing was not possible, the lawyer

263

had asked him if the boy would testify to it, anyway. It had come full circle. The attorneys, knowing their business, had glided like sleek gulls above the righteousness of their clients, assuming corruption and venality in every conceivable and in every inconceivable place. They were no more surprised by the ultimate silence that masked the sin than they would have been by the sin itself.

Herb strode across the lawn and up the steps of George Carr's terrace. George was sitting at a table having coffee and trying not to let *The New York Times* tremble in his hands. When Herb arrived, George folded the newspaper in his lap and looked up.

"I'll make this as brief as possible," Herb said.

"Yes. I would advise that."

"What do you plan to do?"

"Everything I told Cynthia last night I would do. I plan to sue you and Joe on every level I can. What did you think I was going to do, forget about it and invite you and Cynthia to dinner while Michael recuperates?"

"I presume you have an attorney."

"If you were only fatuous, you'd be almost bearable. But in addition to being a fool, you're disgusting. Doesn't it bother you that your wife and child know that about you?"

Soaring like the legal gulls above George's pretensions, Herb said, "I asked if you've been in touch with an attorney."

"Yes."

"Then he must have told you that it would be foolish for you to bring any action against Joe or me if David would reveal Michael's sexual advances toward him."

"Yes. But there weren't any. So I told him that David was incapable of disloyalty. And certainly incapable of perjury. I did not tell him that those were qualities David's father would most highly prize in his son."

"Loyalty? To Michael?"

"Yes."

"David's loyalty belongs to me."

"You mean, his dishonesty belongs to you."

"I mean that David is prepared to testify in court that Michael tried to make David have some kind of homosexual relationship . . . physical relationship with him."

"I don't believe you."

"Would you like me to bring David over here to tell you himself?"

"You would, wouldn't you? How did you get him to do it? I thought more of him."

"George, I don't like you any more than you like me. But can you look me in the eye and tell me Michael never tried to make a sexual move toward my son?"

"Easily. Oh, he wanted to. Not as much as you want to, but it seems to me that since Michael wouldn't have had the burden of incest, it's a tribute to him that he controlled himself. That you controlled yourself is merely what a civilized person would expect. It's not much of a moral victory. Now, I would appreciate it if you would leave." George got up and went into the house.

The blinding agony of the accusation lasted only as long as Herb stood alone on the terrace. When he turned and went down the steps into the gorgeousness of the flowers and the grass and the sunlight, he was trying to forget it had been made. Then he could only remember it as preposterous. Then he could only remember the last time he had seen David naked, in the bathhouse at the lake when David was twelve. Then he could only remember that there would be no suit and that he had won.

Shortly before noon, George went to the hospital. Since Michael had a private room, George could visit him any time between the hours of 9:00 and 7:00. When George had left the hospital several hours before, Michael had been in the emergency room. Now he saw him for the first time in the aftermath of the incident. There was little of him to see. The neat, spotless covers were drawn up to his armpits, and his arms lay free and unbandaged on top of them. His head, tightly swathed in gauze, lay motionless on the pillow. One of his eyes was covered by a white, plastic-taped patch. The other, liverish and bloodshot, was all, except for his hands, George could see of his friend. George had talked to an intern immediately prior to his visit and knew that Michael could not talk. He was sedated, and his broken jaw was wired and bandaged so that he could not move it. A nurse had put a pad and pencil on his bed so that, if he wanted to and were able, he could write messages to whom it may have concerned.

It certainly concerned George, and Michael wrote on the pad, *Hello!* as soon as George came into the room.

"Hello, Mike," George said. "I guess you know you're going to be all right."

Michael made as much of a nod as he could.

"I want to say, 'How do you feel?' but it seems pretty stupid. Are you in a lot of pain?"

Michael made a movement with his arms indicating an injection.

"Ah, in the arms of morpheus," George said.

Michael picked up the pad and pencil and wrote, *Smile.*

"Better than grass?"

Michael wrote, *Wow!* Then he wrote, *If I fall asleep forgive. Did you see them?*

"The neighbors?" George asked. "Only Cynthia . . . and Herb. They asked how you are."

Michael wrote, *It hurts to laugh. David?*

"No, I haven't seen him. I'm sure he'll come to see you when the hospital will let him."

Michael wrote, *Please. Do nothing.*

"What do you mean?" Michael pointed to himself. "You mean legally?"

Michael wrote, *Yes. Last night Joe Herb something about David me.*

"I know."

Michael wrote, *David on spot. Do nothing.*

"You mean you think they'd ask him to lie about you?" Michael moved his head. "You know he wouldn't."

266

Michael wrote, *I know. Don't let ask him. Do nothing. Don't sue. Forget it. Very sleepy.*

"In spite of what they've done to you?"

Michael wrote, *Tell Gianni winter France. Tell George same.*

"I will. I'd like to kiss you, but I'm afraid it would hurt you."

Michael wrote, *Kisses always hurt. Poetry. Hello Kevin. Sleepy. Good night. Day?*

Most of the guests had gone when George got home from the hospital. Only Derek, Arthur, Bob and Kevin remained. Gian-Carlo was there, too. They were having whiskey sours in the den, and George accepted one eagerly. He sat down with his drink and said, "Gianni, Michael asked me to tell you we're going to spend the winter in France. You were right and we . . . no, I bow to you both. You were right, and I was wrong. For whatever it's worth."

"Is he really all right, George?" Kevin asked.

"Yes. I mean, he will be. He asked me to say hello to you. Would you stop to see him on the way into town, Kevin? He'd like that."

"Yes. I'd like it, too."

"You know, you mustn't underestimate Michael's . . ."

The telephone rang. Gian-Carlo answered it there in the room. After a moment, he lowered the phone and said, "It is David Radnor."

George crossed the room and took the phone quite casually. "Yes?" he said.

"May I come over and see you?" David asked.

"No."

"Please."

"What good would it do? It's over. You can tell your father it's over. That should please him."

"Let me come . . . please. Let me come over."

"All right, come," George said and hung up on David as he had on his father.

By the time George had told the others to wait in the

house for him and gone out onto the terrace, David was walking across the lawn. He came up the terrace steps and stood before George, who was standing, too, and with no intention of sitting down.

David knew that any kind of courtesies would have been absurd. He said, "You know what I did?"

"Yes."

"I mean, you know I only *said* I would testify . . . to stop everything. You know I would never . . ."

"No, I don't know that, David," George said wearily. "And I don't care anymore."

"I care."

"Oh, yes!"

"And Michael cares."

"Yes, I know."

"Can I . . . see him?"

"I don't think that's a particularly good idea."

"I want to tell him . . . what I did."

"Why?"

"So he'll understand."

"Understand what? You know he was in love with you. You know he kept his hands off you. You know he meant you nothing but good. Now that you've agreed to accuse him in public of trying to corrupt you sexually, what is it you want him to understand?"

"Why I . . ."

"Go home. You're still a child . . . an ignorant, cruel child. Go home, and let Michael alone."

George turned back toward the French doors, but was conscious of David's still standing there. Just before he went inside, George turned back again and said, "He doesn't know what you did. And I'm not going to tell him. He figured out the problem for himself, and asked me not to bring any action against Joe or your father. He didn't want you put on the spot. Of course, he said he knew you wouldn't lie about him. He's more of a child than you've ever been. So I didn't tell him, and you're not going to, either. Stay away from him, David.

The only reason I've told you this is because it might hurt you more than not knowing. I hope it does. I wanted you to know how pointless, how unnecessary your betrayal was. There will be instructions at the hospital forbidding you to see Michael." George went into the house and got drunk with his guests.

Most of what happened to the nighbors in the next ten days was not visible. Michael could be seen being transferred to Doctors' Hospital in New York City. The Mercedes, loaded with luggage, could be seen being driven out of the driveway of the Cartwright house by George Carr. The gardener could be seen taking out the roses and bulbs from the garden. And eventually, the vans could be seen, pulling up before the elegant old house and swallowing up every piece of furniture.

But there were those things which could not be seen. No one really saw the neighbors return to normalcy. No one could see that George and Michael's return to temporary lodgings in New York was a return to their old life, with Gian-Carlo and Europe and each other. No one could see the sweet resignation with which the Radnors and the Parkers and the Jablonskis settled down once again to their proprietorship. No one could see David's loss or Michael's or Cynthia's or Tom's, for they were as vaporous as the gains of the others. No one saw the contract, zonally illegal, but paid for in every way, by which George Carr vivisected Janet Cartwright's house, only on condition that it be transformed into The Hainesdale Inn, with music and dancing every night in the week.

OUTSTANDING FICTION FROM
PAPERBACK LIBRARY!

☐ **GREEN HOLLY** by Sue Kaufman
A young woman's affair with an older man reveals much about herself . . . and her closest friend. By the author of **Diary of a Mad Housewife**. (65-769, 95¢)

☐ **E PLURIBUS BANG!** by David Lippincott
When the love-hungry wife of the president of the U.S.A. seeks a more perfect union, it's time for E PLURIBUS BANG! A novel of "hilarious and often biting wit."—**The New York Times** (65-709, 95¢)

☐ **GOIN'** by Jack M. Bickham
At 40 (a **young** 40), Stan Pierce set out on a voyage of discovery. Others, earlier, had gone looking for America. Stan was looking for himself. (65-628, 95¢)

☐ **THE TEMPTRESS** by Sandra Shulman
A blazing novel of sex and Satanism set in the framework of present-day London politics. (65-395, 95¢)

☐ **THE HAPPY SUMMER DAYS** by Sue Kaufman
A novel about the tangled lives of a group of married couples summering at a New York beach colony, by the author of **Diary of a Mad Housewife**. (65-670, 95¢)

☐ **GLAD AND SORRY SEASONS** by Carol Evan
A novel about a witty, bright, liberated, over-30 woman. "Funny, sexy, sad, candid, scandalous and very human."
—**San Francisco Chronicle**. (65-606, 95¢)

☐ **THE PRODUCTION** by Daniel Broun
A behind-the-scenes novel about the making of a Broadway hit. "Genuine and fascinating."—**The Hollywood Reporter**. (66-581, $1.25)

MORE BESTSELLERS
FROM PAPERBACK LIBRARY!